Shana Gray is a hybrid author who was first published in 2010. She has written contemporary erotic romances for multiple publishers, including Harlequin Blaze, Random House, and Headline, and is also an indie author. Her stories range from scorching quickie-length to longer full-length novels. Shana's passion is to enjoy life! She lives in Ontario, but loves to travel and see the world, be with family and friends, and experience the beauty that surrounds us. Many of her experiences find their way into her books.

Visit Shana online at www.shanagray.com and connect with her on Twitter @ShanaGray_ or via Facebook www.facebook.com/authorshanagray.

By Shana Gray

Working Girl

WORKING GIRL
THE COMPLETE NOVEL
Shana Gray

HEADLINE
ETERNAL

First published in 2016 as an ebook serialisation

First published in paperback in 2018
by HEADLINE ETERNAL
An imprint of HEADLINE PUBLISHING GROUP

1

Cataloguing in Publication Data is available from the British Library

ISBN 978 1 4722 5455 9

Typeset in 11/14 pt Minion Pro by Jouve (UK), Milton Keynes

Printed and bound in Great Britain by CPI Group (UK) Ltd, Croydon, CR0 4YY

Headline's policy is to use papers that are natural, renewable and recyclable
products and made from wood grown in well-managed forests and other
controlled sources. The logging and manufacturing processes are expected to
conform to the environmental regulations of the country of origin.

HEADLINE PUBLISHING GROUP
An Hachette UK Company
Carmelite House
50 Victoria Embankment
London EC4Y 0DZ

www.headlineeternal.com
www.headline.co.uk
www.hachette.co.uk

I lost my mom to listeria food poisoning in December 2012. She was my champion but after her passing Dad took over, even though he had no clue what publishing was all about. He even read my HQ Blaze, which was a tad uncomfortable because it was steamy. He followed everything I did with gusto. Sadly, my dad died on July 23, 2016. It was right in the middle of wrapping up this fabulous Working Girl serial. I was finishing 'Mr Sunday' when I got the call from the hospital. To say I was absolutely gutted doesn't even touch how devastated I was/ am. Dad was 93, a WWII vet, Polish lad forced to fight for the Germans and had seen a lot of things in his lifetime, even his daughter achieving her dream of being published. This book is for him. My dad, who I love with all my heart and miss terribly. I only wish he was here to see it. xoxo

Acknowledgments

First to my fabulous agent Louise Fury. Thank you for everything! Kristin Smith, aka Hawk-Eye, heartfelt thanks. *Working Girl* wouldn't be possible without Kate Byrne and everyone at Headline! It has been such a wonderful experience working with them in every way – thank you! My family, since for the last four months I've been glued to the computer. I wouldn't have been able to do it without your patience and understanding. Meat Man for not feeling abandoned or jealous when I was busy with my other seven Mr-s and instead, kept singing to me – *Mr Monday me-o-my!* Love you all. xo

WORKING GIRL

MR MONDAY

I settled into the soft leather armchair and quietly took in the posh reception area of Diamond Enterprises. It was all marble, honeyed-colored wood, thick carpets and soft lighting, with one wall housing hermetically sealed first-edition classics behind beveled glass. It gave the impression of an elegant sitting room. Under normal circumstances, I would be drawn to the shelves, eager to see which books rated being so carefully protected.

Not today.

The whole place gave off an aura of old money and, in my opinion, also reeked of arrogance and entitlement. I didn't belong, but that wasn't going to stop me. I'd nurtured my revenge since I was fifteen, when my father died. Just five years earlier, he, only fifty years old, walked into our house, the contents of his office stuffed into a battered cardboard box, and the direction of my life changed. Now that a window of opportunity had finally opened, I'd leapt at it. The head of Diamond Enterprises needed an executive assistant.

In the weeks since I'd seen the job on an executive-jobs

search site, I'd quit my position as corporate librarian for an international mining exploration company, and done my due diligence, researching and cramming as if this interview were the exam of a lifetime, in order to be absolutely ready for it. At the library, I'd done everything from ordering reference materials and tracking down obscure theses on mineral rights to supervising a small staff of archivists and researchers. To leave all that and become somebody else's secretary was a step down, a waste of my degrees and the scholarships that paid for them. But the opportunity to bring down a huge corporation didn't come along often … and I was prepared to do whatever it took. There was nothing they could trip me up on now. I'd learned all I could about the company – at least, what was in the public domain. What wasn't public knowledge was what I needed to find out now, and the only way to do that was from the inside.

From my seat, I had a clear view down the elaborate hall into the mysterious and very secretive inner sanctum of Diamond. The very sanctum in which my father, Charles Raymond, had once walked, moving with the exclusive executive management team, until he'd been let go, falsely accused of misusing company funds, and it had cost him – *us* – everything. He'd been ousted unceremoniously, cut off at the knees, his pension taken away and with no golden parachute to see him through his senior years. It left him with a reputation that haunted him until he died, a bitter old man. (I'd been born when he was forty, rather late in his life, before his fall from grace.)

I pressed my lips together, trying not to let my anger boil over. It wouldn't help; calm and level-headed thinking was the only way to succeed. I glanced at my watch, a delicate piece I loved with all my heart. Dad had given it to Mom on their wedding day, almost thirty years ago, back when they still lived in England. I gently touched the small, round face ringed with exquisitely tooled platinum and a bevy of sparkling diamonds. The second hand ticked and reminded me I was waiting, something I'd become very good at.

I'd arrived the obligatory fifteen minutes before my interview, and only a few minutes had gone by. I glanced up and saw the polished young receptionist's gaze slide away from me. I watched her try to pretend she hadn't been caught in the act of staring and decided I would ignore her. It wasn't important. Instead, I leaned back, crossed one leg over the other and primly laced my fingers over my Kate Spade purse, gazing down the long hall. I could play it cool. But I had to admit I was curious about the timing of the interview; it was well past six o'clock in the evening.

Scheduling didn't matter, anyway; getting the job did.

All I needed was to become a part of the organization, and this interview was my only chance. I was prepared to do just about anything to get my foot in the door.

My nerves were shot, though. I drew in a deep breath, as quietly as I could. I didn't like that I was quaking, deep inside. I felt it, and there was nothing I could do about it. At least it didn't show outwardly. If they found out who I was, I couldn't imagine what would happen. Probably the same thing that happened to my father.

The hem of my skirt rode up above my thigh when I recrossed my legs. I knew it was a dated skirt suit, but I loved my vintage clothing. Glancing down at my feet, I smiled at my shoes. Another great find. The only thing new was the purse. My passion for purses had gotten out of hand and my credit card was crying the blues.

Sounds echoed in the long hall. I looked up from under my eyebrows, glanced briefly at Ms Gatekeeper Receptionist, who was suddenly intent on her appearance, staring into a compact before snapping it shut. I fidgeted with my purse, stricken by the urge to see if I had any lipstick on my teeth. I heard doors open and close and kept an eye on the end of the hall, drawing in a soft breath when a man appeared. My heart fluttered as he approached, my nerves kicking into high gear. I no longer had time to check my lips and so I watched the man approach. He seemed about to explode out of his well-tailored suit. I noticed everything about him, imprinting him into my brain.

He. Was. Gorgeous.

And *big*.

Good Lord, he seemed to fill the hall with his presence. The intensity on his face as he concentrated while talking on his cell phone had me holding my breath. His brows, heavy and dark, just like his closely cropped hair, were drawn together. He was focused and walked with confidence. A fierce scar ran over his cheek, just under his right eye. I had the urge to trace my finger along the angry welt across his cheekbone. All sorts of stories about how he had achieved such a scar raced through my overactive brain. None of them was very comforting.

He entered the reception area, and dwarfed it. I stared at him, my heart pounding. *Was my interview with him?* He turned to the receptionist, glancing up from his phone, and said something to her that I wasn't able to hear. I tried to hold back a frown when she giggled and flirted. He smiled at her and tapped his fingers on the desk a couple of times – he had big hands, too – before turning around. Then he was in front of me, and I stared up at him. I waited for a brief moment before deciding that I should stand. I struggled to get up. It was as if the damn chair had suctioned me in. I wiggled, trying to get my legs under me so I could rise gracefully.

'Ms Canyon?' the dark and dangerously gorgeous man asked. He reached out and offered his hand.

'Yes.' I tilted my head so I could meet his gaze. I'd started using my mother's maiden name when I was in my late teens.

Otherwise, one internet search and all the scandalous gossip about Diamond's betrayal of Dad would be revealed.

Taking his hand was absolutely the wrong thing to do. His touch was electric, and heat rocketed up my arm and into my chest, drawing all the oxygen out of my lungs. I glanced at our fingers to see if there were, literally, sparks flying. I allowed him to help me to my feet.

'Thank you,' came out a little too breathlessly, and I tried to catch my breath.

I adjusted the chain shoulder strap of my purse with my free hand, then ran it down my hips to smooth my skirt, which I knew, without looking, had ridden even higher on my thighs. He let go of my fingers and I curled them into my palms, wanting to hold on to the sensation of his touch. I flicked my gaze to him and nearly fainted when I saw he was staring at my legs. I realized I was still running my hand over my hips.

God, I hoped it didn't seem like a seductive move. I quickly laced my fingers in front of me. He looked up and I was captivated, his blue eyes holding me hostage until I once more had no breath. He smiled and one side of his mouth rose up almost imperceptibly. It made the scar on his cheek follow suit and – holy shit! – rather than being off-putting, it was the most enticing look a man had ever given me. I was rattled, and trying desperately not to show it. I dragged my gaze from him to focus on breathing for a few precious seconds.

'Thank you for coming in so late on a Monday. I realize it was a last-minute request for the interview, and we appreciate your accommodating our unusual scheduling.' His voice held authority, and a slight accent that I couldn't place.

I liked it.

I nodded my head, acknowledging his words.

'Thank you for inviting me for an interview. I'm glad we were able to find a time.'

'As I said, we do appreciate that you were able to join us. Now, let's get started.'

'Of course,' I said, grateful that we weren't going to stand and stare at each other all evening.

He held his hand out, indicating that I should walk before him. 'Please, ladies first.'

A shiver rippled through me. It was as if he had touched me with his voice. I'd never been so acutely aware of a man before. I wasn't so sure I wanted him behind me. I wanted – no, *needed* – to see him, but that wasn't to be. I had no clue where to go and continued forward until he gave me directions. Then everything seemed to take a strange turn as he directed me down a maze of halls to what looked like another elevator, a private one. He inserted a card at the bottom of the sensor and I found myself inside in the blink of an eye.

The doors whooshed closed and, if I hadn't been looking at the numbers showing that we were climbing, I wouldn't have known if the elevator was going up or down.

We were silent, and I kept my eyes glued to the floor numbers. He was a step behind me, and it was as if he had an effect on the air around us. His size dominated the small but well-appointed elevator. I glanced down at the ground and saw his feet just behind me to the right.

My mom used to say you could tell a person by their shoes. His shoes were mighty fine. Polished. Black and large. The elevator was warm – either that, or my body temperature was spiking. How could it not with a man radiating intense sexy goodness in such close proximity to me? When the doors opened to a small vestibule with glass walls, I was surprised to find we were on the roof. I turned to look at him.

'The roof? Why—?' He pushed at the door's handlebar and it swung open, a leaf that had been caught beneath the door-jamb blowing out. He stared at me, clearly waiting for me to proceed. Was he not aware that we were currently over seventy stories above the ground?

'Do you not speak much?' I asked him, and I cringed at the edge I heard in my voice.

Mr Gorgeous smiled. 'Only when words are necessary.'

I didn't really know how to reply to that so I narrowed my eyes, then turned my back to him. Even though I couldn't see him, I was acutely aware of him behind me.

'Ms Canyon, this way, please.'

Wind rushed in, pulling at my hair. Thank God I'd had it cut. I missed my long, loose curls, but I'd had to make the change, and now I sported a short, layered cut, the thick strands dyed so dark they almost held a blue tinge. I'd remembered to dye my eyebrows, and mascara took care of my lashes. My hair's normal fiery red was a dead giveaway, as I took after my father. He'd passed his hair down to me, and I treasured it. His nickname had been Rooster, due to his vibrant, unruly hair. I shoved thoughts of him away and stepped on to the rooftop.

'What's going on? Why am I up here?'

Mr Gorgeous turned to me. 'This is the next step in the interview process.'

I frowned, trying to make sense of his comment.

'What, on the roof?'

Then I heard the sound of an engine and searched it out. To my surprise, there was a helicopter waiting on a helipad at the far end of the roof. A metal catwalk led from the small entryway to the roof and stairs leading up to the waiting helicopter.

'I don't understand.' I turned to face the man, and hesitated.

Going up in a helicopter was not on my bucket list. I never flew if I could avoid it, because of my fear of heights.

'As I said, this is the next step. You either move forward or you turn around and consider the interview over.'

'What? Just like that? No helicopter, no interview? This is certainly unorthodox.'

Fear started to tighten around my heart. All my strategic plans had, up until this point, gone flawlessly, almost too well to be true.

I gritted my teeth and quickly weighed up my options. There were only two. Turn around and leave, never find the retribution I'd been gunning for all these years and live with regret for the rest of my days, or . . . I turned and looked at the helicopter: get in that thing and fly off to God knows where and keep my plans on track. The company had accused my father of padding his expense account and spending company funds on a mistress, and my plan was to locate expense reports and any other financial records for the executive team back then and, if lucky, perhaps find some recent ones as well. I'd release the documents to the media, prove the executives were all hypocrites. There's no way my dad did what they said he did; he was honorable to the core and he adored my mother, so the implication that he was having an affair shattered them both. I don't think my mom ever truly got over it, and I think she believed that he had had an affair. I, on the other hand, was adamant that he was innocent.

Do I follow the white rabbit down the rabbit hole, or do I let the adventure end now? There was no decision to make. I'd made up my mind long before this moment. I would follow the rabbit. I moved toward him and stared at the man head on.

'Lead the way,' I told him, and did my best to keep my voice from revealing the panic that had started to build in me.

He smiled and allowed me to pass. I went on to the catwalk. Heights. God, how I hated heights. Rivers of fear barreled up the backs of my legs, over my ass, and clutched my back in a fierce grip, nearly squeezing the breath from my lungs. I stared down at the concrete canyons of New York City, sparkling innocently in the evening twilight. Bah, not so innocent. Far from it.

I started to hyperventilate at the pull of the abyss below.

Slowly and very cautiously, I placed one foot in front of the other, keeping my knees slightly bent, much like a drunk being directed by a cop to *walk the line*. Seventy-five stories up.

Outside.

Shit, this was a nightmare coming to life. If only I could wake up and things were back like they were. I wavered, and a steadying hand rested against my waist. 'Careful, ma'am.' His deep voice in my ear wasn't as far away as I had thought it would be.

His presence behind me was comforting, in a way, but I would not thank him for it. The polarizing touch of his finger-tips didn't help my breathlessness. Heights and him. What a dizzying combination.

'Try not to look down, it's easier.'

'I'm not looking down,' I snapped, lying as I flicked another glance toward the edge of the building.

I climbed the last few steps to the platform. My skirt hiked up my thigh a bit and I jerked it down. *Should have worn slacks, but how the hell could I know I'd be flying off in a helicopter?*

I'd told myself I was prepared for anything, so I had to buck up. I'd come this far and I wasn't about to quit now. I needed to find out the truth and clear my father's name. I hesitated at the top of the platform.

He asked, 'Have you made your choice?'

Brushing past him, I walked toward the ride that would be one of the most terrifying things I'd ever done. There was no way I would turn away and forget that this company had, basically, killed my father. Fired him, devastating our lives. He was too much of an honest man to misappropriate company funds – and for a mistress! He loved my mother, and I simply couldn't believe he'd jeopardize everything he'd worked so hard to accomplish. I needed to clear his name and make Diamond Enterprises pay.

I stopped by the open door and looked into the sleek interior. This was no touristy helicopter. This was class. Style. I turned and gave the man a determined look.

'That I'm here on a skyscraper about to board a helicopter that will take me to an unknown destination should tell you how badly I want this job.'

Mr Gorgeous walked toward me. My heart leapt into my throat when he reached out and took my elbow. His touch was just as electric as it had been moments ago. He leaned toward me, and my gaze roamed over his face, seeing him up close for the first time. The ice blue of his eyes under his dark brows, and his lips, full and inviting, caused me to part my lips in anticipation . . . of what? A kiss? I could almost imagine the feel of his mouth on mine, and my muscles weakened at the butterflies that filled my belly. I found myself gripping his arm. His very muscular arm. But he didn't lean in to kiss me. I felt foolish and angry for even entertaining the thought.

'Get in.'

His assured tone left no room for argument. It took all my reserve to keep from falling any further under the spell he seemed to have cast over me. From the minute I saw him, there was a special something that had me short of breath, as if I were waiting for something to happen, and did all sorts of good bad things to my already heightened nerve endings. I stood taller and pulled from his grip.

'I can manage.'

Turning away from him, I tried to step up into the helicopter. My tight skirt had been a perfect choice for an office interview but not for this unanticipated adventure. I tried again to get in, and the toe of my shoe caught on the step into the helicopter. It made me feel even more unraveled. The crowning glory was when his hands gripped my waist and he lifted me into the cabin. I was embarrassed that I needed his help, and hated how much I enjoyed his touch.

'Thank you.'

Once inside, he let me go, and I found a seat. He jumped in as if riding a helicopter were a normal, every-day event. Maybe it was for him. He filled the interior with his dark, very dangerous and totally enticing aura.

'Here,' Mr Gorgeous said, and handed me a headset; it would drown out the noise and allow us to hear and speak to each other. 'Put them on and do up the seat belt.'

I did as he instructed and watched as he reached into his pocket and pulled something out.

'Now this.'

I looked at his hand and furrowed my brows.

'What's this?' I leaned forward to see what he was holding.

'Blindfold.'

'Wh-hat? A blindfold? What on earth for?'

I looked up at him, cold dread slipping along my spine.

He smiled. 'What are they normally for?'

That was a loaded question. My mind fell down that rabbit hole again and I had a flash of being blindfolded on a bed, with him above me, in me, making love, and I almost moaned. He was hot, sexy, and my body had reacted to him since the first moment I saw him. I closed my eyes and squeezed my thighs together, trying not to get carried away. I was here for a purpose, one reason only, and sex was not on the to-do list. I silently cursed him.

'I really don't understand why I have to wear one.'

He sat next to me.

'It's the rules. You're here for a job interview and this is one of the criteria.'

'That's such bullshit.'

I felt myself getting pissy, which was a welcome change from the desire I'd felt moments before but not at all a good thing in a job interview. Nor was the swearing. He laughed, and I liked how it sounded.

'Be that as it may, either put it on or get out.'

What the fuck had I gotten myself into? I hadn't established an emergency plan. No one was waiting for my check-in phone call. Mom was back in England, which was what had made this whole venture possible. No one knew I was here. My former co-workers thought I was taking a trip to London to see my mother and the Harry Potter studios, and I'd lost touch with the few friends I'd had in college. Plotting the best way to reduce a company to figurative smoking rubble didn't leave me with a lot of time to socialize. If something happened to me now, there wasn't a soul on earth who would notice any time soon. Panic filled me and I glanced at the now closed door. I could leave if I wanted to, but I couldn't give up. I eyed the blindfold. *Really?* Then I pressed my lips together and switched my gaze to his face.

'Give it to me.' I held out my hand. How much more control was I to give up? It was bad enough that I'd soon be thousands of feet up in the air, and now he wanted me to put my fate entirely in his hands.

He ignored my hand. I kept my gaze pinned on him and refused to look away. I was beginning to wonder if he knew who I was. If he – or *they* – did, then my plan would be shot to hell, but if they didn't, then I was one step closer to making my way inside the organization.

'I'll handle the blindfold,' he said, and moved toward me.

I shook my head and leaned away from him, keeping my hand outstretched for the blindfold. 'I'd prefer to put it on myself, if you don't mind.'

'I do mind. The sooner you let me, the sooner we're on our way.'

I shifted forward, not wanting to comply but knowing I had no choice. When he placed the blindfold over my eyes his fingers were warm against me, and when they brushed my skin I'd never had such a reaction to a man's touch before. I could barely keep myself still on the seat as the shock of arousal swept through me. The blindfold was soft and silky, and the most seductive male cologne I'd ever smelled wafted around me. I raised my fingers to touch it; they trembled as I felt the bottom edge of the blindfold against my cheeks. Leather. The outside was leather, and the inside was lined with satin. Something about that combination got my blood pulsing thick and slow, whirling in a seductive heat between my thighs.

This man was more than I'd bargained for.

'You're trembling.' Hearing his sultry voice, it felt like he was inside my head. In every crevice and corner. Filling me until I was all him. Distracting me. And I was letting him . . . oh God, I was letting him.

I turned to him, unable to see his face and excited that I couldn't.

'I know.' My voice was weak, and all I could do was whisper.

'I like that.' I felt his breath next to my neck, warm and inviting.

Holy shit. This man exuded sensuality. I was confused. How could he have me in such a state? I was not normally a fool for a man, but this one was making me forget the importance of what it was I was here to do. That couldn't happen.

Then he must have leaned closer, because I felt him all around me. He filled my senses. My body and my soul. I knew instinctively that he would be amazing in bed. Would that opportunity ever present itself? *Oh, I hope so.*

I couldn't sit still. He was so close I felt his body as if an electrical current were crackling between us and I squirmed on the seat, trying to ease the ache building in me. I turned my face to the window, hoping for some air to cool my flushed skin and help me refocus. I had to pull myself back together.

Was being blindfolded better than being able to see him? I wasn't so sure. To see him in the dark, so intimate and close, would be almost as seductive as not being able to see him but knowing he was there. Especially not knowing how close he was sitting to me. Was he looking at me? I breathed in and caught his scent again; it mingled with that of the blindfold. I was overcome and drew in a breath when the helicopter lifted off. It tilted. I wasn't prepared for it and I flung my arms out in attempt to keep my balance. My body lost its sense of up versus down and panic hit me in the chest. I knew I was high in the air, with nothing between me and the ground but the shell of this tin can of a helicopter.

One hand hit the window and the other hand *him*.

'With great risk comes great reward. Just chill. We'll be there soon.'

His voice filled my headset and I wondered if the pilot could also hear him. Would they both be able to hear me if I spoke?

Could they both hear my rapid breathing? It sounded like a roar in my own ears. I settled back into the seat, but I couldn't relax my muscles. Tension built in my neck and shoulders as I held myself rigid.

After a few minutes, I felt myself calm as the helicopter settled into a steady flight. It wasn't choppy or jumping around in the sky, like I thought it'd be, and I let out a slow breath. *It was going to be okay.* I didn't really feel like talking, so when music filled my headset I felt myself calm a bit. It lulled me. My sense of hearing was heightened by my lack of vision, and I swore I could hear the man next to me breathing through my headset, even with the music in the background. It was seductive. The image I'd had moments before of us making love flashforwarded to one of us sated after a night of sweet love. Falling asleep, intimately, in the dark, wrapped in each other's arms. I could see myself inhale, liking the scents of him that swirled around me. I knew I would never forget it and, should I ever smell it again, I would be forever reminded of this night. Of him. This strange and enigmatic man who had tipped my world off-kilter in such a short space of time.

I rested my head back on the seat, allowing my senses to take over. Behind the blindfold, I closed my eyes. It helped to see him in my mind's eye. I wondered if he was looking at me, and I felt a flush sweep through my body. My mouth opened as I drew in yet another shaky breath and I could've sworn I heard him breathe in at the same time. It told me that maybe he had been watching me, and that excited me more than I cared to admit. His presence gave me a bit of comfort, though, and I felt my fear fading a little.

We sat in silence, but it was as if our bodies were speaking to each other. I opened my mouth, about to say something, but snapped it shut again, remembering the pilot. Then the cadence of the helicopter changed. It was descending and I curled my fingers over my knees as my stomach dropped with the descent. The touchdown was gentle, however, and the engines were turned off.

It appeared I would be staying here – wherever *here* was – for a while, otherwise why would the engines be shut off? I touched the blindfold, desperately wanting to rip it off. But I waited. Positive there would be a further set of instructions.

'We've arrived.'

The announcement came from the pilot through the headsets.

Then my headset was removed, the man's fingers brushing over my hair and behind my ear. A delicate shiver overtook me, and my nipples hardened. Thank God I had a jacket on.

Still blindfolded, I tipped my head to listen. The door was unlatched and opened, and a rush of sea-scented air filled the cabin. I was baffled by everything that had transpired so far. Why on earth would he bring me to the seaside?

Then my blindfold was gone.

He stepped out of the helicopter and offered me his hand. I took it, but hesitated, hoping we weren't on a sky-high helipad again. Damn my fear. After marshalling my courage, I exited the helicopter. I gasped at what I saw. We'd landed at ground level but a magnificent house sprawled beyond the helipad, perched on a cliff overlooking the ocean. I felt a jolt of vertigo, just seeing how the house stood right on the edge. This interview was getting stranger with every passing minute.

'Where are we?' I asked, looking down at him. 'This is incredible.'

'Come.'

He dropped my hand to take hold of my waist. He lifted. I steadied myself by gripping his shoulders. He lowered me slowly. I held my breath and our gazes locked. Time stood still until my feet touched the ground, and I tipped my head back so as not to break eye contact. Only then did I realize that I'd slipped down his body, intimately, and we didn't part, lingering flush to each other with his hands at my waist and mine on his shoulders. I swallowed and stepped back. This was all wrong. I needed to get a grip and stop obsessing about him, especially as it was a job interview.

My legs were a little wobbly and I stumbled along the flagstone pathway to the house. He took my elbow and I glanced up at him. He was watching me with an unreadable expression. It didn't unnerve me, but it did make me wonder what he was thinking. I was curious about this man, whom I'd met such a short while ago. I liked his touch; it had an element of possession which was rather exciting. It was as if we were both magnetized, being drawn one to the other, and it took everything I had to resist the pull. Yes, I acknowledged to myself, he made me feel like a woman. No man had ever taken the time to do that before, because I tended to go for the one-and-done guys. It was less time-consuming – and less emotionally demanding – that way. This feeling was new, but I was enjoying it.

Once inside the house, I was led to a study. All the drapes were drawn. The furniture was old, heavy and very masculine. I knew my antiques and was stunned by some of the pieces in the room. There was no one there but us. He touched the back of the chair by the desk, but I stopped in front of a tall, multi-paned window, one of many that lined one wall of the study. Very old but elegant drapes hung behind the ornately carved window valance. The ceiling took my breath away, it was so high, like in a cathedral. It seemed that everything was making me breathless tonight.

'Please sit.'

Especially him.

I did as he asked and watched him walk to the sideboard and pour golden liquid into a beautifully cut crystal tumbler.

He glanced at me. 'Ice?'

I shook my head. 'No, neat.'

I could barely contain myself. It was hard to stop myself bursting out with a million questions. I was frazzled, aroused, confused, and I needed that drink something fierce. But having a drink at an interview was oh so wrong. I took the glass from him in any case, our fingers touching. I gasped and gulped a mouthful, welcoming the burn as it slipped down my throat.

'It was a pleasure.' He bowed his head and, before I could comment, he left.

Disappointment filled me and I stood up.

'What the hell?' I looked around and froze when a voice filled the room.

'Ms Canyon. I've been looking forward to meeting you.'

The speaker's voice sounded odd – being piped into the room, like that of a visitor from the Great Beyond.

Tentatively, I replied, 'I'm sorry, you have me at a disadvantage, Mr—'

There was a sly amusement in his tone when he said, 'You may call me Mr King. Welcome to my kingdom.'

I remained silent. One thing I'd learned from my father was to let the other person do the talking. Let them expose themselves or give away their intentions. So I sat quietly, trying not to explode with impatience.

The voice filled the room, and it rather unnerved me. How do you have a conversation with a disembodied voice? I listened, focusing on the words, while keeping the expression on my face blank. If the voice was coming via speakers from another location, I had every expectation that there would also be a camera watching me. I let my need for revenge fuel my patience. I'd come too far to screw it up now.

'Your résumé is impressive. If it weren't, you wouldn't be sitting in my study. Your degree and the years you spent as a corporate librarian are good background for what I am looking for. Your discovery of the antiquated geological survey that allowed your former employers to snatch up untapped ore veins on the cheap was quite impressive. I also enjoyed the digital gallery you created of the fossils discovered in the Montana quarry.' He paused, and I wondered if he was trying to bait me. I wouldn't let him. 'However, this interview process is not going to be what you would normally expect.'

I couldn't sit quietly any longer. 'What exactly do you mean?'

A deep chuckle echoed in the room. 'You are inquisitive. I like that. In order for you to be considered further for this position, you need to agree to complete the tests that will be assigned to you.'

'How can I agree when I have no idea what the tests are?' I was beginning to feel frustrated by all these games.

'It comes down to trust and to how badly you want the job. Enough to take a risk?'

'I don't even know you.' I wasn't about to reveal how much I didn't know about the company. And what I did know screamed at me that trust was something they didn't deserve. Especially after what they did to my father.

The room seemed to close in around me as the heaviness of what he was asking me to do pressed down on me. I realized I had to take a leap into the unknown if I wanted to continue with the job interview. I had to take the risk. It was hard going along like this, blindly, without being given any explanation. It scared me, just like letting Mr Gorgeous put the blindfold on me and getting into the helicopter, so desperate not to show my fear and doing it anyway. It was why I was here now, with another decision to make that would either take me closer to my goal or ruin everything.

I sat back in the chair, processing this information.

'You look skeptical, Ms Canyon.'

'How can I not be? Have all the candidates performed these tests? With everything that has happened to me so far tonight, if what you are expecting isn't *misguided* trust, I don't know what is.' I paused and looked around the room, trying to find that damn camera. And yeah, I heard the tone in my voice when I answered him. Not an overly respectful way to speak to a potential boss.

My legs were trembling with both frustration and uncertainty about what lay ahead. I was a hot mess of emotion. I stood and paced the room, prowling like a caged animal trying to find an escape route. This was the weirdest thing that had ever happened to me. To think I was the one that got this adventure rolling by applying, and now I felt the tables were turning on me. Only in which direction? I clutched my purse in front of me to keep my hands occupied. I was still me, and I did have a choice. Follow the rabbit? Don't follow the rabbit. It appeared that Mr King didn't mind my renewed silence as he was also quiet – probably because he was watching me. I felt his eyes on me and, even though I couldn't see him, I knew without a doubt that my every move was being monitored while I was in this room. Was Mr Gorgeous with him, watching me? What if Mr King *was* Mr Gorgeous? Holy shit, what then? There was no way of recognizing the distorted voice.

I eyed the desk and my glass of Scotch. There was one last

swallow and, boy, did I want it. The silence lengthened, filling the room with its oppressive weight. I was a little surprised that Mr King hadn't spoken again. He seemed the sort who liked to hear himself talk. I peered out of the window. It was now dark as pitch and I couldn't see a thing, but I was pretty sure this set of windows overlooked the ocean. And the cliffs, too. I was glad of the darkness, because then I couldn't see how far we were above the pounding waves below. Just the thought of it worried me. Remembering the glimpse of the house I'd gotten debarking the helicopter, I shivered. It was all so very gothic. Now that I thought about it, I was sure I could feel the pounding waves resonate up through the rock, into the foundations of the house. I didn't like that idea at all, but I started to imagine secret caverns and tunnels underneath the building. Places where people could easily get lost.

I placed a palm on the window to steady my crazy imaginings. It was cool, and I drew in a few calming breaths. How could I have missed the existence of this house in my research? But obviously, there would be things buried too deep to find, and this house was one of them.

'It's a spectacular view in the daytime.' The words boomed, and I nearly jumped out of my skin. This hiding-behind-a-voice façade was getting a bit annoying. It was time for him to show himself.

I spun around. 'I'm sure it is. What I saw when the helicopter landed was quite beautiful.'

'I'm glad you liked it. If you pass all my tests, and I hire you, then you will be able to enjoy this view often.'

'Is this where your executive assistant will be based? Would I have to come here every day?'

There was silence again. Why wasn't he talking? A few minutes passed and, when the speaker made a series of clicks, I realized I'd been breathing shallowly, waiting for the next words from the Great Beyond.

'The details will be provided.' The voice sounded tired. I could hear it through the distortion. I walked back to the desk and picked up the glass. I swallowed the last of the Scotch. I needed another drink, but I didn't feel comfortable helping myself.

'Please, if you'd like another, by all means help yourself.'

He knew every move I was making. Looking out the window. Finishing my drink. I huffed out a breath, then cast a look around the room. 'I know you have cameras in here. If this is some kind of weird audition for *Big Brother*, I'm not amused.' I walked over and poured myself a generous splash. I kept my face toward the elaborate bar, my back to the room. I held the glass, not taking a sip. Then I turned to scan the room again. 'I'm not sure it's entirely fair that you are keeping yourself hidden from me.'

'There are many things in life that aren't fair, Ms Canyon. Something to which I can attest.'

'As can I.' His comments pissed me off. I wanted to scream at him, but I bit my tongue. Literally. Otherwise, I would probably find myself saying something inappropriate and being escorted off the premises. Oh God, that simply couldn't happen. I'd moved heaven and earth to get here. The words hung heavy on my lips. How could things be so unfair for him? Didn't he have it all? A lavish house like this, full of valuable possessions. No money worries. The power he wielded, power that my family had experienced first hand. I put the glass back down on the bar, no longer wanting to drink his Scotch.

'I'm sure you can, Ms Canyon. Attest to it, that is. Most people feel they are dealt a raw hand.' How could someone as rich as him ever know what that was like? Then I thought of something and an icy chill gripped the base of my spine. I narrowed my eyes, because the way he was speaking gave the impression that he knew who I was. If that was the case, then did he know why I was here? The thought was utterly terrifying; it could jeopardize all the strategic and careful planning I'd done to get here. I had to breathe deeply in order to hide how freaked out I was. I needed to leave. The sooner I accepted his offer, the quicker I could get out of here and start this ridiculous process.

'I am still waiting for your answer, Ms Canyon. Will you participate in the tests?'

I stood quietly in the room, my thoughts in turmoil, but I wouldn't let anybody see. I had to remain strong, keep my determination ripe. My hesitation was only a way of playing the game. To make him wonder if I would accept his terms. I did want the job, there was no doubt about that. I needed to readjust my attitude and behavior before I completely shot myself in the foot. I had to give myself time to see how this was going to play out. I drew in a deep breath and pressed my fingertips into my thighs. So this was it, then. I knew what I had to do. I opened my mouth to answer, but the words weren't yet ready to come. I swallowed and tried again.

'Yes, I do want the job.'

'Excellent. I was hoping you would agree. How well you do on the tests will be the deciding factor on whether you're suitable for the position.'

'Fine.' I kept my voice firm.

'Now, I know you were concerned about being flown here this evening. I can understand that. But it was a necessity.'

'I'm sorry, but I don't understand. How could you know I don't like flying?'

Mr Gorgeous must have told him. Yes, that was it. This

reassured me. That was how Mr King knew, because there was no way they could know who I was even if they did know about my fear of flying. I felt more and more nauseous as my mind ran away with itself, yet again. I needed to get a grip! I didn't want to even think about the implications if he ever did learn that I was the daughter of a man he'd fired for alleged misuse of company funds. I heard him sigh, and thought it an unusual thing for him to do, considering the no-nonsense attitude he'd assumed during our conversation. I listened intently, waiting for him to speak, trying to interpret what he was *not* saying to me. If I could only read between the lines. I was waiting for another shoe to drop, and prepared myself.

Without missing a beat, Mr King continued talking. 'On the desk is a manila folder. Please open it and sign the non-disclosure agreement inside.'

I walked over and flipped the folder open. I touched my fingertips to the papers and spread them apart, scanning the document. I had to sign it. No way could I get around it. I took the pen clipped to the top of the folder and signed where indicated.

'There,' I said to the empty room.

There was a moment of quiet. I walked over to the mantle, and there I spied the camera. I touched it, knowing Mr King was on the other side. I boldly looked into the lens. Damn this man for his twists and turns. The silence continued.

'Hello?'

Nothing. I shook my head and turned my back to the camera. Now what? I was exasperated beyond belief. Then the door behind me opened and I spun around. Mr Gorgeous pushed it wide open. His gaze caught mine and he didn't smile. My belly lurched. I couldn't even begin to think why he'd have such a stern look on his face. He propped the door open and went back into the hall. I stood rooted to the spot.

I blinked and took a step back when he came into the room, pushing an old man in a wheelchair.

'Mr King?' I asked.

'One and the same, Ms Canyon,' he answered. Gone was the booming distortion and in its place a deep but weak voice. He was old, frail and only a slip of a man, but I could tell he'd been a formidable force in his younger years. He looked as if he'd been tall. His knees, covered in a heavy blanket, jutted out from the chair. His shoulders, though drooped, were still wide. His cardigan, as my mom would call it, was a thick black cable-knit lined along the placket in a strip of bright yellow tartan. His gaunt face looked tired, but his hair was perfection, silver-grey and thick, just like his closely cropped beard and mustache. I was sure he'd once been a very handsome man.

I walked over to him and stretched out my hand. 'Good evening.' So this was the elusive CEO of Diamond Enterprises.

He raised his hand to mine, the skin almost translucent and showing the delicate veins underneath. He had numerous purple bruises on his flesh and I wondered how he'd gotten them. His grip still held an edge of power. He let my hand go and looked at his hands, which trembled a little. 'Not the prettiest sight, but blood thinners will do that to you. The slightest knock or bump and I bruise.' He slipped his hands under the blanket as if ashamed, and I felt a flash of empathy for him. 'Now, then. I can understand your confusion – a lot has been thrown at you – but I sensed you would be able to handle it.

'Ms Canyon, the reason for the stratagem we employed tonight was valid and important for the process. The interview needed to be away from the corporate offices because I'm ill – dying, in fact. It has not been made public yet, and I'm sure you see the potential ramifications if it were to get out without another CEO having been firmly established to create a seamless shift of power. I can't stress enough how important it is to keep this confidential. Should any whisper of my medical condition leak out in any way, then your interview process will cease. I will know that you leaked it and, now that you've signed the NDA, there will be consequences.'

I was stunned by this revelation and by his open threat. I shouldn't have been surprised about him dropping such a bombshell once he'd made sure I'd signed the NDA. Clearly, Diamond worked through subterfuge, given both their manipulation in firing my father and the way in which they were treating me now. Now, the unusual interview time and the mysterious helicopter ride made sense.

My mind raced. This only cemented my urgent need to get to the inner sanctum of Diamond Enterprises – before Mr King died and this opportunity with him. I did feel slightly ashamed because my only concern was how the man's impending death would affect me. I know how devastated I was by my father's decline, and by not being able to help him. Dad died when I was fifteen. Growing up, I'd been his special princess, but our relationship had changed after he was fired from Diamond. I laid that directly at Mr King's feet. After he was fired, the life my mom and I had become accustomed to had changed rapidly. We'd watched helplessly as Dad withdrew from us and became bitter with hate. His deterioration – emotionally, physically and financially – was more than we were able to handle. It had been a difficult time for us, causing me to mature far too quickly; it was the driving force behind my need for revenge. I tightened my lips. I needed to harden myself to achieve my long-planned goals. I couldn't feel sorry for the man responsible for me missing out on so much with my dad. I needed to get access to those documents before Mr King no longer needed an executive assistant.

'I'm not sure what to say. I'm so sorry.'

'There is nothing to say. It is what it is. I need to ensure the survival of the company, and that's where you come in.'

'Me?' I was more confused than ever now.

'Yes. I need someone smart, someone who understands my vision. Your experience with non-profits in your previous role and your background as a librarian are valuable to me.' I realized I was nodding when he paused, as if to add drama to the situation. I held my breath, waiting for his next words: 'I need someone to take over as CEO, someone who will take this company to new and exciting levels. I devoted my life to building Diamond, and now that I'm dying, I'm looking for the right person to continue my legacy. Someone young, with a fresh perspective and new ideas. Someone with a breadth of experience who can think outside the box. However, this will not be your typical interview.'

I got stuck on 'CEO'. 'Excuse me.' I raised my hand, one finger pointed in the air. 'Aren't I being interviewed for the position of executive assistant? How does your need for a CEO affect me?'

'Well, as I said, I have no doubt you are capable, with a bit of added training. You've demonstrated creative thinking and leadership qualities in your previous roles. You see—' He paused again for effect. His piercing blue eyes caught mine and I held my breath: here it was. He continued, 'I am considering you to be my new CEO.'

I was speechless.

'Me? CEO?' I managed to croak.

I cast a glance at Mr Gorgeous. He gave me a slow grin, which reached right inside so that, even in the face of this life-changing opportunity, it made my belly flutter. I pulled my attention from him, focusing on Mr King.

'Yes, Ms Canyon, you.'

Certainly I had the education, some of the experience – which I was glad Mr King had recognized – and the tenacity, but … CEO? It was quite a leap, to say the least. Not what I had prepared for. Could I really do it? My mind was a whir but, despite my incredulous state, I realized the possibilities. If I was being interviewed for the position of CEO, and got the job, then I would have access to every aspect of the company. It was like being handed the keys to the kingdom – and on a silver platter! I couldn't screw this up. All I could hope for was that I wouldn't be asked to do anything questionable, offensive or immoral. Lord help me.

I stood straighter, keeping my gaze on the upturned face of Mr King and doing my damnedest not to *feel* Mr Gorgeous oh so close to me. I stared directly into the old man's eyes and answered him.

'I accept.'

The smile that broke out over his face was brilliant. 'Most excellent.' His voice seemed to strengthen, and I heard a tiny bit of a Scottish lilt. 'The interview process takes the form of seven tests over seven days. I'll see how you perform during the tests and, if you do well, you will move forward with the interview process. Now then, I'm tired after all this activity. You will continue tomorrow. But first—' Mr King glanced at Mr Gorgeous and held out a slightly shaking hand. I watched as the sexy devil placed something in Mr King's palm, then he walked to the fireplace and pulled a silken cord, like they do on *Downton Abbey. Seriously? Calling for a maid?* 'A car will arrive at your apartment to pick you up at 7 a.m. sharp tomorrow. Be ready.' He held out a small card.

I took it and turned it over in my hand. It was black on one side, with an embossed 3D image of a diamond. The other side was blank. I ran my fingertips over the slightly raised diamond shape. 'What's this?'

He chuckled, and I glanced at him. 'It is your prize. Today was the first day, and you've passed the first test.'

'I have? What was the test?' No one had told me I was being tested. What if I'd failed? It seemed hardly fair, and only proved my point about how deceitful the company could be. I would have to be on my toes all the time. If I had been tested without knowing about it, that meant the next tests could be pretty much anything. I cast an accusatory look at Mr Gorgeous.

'I mentioned earlier that there are seven tests. This first one was courage.'

'Courage?' I parroted, and shook my head, more confused. 'What do you mean? All I did was show up for a job interview.'

'Your fear of flying and heights.' He paused and looked at me. 'You proved your courage by agreeing to get on the helicopter, despite your fear. You took the added risk of allowing yourself to be blindfolded for the journey.'

Again, I wondered how he knew about my fear of flying and asked him straight out. 'H-how did you know I was afraid of flying?'

This time, Mr King gave a mischievous smile. 'Do you really think I'd tell you that? I have my secrets, too, you know. I may be old and addle-brained—'

'That's a joke. You appear far from addle-brained.'

'I do, don't I?' He smiled again, and I felt a little out of my depth.

Before I could inquire further about where he had learned about my phobia, the door opened and a nurse came in. I wasn't the least bit surprised to see how lovely she was. Mr King had an element of Hugh Hefner about him.

'Regardless. There are some things best kept to yourself. So, I bid you goodnight.' He nodded at Mr Gorgeous.

'Sir.' He acknowledged Mr King and stepped to my side.

I felt the heat of his body, like being kissed by the sun. His delicious scent tickled my nose and I inhaled, almost sighing with appreciation. My earlier arousal for him came roaring back and my knees wobbled. I stood like a statue and clasped my hands in front of me. We watched Mr King as he was wheeled away.

'The helicopter is waiting.'

I lifted my head and drew in a quick breath at the sudden exhaustion that dragged at me. Emotionally, I was wrung out, yet thrilled to be one step closer to the goal I'd been working toward for so long. I could also thank Mr Gorgeous for keeping me on a knife edge of sexual arousal without any likelihood of easing the ache. So much had happened this evening. I glanced down at the card in my hand. It was a more glamorous version of a hotel key card and I wondered if it opened anything. I supposed I would find out tomorrow. I had accepted my assignment, much like James Bond, only I didn't have a license to kill. I ran my thumb over the surface of the card. It sparkled from the lighting overhead. I looked closer, and gasped.

'Is there something wrong?' asked Mr Gorgeous.

I shook my head. 'No, but when the light hit the card I swear it looked like there was a tiny diamond in the center.'

'Perhaps there is. You never know where Mr King is concerned. Anything is possible.'

I raised my eyebrows and tucked the card inside my Kate Spade, which was still slung over my shoulder.

When Mr Gorgeous took hold of my elbow, I started and looked up at him. He was tall, and handsome as hell. So mysterious and perfect. I didn't think I'd ever been so close to such a fine specimen of a man.

'Time to go,' he said, and I was lost in his eyes. My mouth

went dry and I moistened my lips. His gaze dropped to my mouth and lingered. Heat rushed through me and settled, as it had before, between my thighs. I bit my tongue to keep a moan from slipping out. This man, he had a way about him, and I liked it. I found the inherent confidence with which he moved unbelievably sexy, and he oozed power, it seemed to vibrate on the air, and oh Lord, the looks he gave me. I shivered with delight. Whatever spell he had cast, I'd caught it.

'You were my tester,' I said, talking to help cover up my reaction to him.

'What makes you say that?' His voice was hypnotic, sultry and terribly sexy.

I did like hearing him talk.

'How else would Mr King know about my, umm, fear of flying and heights?'

He glanced down at me, and I nearly died when I saw the subtle look of compassion in his eyes. 'It's nothing to be ashamed of, you know. We all have something we're afraid of.'

I couldn't have been more surprised by this moment of empathy. He showed me a glimpse of a man I hadn't yet seen tonight. I searched his face for more of the real him, but it shuttered before I had the chance. *Pity.*

'What are you afraid of?' I asked him, not really expecting an answer.

He smiled, and it was breathtaking. 'I'm not the one being tested.' As I thought: non-answer.

'So, why the secrecy, then?'

'Mr King explained that to you. Come, enough talk. Let's get you back home.'

I allowed him to lead me from the study, back into the stunning, grand foyer. This time, I noticed everything, and it distracted me from drilling him with more questions. The wide, arching stairs with their exquisitely crafted wrought-iron banisters and the vast windows either side of them, which probably offered fantastic views in the daytime. The house was so opulent, and all the furnishings were so breathtaking, it could easily have been a museum, much like the castles I'd visited in Britain which were now set up for tourists. Only this place didn't need to open itself up to tours to manage its costly upkeep. There was no shortage of money here.

'What a place to grow up in. I just can't imagine.' I hated that I felt jealous of Mr King's kids and grandkids, who probably had all the money in the world to do whatever they wanted with, and no worries. I'd made a decent living at my previous job, but now I had no income coming in I had to be careful with money. Charging to-die-for handbags to my credit card was a habit I had to try hard to break.

I thought I felt Mr Gorgeous's fingers tighten on my elbow and glanced at him. He was looking ahead, and there was no angry scowl or any expression at all on his face, but a muscle twitched in his cheek.

He led me to the door and, without a last look at the house behind us, we left the mansion. I let him guide me down a path with hidden lighting in the flowerbeds and alongside that illuminated the way and gave the shadowed flowers a vibrant colour. It was a magical night: stars overhead, surf in the distance and the smell of the air – such a sultry summer night. I would remember this for ever. It was too beautiful and momentous a night to forget. When we arrived at the helipad I was determined to climb into the helicopter on my own this time. Even if my skirt did show him some ass, an ass that belonged to me, an ass that only I was in charge of. No one else. Mr King said I'd passed the courage test, so yeah, he would soon find out just how courageous I could be!

I sat in the same seat as on the inbound flight, fastened the seat belt and turned my face from Mr Gorgeous, almost daring him to hand me the blindfold, but he didn't. I gripped my knees when the helicopter took off, tilted and then zoomed through the night sky. I didn't make a sound and closed my eyes. I'd rather not see out of the window – my courage was wavering a little – but no way would I show him that.

I felt him next to me, much like I had on the earlier flight. Then it occurred to me how important he was in this whole process. He'd be watching my every move, testing me. He was a visual distraction, but the fact that he was the main tester was an even greater one. I fueled that thought, despite being so drawn to him. He could be dangerous. He was clearly a bad boy, and he did it very well. There was definitely a sexual connection between us. And it was electric.

I did my best to ignore him until he saw me into the limo. It wasn't until I was safely locked behind my apartment door that I realized I hadn't given my address to the driver. Mr Gorgeous hadn't said a word either. This was all becoming very intriguing and unnerving. Perhaps they'd researched me just as well as I'd researched them. That was a very unsettling thought indeed.

* * *

The next morning I stretched luxuriously. I'd treated myself to a fairy-tale bed, kingsize; my mom had given me it before heading back to England and I'd splurged on pillows, high-thread-count sheets and a duvet that pluffed up around me like a cloud. I sighed, enjoying the sense of well-being that filled me. I couldn't quite figure out why I felt so good and tried to recall any dreams that may have been responsible. Nothing. I'd been dead to the world and glad of my loud alarm clock when it pulled me up through the deep layers of sleep. I turned to look out of the window and smiled: it was going to be a glorious day. The sun shone bright, casting golden rays over my bed, even at this god-awful hour. Six o'clock was a criminal time to wake up. I blinked and sat bolt upright. Today was the day. My first day at Diamond Enterprises. The first day of my infiltration into the organization through this bizarre interview process.

I was jazzed and rolled out of bed, curled my toes into the thick rug on the worn wooden floor. My apartment was an older walk-up. I was lucky to have found it; even with its cranky radiator heating and cramped space, I loved it. It was my private place. I did a few yoga stretches, thinking about the day ahead, and couldn't stop my excitement growing. Then I padded to the bathroom and took a shower to clear the cobwebs. I wasn't a 6 a.m. kind of girl, and I needed to get the fog out of my sluggish brain.

I saw my Kate Spade bag, which I'd left last night on my antique dresser, and smiled. It reminded me of Mr Gorgeous.

My heart tumbled a bit when I thought of him, and I had to catch my breath. That man was sex on a stick. I'm sure, under normal circumstances, he would have been the first thing on my mind when I woke up; instead, I was already consumed by thoughts of Diamond. Even so, a throbbing warmth started up between my thighs, shocking the hell out of me.

I played the events of the previous night over and over in my head as I got ready: the secretiveness, the deception they used to get me to the interview, Mr King justifying it – and, for a brief moment, I had been excited about it, thinking that perhaps his reasoning had made sense . . . at first. Now I could see the flaws – or was I just jaded? I had accepted his offer. So that meant I was committed. I was a woman of my word. Yet now, in the light of day, I was having second thoughts.

While I'd been on board with the whole CEO idea at the time, now I wasn't so sure. All the hard work I'd put into preparing for my interview for the job as executive assistant hadn't resulted in what I thought it would. It had opened the door to so much more. I knew I could do the assistant job without any difficulty. But could I handle the position of CEO? That was huge. So much responsibility.

Plus, was Diamond the kind of company I wanted to be CEO of? *CEO!* But it was a company with questionable leadership. With a lying executive team that went right up to the owner. I reminded myself that this was why I was doing this. To knock down that ivory tower and expose the lies. My original goal of becoming an executive assistant would've given me access to the documents I wanted, but being CEO would open up a whole new world of possibilities. I wiped the steam from the mirror and combed my fingers through my hair. I looked at my reflection and tried to decide if I'd be able to continue to look at myself in the mirror without shame if I took the job as CEO because, no matter how you looked at it, I was being deceitful as well, albeit for justifiable reasons of revenge. On a positive note, I would have the power to change the company. Make it better, fire all the lying executives and bring the company out into the light.

But if it all went wrong, then what? Plus, if anyone ever found out who I was I would be out on my ear, just like my dad. It would all be over.

I shook my head. I was having a difficult time digesting last night. It was surreal.

I finished getting ready and went from my tiny bathroom, grabbing my purse on the way, to my slightly larger living-room-and-kitchen combination. It depressed me for the first since I'd moved in here five years ago. My apartment would have fitted into the foyer of Mr King's home.

As I left the apartment, I paused and turned back to gaze around the little place I called home. The shabby-chic decor, filled with little treasures I'd found at flea markets and garage sales and then refurbished myself, was where my heart lay. Absolutely nothing like that big mansion on the cliff. But I swallowed the lump in my throat and pushed down my self-doubt. Hell, I knew I could do this! The flutter of excitement in my belly made me nervous. I was okay with that. After all, I'd passed the first test even without any inkling I was being tested.

Would participating in the next tests mean I would have the chance to see Mr Gorgeous again? Hopefully, at least six more times. *God bless the small miracles if it did!* He would be a temptation, and I knew he would be so hard to resist. It would be way too easy to get distracted or, worse, fall for him. My life was too complicated at the moment for there to be room for a man.

I sighed and pulled my door shut carefully, locked it, then walked down the two flights – that's right, no elevator – and out into the early-morning sun. It was going to be a hot day. I felt the humidity already and again I was glad of my short hair-cut rather than my long red curls.

I stood on my pretty tree-lined street and looked up and down. It wasn't long until a car pulled up alongside the curb. I checked my watch. Dead on 7 a.m. Part of me hadn't been entirely sure a car would pick me up. Perhaps the night before had been an elaborate joke to amuse a dying old man. But there it was. Long, sleek and shiny. I shuffled backward on the side-walk, putting distance between me and the car which would lead me to a destiny I'd been thinking about since I'd woken up. No matter how hard I tried, there was no way I could avoid this next step. Could I?

The back passenger door swung open, and I held my breath.

Was Mr King in the back? No, that wasn't likely, given how frail he'd been last night. So who was it? I saw the outline of a man's leg. A well-muscled thigh clad in black slacks and feet encased in shiny shoes. I immediately knew who it was. I didn't have to see his face to know I was lusting for this man. The mysterious Mr Gorgeous. He stepped out and stood tall in front of me. For the first time, I saw him in the brilliant light of day. He was shiver-worthy. I swallowed and blinked, moment-arily at a loss as to what to say. I knew I was presentable and ready for the first day of the interview process, but now I wish I'd given my appearance a little more attention. He didn't seem to notice anything, though. His eyes fixed on mine and it was as if he had reached across the space between us and touched me. My heart pounded like I'd just done a high-intensity work-out, and I couldn't catch my breath. Shit, who needed the gym with this sexy devil around to make your heart pound as much as it would after a cardio workout?

Here he was. That made happy. Right now, I didn't want to think about tomorrow, or if there would even be a tomorrow. I would have to pass today's test for that. I didn't quite know what to do, seeing him standing there in all his wonderful maleness. He draped his wrist over the top of the door and smiled. I melted. He spoke, and it was hard to focus; I was too caught up in my lustful haze to hear him properly. He didn't look away from me and raised his eyebrows.

'I'm sorry. Pardon? I-I didn't—' I tipped my head slightly and let myself get lost in his blue eyes. No point in telling him I hadn't heard a word he'd said because he was just too damn gorgeous to be legal. But I think he knew when he smiled and spoke again.

'Good morning, Ms Canyon.' His voice was just as silky and seductive as it had been last night.

I was doomed.

'Good morning.' That's about all I could muster. I tried not to croak like a toad. My body was betraying me; my muscles trembled and my blood pumped slowly, sensually. This was ridiculous, my reaction to him.

'Are you ready?' He smiled more widely and my heart faltered, and tingles spread throughout my body, only to centre low in my belly in a delightful flush. I drew in a soft breath and enjoyed the feeling.

'Well . . .' What could I say? I needed to sound as confident as possible, and the last thing I wanted was to show him how much he aroused me. I needed to summon the confidence I'd had the night before. It was difficult this morning – you know, waking up in the light of day, when everything seems so different? Words tumbled out in a hot mess. 'I'm not sure. I've had time to sleep on it, and I have questions. The tests, what are they?'

'I would be disappointed if you didn't have questions. As would Mr King. But time is moving on, and there is traffic. So, please, can we be on our way?'

He said exactly the right words, reassuring me, even if he didn't know he was doing it. I adjusted the strap of my purse on my shoulder.

'You're rushing me.'

'No, I'm not. This was the designated time. You were waiting, and I am here. On time.' He looked at the watch on his wrist. I craned my neck to see it; it looked like a Rolex. 'Your first meeting is at eight thirty. If we don't get moving, we'll be stuck in traffic.'

I didn't like him telling me what I had to do. Even if that's what he had been doing since we first met, last night.

'Is this what it's going to be like, then? You giving me

instructions? Telling me what I need to be doing and when? I thought CEOs ran their own schedule.' I tried to speak in a teasing tone but swallowed nervously when he looked at me from under his dark brows. That damned scar didn't look so intriguing right now. It looked rather menacing. I held my breath, wondering if I might have been a tad too cheeky.

'You're not CEO yet. Remember that,' he informed me. It was something I was well aware of. 'And if you complete all the tests and become CEO, you will have an executive assistant who will be running your schedule for you.'

'That's right. I'll be able to interview and select my own assistant, one who fits with my personality.' One who I can trust, who doesn't have allegiances to others in the company. 'And one thing I'll make sure of: no more helicopter rides in the middle of the night.'

He laughed out loud and stepped up the curb on to the sidewalk. I decided I could watch him all day. The way he moved transfixed me, and his laugh was deep, throaty and so delightfully naughty. 'It was hardly the middle of the night.'

'Close enough.' I put a hand on my hip and lifted my chin.

'If you say so.' He reached for me. A horn blared, piercing and long. I jumped, and he turned with a scowl.

A cabbie drove by, yelling out the window. 'Move it, asshole! This isn't a parking lot.'

Mr Gorgeous turned back to me and I let him take my arm, liking the way his fingers felt on me. He leaned closer and my breath froze in my lungs. 'And on that note, I think we should be going.'

'Well . . . I suppose.' He didn't let go of my elbow. This time, it was skin-to-skin, because I was wearing a cap-sleeved blouse. His fingers were firm, I felt his controlled strength, and the sparks flew. He paused, and I looked up at him. Had he felt it, too? He dropped his gaze to me and we seemed to freeze in time. It stretched out, with us simply looking at each other. Tingles raced along my nerve endings and I felt my nipples rise up. His gaze dipped and I was horrified to see that he'd noticed. But I couldn't move a muscle.

His eyes found mine again. He cleared his throat and gave me a gentle tug. 'Shall we get this day started?' I found myself beside the limo. 'Hop in.'

I pulled my attention from him and looked inside the darkened interior. It was like a living room on wheels. I sniffed, smelling the wonderful aroma of coffee and pastries. I nearly died.

'There's coffee?' I asked stupidly.

He nodded and raised one eyebrow. 'Costa Rican, and bagels with cream cheese and lox.'

'My favorite.' That sent my alarm bells clanging. Another indicator of the possibility that they knew who I was. But how? I had been careful with all my personal information. I'd chosen not to use my father's name, assuming my mother's maiden name instead. I reassured myself with the thought that I wasn't the only one in New York City who liked bagels with cream cheese and lox.

'I must insist that we get moving. Please.'

I chewed my lip and stared at him, then into the car. Everything was so utterly convenient. Events ticking along, carefully planned out. I was the one who was supposed to have everything under control. Yet I didn't feel like that at all. I groaned and straightened my shoulders. If I did this, then I had to grow some balls. I put my hand on the edge of the door and leaned into the car, lifting my foot to rest inside the limo. All I had to do was get in. Sit back and have breakfast. There was absolutely no reason for me not get in, especially since I'd given my verbal acceptance of what lay ahead the previous night. Oh Lord – *and* signed an NDA. I was bound to silence and to my word.

Climbing inside the limo with Mr Gorgeous would be a step along the path from which I would never be able to come back. My revenge plot would jump from the planning stage to being on the way to actually happening. There would be no turning back. The endgame of all my years of fueling the desire to right the wrong done to me and my family lay in front of me; it was through this car door, and then the ride that would take me into a new world. A world I had plotted against and readied myself to face for so long, it was as much a part of me as my own flesh and blood. And that scared the shit out of me.

MR TUESDAY

ASH TUESDAY

I got in. The delicious smell of coffee lured me. Limos, while very extravagant, are, however, a bitch for a woman in a skirt. I held my hand over my ass as I ducked inside the car, pinching the hem with my fingers so it didn't rise up and give Mr Gorgeous a view I wasn't prepared for him to have just yet. I slid across the leather seat and checked out the inside of the car. The aroma of coffee and freshly baked New York bagels almost had me drooling. A basket sat on the small ledge across from the seat and I lifted the edge of the linen that covered it. The bagels were tucked inside. I was starving and dying to have one but thought it best to wait until Mr Gorgeous was in the car with me.

I looked through the limo door. He stood outside, one hand on his hip. I noticed how long and tanned his fingers were. It made me wonder what he did when he wasn't working, then I speculated what he and Mr King had in store for me today. What test would I be assigned? I couldn't possibly even guess, so I didn't bother trying. I would know soon enough.

I took the opportunity to enjoy the view of him as he leaned against the limo. He was talking on his cell phone. His white shirt was neatly tucked into his pants, an expensive-looking belt hung around his hips and a slim silver buckle caught my attention. There was a small, diamond-shaped emblem on it. Corporate swag, I guessed. I couldn't help myself – I looked lower, and felt my cheeks flame. He was impressive, in all places. He wasn't hard to look at, that was for sure: slim hips, lean torso, wide shoulders and muscular arms which I could easily fantasize being held in. I had the urge to reach out and hook my fingers around his belt, and pull him inside the limo. The visual that accompanied it seemed so unbelievably real I blinked a couple of times to make sure my fantasy hadn't actually taken place.

His call finally over, he climbed in, and I watched as he folded his body into the seat next to me. The odd thing was that he had on no tie; perhaps it was in his pocket to put on later. The top button of his shirt was open, and his skin in the V was tanned. I could see a hint of dark chest hair, which I found terribly sexy. His presence filled the interior of the limo, and I felt him, almost as if we were touching. It reminded me of last night, when he'd helped me into the helicopter, his fingers at the small of my back as he guided me. This man was all male. A man's man that a woman could lose herself in. And if I was, or wasn't – depending on how you looked at it – careful, I'd be lost for sure.

He sat back and lifted his hips to slip his phone into his pocket. The movement accentuated his powerful chest and taut belly under the expensive cotton shirt and that wonderful place below the belt buckle that bulged, not so innocently. I squeezed my thighs together and imagined him between them, me cradling his weight as I ran my fingers over his naked back, thrusting my hips up to meet his. I blinked and brought myself back to reality in a hurry. Thinking about him in this very naughty manner made me want him as much as I wanted a bagel and coffee.

He sighed, and I imagined how he would sound in bed after a night of mind-blowing sex. I cleared my throat and pushed the seductive thoughts aside. I couldn't let myself fall under his spell. I continued to watch him until we made eye contact.

All thought fled from my mind when he looked at me.

'Help yourself.' He pointed to the cornucopia of breakfast fixings on the ledge in front of us. I noticed that the privacy glass was closed. We were sealed inside, alone. Together. I drew in a quiet, deep breath and tried to keep myself calm.

'Thank you,' I said to him. I was hungry and slid forward on the seat. I wasn't going to be shy about the food. 'Is this a regular morning for you?' I asked him as I selected a rather fancy-looking travel cup.

'Not generally, but when I take the limo, yes.'

I put in a generous dollop of cream and filled the cup with the most aromatic coffee I had ever smelled. 'I suppose it would be easy to get used to.' I glanced at him to see if he was going to be critical of the amount of cream I took with my coffee. Most people were, but it was one of my downfalls. I adore creamy coffee. With a mysterious smile, he watched me drink and said nothing, his eyes capturing my every move. I was breathless under his gaze.

'I suppose.' He wasn't much of a talker: I'd figured that out last night.

'Quite the whirlwind, what with the helicopter and, today, a limo. What else is today going to bring?' I asked him as I lifted the cup and took another sip. 'Mmm, this is so good.'

'Fresh roasted and flown in from Costa Rica this morning,' he informed me, and put his hands behind his head and stretched. I nearly choked on the coffee as I watched him. He was very at ease with himself, which helped me to settle down a bit. Even though I knew, from the outside, you wouldn't be able to tell I was nervous, my insides were quaking.

'Seriously? The coffee was flown in from Costa Rica this morning? That seems awfully indulgent.'

'If you have the kind of money Mr King does, it's no big deal to fly in anything you want.'

'Well, it certainly is good.' I sipped again, and then asked him, 'Can I pour you a cup?' I fully expected him to say no.

'I would like that very much. Thank you.' A man with manners. Even sexier.

I turned back to the ledge and, before I poured the coffee, glanced at him and inquired, 'Cream? Sugar? One lump or two?' I blushed. It sounded very seductive and suggestive . . . Perhaps I should have said, 'Coffee, tea or me?' I knew exactly what I would want him to choose. Me.

He chuckled. 'Like you, I enjoy a lot of cream.'

I gave him a wide smile. Finally, I had met someone with the same taste in coffee. I was happy that we had something in common, however small it might be. It made me feel more connected to him. I poured the cream in first and then the coffee. 'My mother always said the milk or cream must be poured into the cup first, so I guess I've adopted her preference.' I glanced at him and smiled.

'Does it make a difference?'

I shrugged. 'I think so.'

I leaned over and handed him the cup. His fingers brushed mine. We both had the same reaction, and drew in a breath, as if we were in sync. Our gazes met and held. I felt the same sizzle of excitement as I had the night before, and I wondered if he did. His expression was unreadable, but I could see something in his eyes. He was feeling it, too. Knowing that made me breathless. He seemed to lean a little closer to me, and I was drawn in to him. The silence stretched between us, but the chemistry was definitely there.

The car bumped over some potholes, breaking our trance. I blinked and sat back, as did he, and he lifted the cup to his mouth. I followed the movement and the way his lips pursed next to the rim of the cup. Every move he made was seductive, even if he didn't realize it.

'So, do you have a name?'

He looked at me, and I held my breath. After taking a slow sip of his coffee, he smiled, and I waited, dying to know what his name is. 'You can call me Mr Monday.'

I rolled my eyes. 'Seriously?' I murmured under my breath. 'Whatever – nothing about this is normal.'

'Pardon?' he asked.

'Never mind. I mumble to myself sometimes. Did you grow up in the city?'

He gazed at me, and I got the distinct impression he was trying to decide what to tell me. How honest he was planning on being. 'Yes, both here and outside the city, in the boonies. How about you?'

'Mainly in suburbia. You know, the typical childhood, playing Hide and Seek on the street, Red Rover and the like, with the neighborhood kids.' Taking another sip of coffee, I waited for him to answer. He looked out the window of the limo, then back at me. I swear I saw a mix of sadness and anger in his eyes.

'No, no typical childhood for me. Living in the city meant no street games like road hockey or playing with a bunch of kids. Time spent outside of the city, and in the country, was also very different.' He shrugged and didn't go on.

'A country boy?' I murmured. I liked that thought. 'Bet you

rode horses, chased bunnies and spent hot days in swimming holes.'

He smiled, and my heart swelled. 'It wasn't as idyllic as that. More along the lines of golf and sailing. But sure, country living had its benefits.'

'Did you have your own boat?'

'It belonged to the family, and I sailed on it from time to time.'

'I've never sailed. Have you ever raced?' I turned a little to face him, and he met my gaze, which gave me a thrill of excitement. 'Or gone on one of those impossibly long trips where you spend ages on-board?'

He shrugged but didn't look away from me. 'I've not circumnavigated the globe or taken part in the America's Cup, if that's what you mean.'

After waiting for more details, which did not come, I narrowed my eyes. 'Apparently, you belong to one of the rare species of men who doesn't like to brag about themselves.'

'Remember what you said last night? I don't talk much? Well . . .' He shrugged and smiled again.

'Okay, I get it. Off-limits conversation.' I decided to let it go. He clearly didn't want to talk about it. We all had secrets. 'Disappointing childhoods can leave nasty scars.' I wondered again at his scar and what it was that had permanently marked him.

He shot me a look, and I worried that I might've offended him. 'What makes you think that?'

I lifted one shoulder and frowned slightly before carrying on. 'Oh, I don't know. Just a feeling. I had some good and not so good times, so I understand.' I hoped he could see in my eyes that I truly did get it. I couldn't tell him why, of course, as it would blow everything. But I understood the hurt in his eyes.

'Maybe we both have some childhood baggage.' His gaze searched mine and we hung like that for a few minutes, looking at each other and maybe seeing each other behind the walls that surrounded us.

I drank some more coffee, deciding to change the subject. 'I could get used to this kind of treatment.'

'Well, don't get used to it too quickly,' he warned.

'Perhaps this is like the Last Supper?' He laughed once more, and I smiled, liking the timbre of his voice. 'What's so funny?'

'You *are* dramatic.'

'Hmph.' I gave him what I hoped was a sassy smile. I must have succeeded, because he chuckled again.

The car headed off the side street into the heavier traffic, reminding me of what lay ahead. The unknown. The only thing for certain is that I would have seven – well, six now, since I'd passed the one last night – tests to do, and I'll admit it: it had me on edge. Not knowing what to expect was killing me. I was a creature of habit with a burning desire of *needing to know.* That, mixed with the mood in the back of the limo, was a recipe for a beautiful disaster.

'It is tricky, you know, going into all this without knowing what is going to happen.'

'You'll manage.' Not quite the answer I was expecting. His cell buzzed, and I was delighted that he ignored it and kept his attention on me. This man was intensely focused and fascinated me to no end. Right now, it seemed he had no other interest except from me. I liked it.

'Where are we going?'

His deep voice filled the space between us. 'To the offices of Diamond Enterprises. Please, help yourself to some food. I know you like New York bagels.' Another bit of personal info they knew, which put me on edge again.

I placed my cup in the recessed copper cup-holder and took the basket, putting it on the seat between us.

'I don't really like to eat alone,' I told him, as I carefully spread cream cheese on half a bagel that I'd placed on a linen napkin. The basket housed all sorts of treats. A dish with ice sealed in the bottom so that delicate slices of smoked salmon remained chilled. Using a small silver fork, I lifted a piece and laid it across the cream cheese. There were even capers in a little bowl.

'Here you go.' I held the bagel out for him.

Watching him eat and drink morning coffee seemed almost domestic, like a morning ritual, and terribly intimate. I turned away and busied myself preparing the other half for myself, trying not to let my thoughts go down that road.

The bagel was yummy. I could easily have eaten the other half, since Mr *Monday* and I had shared one. *Like a married couple would.* I froze. I shouldn't be thinking such nonsense. He didn't look the marrying kind, and I certainly wasn't looking for a husband. I took a bite, trying to forget the ridiculous notion. Marriage and relationships were the last thing on my mind. Now, a bit of fun, a roll in the hay, a one-night-stand – *that* I could get down with. I had a priority project, and time was of the essence. There could be no complications.

I slid back on the seat again, finishing my half of the bagel and washing it down with a last gulp of coffee. If this tasty snack was any kind of example, working for Diamond would be a foodie's dream.

'So do you have anything to tell me? Any instructions? About what I'm supposed to do?' I waited quietly for his reply, watching him for any give-away facial expressions. He seemed relaxed. No expression at all. I was disappointed; I had hoped for *something.* He still maintained that air of mystery and ease, even after our bonding moment discussing our childhoods.

He slowly shook his head. 'Nothing. I'm not the one who will be giving you the tests. My role for today is to make sure you arrive at the office without any incidents. Your schedule has already been set up.'

'Schedule? Really? And you have no idea what my tests are going to be?'

His mouth lifted on one side, making his scar curve enticingly. 'You'll find out as everything progresses. Providing you pass each day.'

I blew out a puff of air. I wondered how deeply Mr Monday was involved in the deceit of the company. Had he been around when my dad was fired? I assessed his age to be late twenties, maybe early thirties, so unless he had started when he was a teen, he probably wouldn't have been there the same time as my father.

I pressed for more details, but he didn't budge. It was clear he was a vault and would give nothing away. I closed my eyes, letting my thoughts run around for a while. I could hear him beside me, much like last night in the helicopter. I'd been blindfolded then. Remembering made me shiver with delight, and I realized I wouldn't mind him blindfolding me again – for a very different reason.

'Will you be my guide throughout the day?' *And after?* I was hoping for more time with him. He was intriguing, and I wanted to have the opportunity to get to know him better.

He shook his head. 'No. That's not in the schedule.'

Alarm flashed through me. 'You're not staying with me?'

'No.' He gave me a long look, which threw me off kilter. I couldn't look away from him, and my mouth dried up.

I didn't know what to say. In order to pull this off seamlessly, I had to remain strong, confident and alert. We seemed to stall somewhere between chatting and staring. I felt magnetized by him, unable to focus on anything else. Maybe it was a good thing he wouldn't be staying with me. I needed to focus on my revenge, and he would be a sweet distraction indeed. It wasn't until the limo turned and the morning light suddenly dimmed that I was able to shift my focus. I craned my neck to see.

We drove into the shadow of the building. It was different in the daylight, not so ominous and glowering. It was actually quite bright and cheery and very upscale. I had to admit, it really was impressive. A renovated New York skyscraper that touched on the architecture of the new millennium. The way they'd built a private driveway through what had obviously been a main floor before the renovations was unique. It allowed cars to drive up and allow their passengers to disembark, just like valet parking. To think, I could be in charge of it all. The surge of excitement was exhilarating.

The doorman approached the car, in livery no less. I didn't wait for the limo door to be opened for me. I pulled the handle and pushed, swinging my legs out. I stood and looked at the gentleman waiting to assist us. Magnificent summer flowers cascaded in a riot from massive iron urns placed at each side of the entrance. It was perfection. The brass handles and glass panes on the doors were spotless. I stood to the side of the car and waited for Mr Monday.

'This way, ma'am.' The doorman held his hand out, indicating the front door. I glanced over my shoulder to see if Mr Monday was coming, but he was on his phone again. The doorman lifted his chin toward the revolving door, so I entered the lobby and waited.

The area dripped with wealth, much like the waiting area last night, only not as over the top. A security guard, who was all business, stood when I entered. He rounded the security desk, and I was stunned by his size. A mountain of a man, he seemed to fill the lobby. Behind him, I saw a bank of monitors, each with

smaller, framed videos running within them. This whole building was monitored. I nodded to myself, expecting no less.

'Stanley, good morning.' Mr Monday came up behind me and
greeted the security guard. I almost snickered but bit it back. He
so did not look like a Stanley. 'This is Ms Canyon. If you see her
wandering around lost, please direct her. Today is her first day.'

Stanley swung his dark eyes toward me, and I caught my
breath. He was an interesting-looking man, probably in his fif-
ties, yet very buff. He was impressive. 'Ms Canyon. Just dial 51
from any phone in the building and you get Security. We're
here to help.'

'Thank you, Stanley.'

'Ms Canyon, if you would step over here, please. You need to
sign in.'

I leaned against the security desk, putting down my purse,
and took the opportunity to scope out the security system. It
was tight, and I knew I'd have to be super careful when trying
to sneak around. As I placed the pen back on top of the security
ledger, I knocked my purse off and the key card fell out.

Mr Monday bent down to retrieve it. 'Don't lose this, or
you'll be stuck inside the building. Shall we?'

He took my elbow and – *zing* – there it was again. The *feeling* that made my legs wobble, my heart do double time. I
blinked and drew in a slow breath, against my better judgment
loving what he roused in me and doing my best not to show the
physical reaction he caused.

'Um, I have no idea where to go. Are there instructions or
something that will instruct me? I thought Mr Ki—'

'This way, Ms Canyon.' His fingers gripped a little tighter
and he led me past the security guard to a bank of elevators.

I looked up at him. 'What was all that about?' I asked. He'd
cut me off.

He turned and looked down at me. 'I thought you would have understood.'

'Understood what? I've had no instruction, no do's or don'ts, so how do you expect me to understand?'

'You're a smart woman – think about it.' His voice held a tense edge that reached up to his eyes. I guessed our bonding moment in the limo was history.

Had I failed already? Panic flared in me and I snapped my head away so he couldn't see my face. I started to think furiously. What had I said? The elevator door opened and he ushered me in. I watched as he put the card in the slot, the lights on the buttons lit up.

He smiled at me and handed the card over. I took it, our fingers brushing again. My heart leapt at the way his face softened. He was a complicated man, frowning one minute and smiling the next. God, he seemed to push all my buttons.

Jeez, my emotions were all over the map. I needed to keep things calm and steady. It really bothered me that, somehow, I'd upset him. I didn't like it. Not only because of the job, but there was something else. He had a different way about him which I liked; he seemed a deep and very complicated man. I wanted to know more about him. Would the opportunity ever present itself to explore this connection we had? *Oh, I hope so.*

He pressed the button for the twenty-eighth floor.

'One card, one floor.'

I understood what he meant. I tried to tell myself I shouldn't be annoyed by the limited access, but I was. My movement around the building would be severely restricted. I began to worry how I'd be able to find the information I sought: the restriction would be a serious problem but not *if* I became CEO. I needed to have free access. I deflated, knowing I was at a distinct disadvantage. It didn't matter how much pre-research I'd done; the company still had the upper hand. It would remain that way until I could infiltrate and bring this empire crumbling down.

'Is there anything at all you can tell me about today, or what I'll be facing?'

A bell chimed as the elevator arrived at the twenty-eighth floor.

He hesitated before stepping out and looking at me. 'Just trust in yourself.'

I nodded, not too sure what to think. Was he warning me about something?

It took all my resolve to control my nerves. So much could go so terribly wrong, and so quickly. My muscles betrayed me, starting to tremble, and I pressed my teeth together so they wouldn't chatter, lacing my fingers to keep my hands steady. The fabulous breakfast of Costa Rican coffee and New York bagel sat like a stone in my stomach. I had to swallow a few times to quieten the nausea that was bubbling up. I needed to get a grip. I followed Mr Monday through the floor lobby.

I looked around and, again, the decor wasn't lost on me. The doors were of honey-colored wood and ornately carved, with brass knobs and kick plates. Even the lighting was golden, subdued, and cast a rich glow over a pair of wing chairs. I followed Mr Monday.

'This way, please.' He took the card from me and slid it into the slot in one of the two doors in the lobby. The door swung open and he held it for me as I passed, enjoying my close proximity to him. I took a few deep breaths and loved being able to smell his wonderful scent.

This floor had an array of drafting tables and another large, wide table in the center of the room with rolls of paper at one end and rows of shallow, wide drawers underneath it. As we walked by, I saw that there were blueprints on the tables. This was the kind of setup you'd find in an architectural practice.

'What's this department?' I asked Mr Monday.

'Mergers and Acquisitions.'

'These look like drafting tables for architects.'

'We buy 'em and build 'em on this floor. Here.' He handed my key card back.

I followed him, doing my best to look as if I had a purpose. As if I were here for a reason and not just a fish out of water. As we passed some desks, I took the opportunity to look at any paperwork on them, trying to read file names or glean anything that might have any importance to my plan for revenge. Even though I didn't expect to find anything of interest out in the open, it didn't hurt to be vigilant and alert. I also tried to listened to any conversation among the staff, trying not to be obvious and remembering to smile. Most nodded, acknowledging me. Some watched me with curiosity; others ignored me. I didn't care either way, because I had my own agenda.

'Tess Canyon!' A booming voice echoed across the floor. I froze mid-step, stunned that someone had shouted for me. I glanced at Mr Monday, then looked around to see the expression on other people's faces. They didn't seem surprised in the least, simply looked up to see who Tess Canyon might be. The voice belonged to someone standing in an office doorway at the far side of the room. Mr Monday seemed to tense. Was there an issue between these two men?

Mr Monday scowled, and I swear I heard him growl.

The man raised his hand, and I could see his smile from where I stood, white teeth against his deeply tanned face. The man was huge, and seemed to get bigger the closer I got. He crossed his arms against an impossibly wide chest as he watched me approach. I shivered when his smile widened, and I couldn't help put a little extra swing in my hips. He was seriously built. This company clearly nurtured giant men. I stopped in front of him and was thrown a little off balance by the sexy gleam in his eyes, but I couldn't help comparing them to Mr Monday's crystal-blue eyes and intriguing scar. One day I would find out how he'd gotten it, I promised myself. I glanced at him swiftly, as he'd been awfully quiet, more so than normal, since getting out of the elevator.

We walked into the corner office, which had windows on each side and a completely awesome view of the city beyond. The man came forward to meet me. He had the broad body type of a college football player, the fabric of his designer suit perfectly framing his muscular torso. I looked up, and my whole vision was filled with him.

'Hello. Pleased to meet you, Tess.' He stuck out his hand, and I shook it, my hand engulfed by his. The first thing I thought of was . . . *no spark* . . . He glanced at Mr Monday and acknowledged him.

Yes, there was tension. I felt it.

Mr Monday turned to me. 'Ms Canyon, I'll leave you now. Enjoy your day.' And then he was gone. I was a little surprised at his abrupt exit, and it must have shown on my face.

'Pay no mind to him. He's an intense sort of fellow,' the man said. I faced him as his very dark eyes settled on me. 'Welcome to the think-tank floor of Diamond. I'm your Tuesday man.'

'Nice to meet you. Tuesday man?' I found that humorous and tried not to smile.

He laughed. It was big just like him, and very infectious, as I couldn't help the smile that curved my lips. I decided I liked him. He seemed genuine, and his mannerisms made me feel relaxed. I let out a nervous breath. He pointed to a chair. 'Please, make yourself comfortable. Today is Tuesday, yes? So call me Mr Tuesday.'

I sat and crossed my legs, keeping my fingers pressed to the hem of my skirt. His gaze flickered to my thighs and then to my face. I tried not to feel surprised, or show the sensual heat that fired through me. There may not have been any spark a moment ago, but the way this man looked at me was anything but dull. I watched him fold his super-tall body into the leather chair the other side of the desk, surprised that it didn't groan under his muscular physique. I drew in a quiet breath and made direct eye contact with him, hoping the flush on my cheeks wouldn't give me away. I raised my hand off my knee a little, about to pat my cheeks to cool them, but that would have been a dead giveaway.

'Well, then, Mr Tuesday, I suppose you know why I'm here. Which is more than I can say.'

He laughed again and leaned back in his chair, lacing his fingers behind his head. Every move he made was effortless, calm, and the feeling washed over me: *it's all good.* His dark brown eyes were expressive and drew me in. His easy nature was comforting, in contrast to the constant on-edge arousal I seemed to feel around Mr Monday. 'Everything has been rather whirlwind.'

'Yes, yes, I'm sure it has. The important thing is, you're here. Now, time's a-wasting. We have a lot to do. You have a lot to bone up on before we leave.'

'Leave? Where are we going?' I ask, rather startled that were going somewhere so soon after I had arrived.

'Yes. We're leaving, oh –' he pulled his phone out of his pocket and glanced at it – 'in about twenty-five minutes.'

'But where are we going?' I asked, starting to feel my alarm building back up. Where had the calmness I felt only moments ago gone?

The man was full of big smiles, and he rocked in his chair a little. It reminded me of when I was a little girl and my dad used to tip his chair on to its back legs when we were at the dinner table. It would drive my mom crazy. He would laugh, give a big smile and crash the front legs on to the floor, making both Mom and I squeal with surprise. Then he'd jump out of the chair and tickle us until we were laughing so hard we cried. How could a man like him, once so happy and loving with his family, become such a bitter shell of his former self? But Mr Tuesday had such an easy air about him, it helped me to relax again. 'Road trip,' he said, and laughed once again, before getting out of his chair. 'Come with me.' I noticed he picked up a file as he rounded the desk and exited his office. I followed him. He stopped suddenly and I stepped right into his back. 'Whoa, now. Okay?' He turned and grabbed my elbow as I stumbled.

'Yes, I'm good. But next time you decide to put on the brakes, you might at least give a girl a heads up.'

'Point made. Take this.' He handed me a folder. 'Find a desk around here that nobody's using and start reading this file. It should become self-explanatory as you go through it. Feel free to explore the floor if you have time, but I doubt you will. If you want a coffee, you might be able to sneak in a quick one, but remember, we're leaving here promptly – in twenty minutes now.'

I clutched the file. He strode off toward a group of people crowded around a drafting table. I could hear his loud voice, and I smiled at the way everybody laughed after some remark he'd made. Obviously, he was the boss. And a well-liked one, too – except, perhaps, where Mr Monday was concerned.

I found a desk one over from the window and sat down, glancing at my watch to judge how much time I had. Mr Tuesday seemed to have every minute accounted for. I tried to focus on the file, but kept looking at my watch. I turned back to the first page, which had got stuck to the inside of the folder.

It was a cover page. I didn't say much. But what it did say meant a whole lot.

'Acquisition Proposal. Northbrook Industries.'

Wow, Diamond wanted to buy Northbrook. I'd heard of them. They were a family-owned business, big in the tech world. Intrigued, I flipped over the page. I wondered what they had that Diamond wanted. I scanned the file, then checked my watch once more. I had no more time to read, and I didn't fully understand the situation, which made me feel at a huge disadvantage. I was suddenly panicked at how quickly the time was going. It was five minutes before ten. I snapped the file shut and dashed over to meet Mr Tuesday.

'Tess!' I had a feeling this man would be yelling for me all day, and I sighed. Once he caught my eye, he vanished through the doorway and I had to hurry to catch up with him. His energy left me breathless. How was I going to survive today, the way he dashed around all the time? When I finally caught up with him at the elevator, he asked, 'All set?'

'As much as I can be after a twenty-minute cramming session.'

He burst out laughing, not seeming the least bit concerned. 'Come on, then. You can read it over again in the car.'

Minutes later, we were roaring out of the city in his Porsche Panamera. It was an amazing car. I'd never seen anything like it. I was having a hard time believing everything that was happening to me since I'd walked into Diamond Enterprises last night. Here I was, flying through the city in a Porsche, heading to a mystery destination. This wasn't normal for me, to be so reckless and wild. I was beyond control now, out of my comfort zone. I had to try to regain control, though; otherwise, everything could fall to pieces. I decided to try to enjoy whatever lay ahead. It was just too bad I had to study the file, because it kept me from fully enjoying the ride.

'How about taking a few minutes to go over the deal?' said Mr Tuesday.

'I think it's going to take a lot more than a few minutes to familiarize myself with this.'

'I have faith in you, Tess.' He glanced at me, his dark eyes like chocolate – but was that a tinge of hardness in them? Maybe he wasn't all smiles and chuckles. I suspected he had an edge to him.

'As do I.'

He tossed his head back and let out a great, hollering laugh. 'Excellent.' He certainly did enjoy life. 'It's about an hour-and-a-half drive.' *Now, that was news.* 'I won't say anything while you're looking over the notes.' *Much appreciated.*

We fell silent for a while as we drove out of the city. I couldn't begin to guess where we were heading. I wanted to sit back in this luxurious car and enjoy the ride, but I had a file on my lap that was calling my name.

The folder was a lead weight on my knees. I knew I should open it. A shiver of alarm ran down my spine. Was I in way over my head here? I was beginning to wonder what I'd gotten myself into. I glanced over at Mr Tuesday. He was focused on the road, his large hands holding the steering wheel lightly. He must have felt the weight of my stare because he turned and gave me a slow smile. It was almost seductive, and I wondered if he was flirting. He was definitely attractive, and a tingle of awareness bloomed inside me. Since last night, I'd been thrown together with two sexy, attractive men, and my libido was on high alert. Every moment brought a new stimulation, whether it be mental, like from the unknown challenges of the tasks ahead, or physical, like the adrenalin rush that came from being a passenger in a speeding car. I was living on the edge. If life kept up at this rate, I'd be in sensation overload.

It certainly didn't feel like I was having a job interview any more. At least, not right now, as the wind blew in the window and my hair flew around my head, refusing to obey, no matter how many times I pushed it off my forehead. I felt my smile widen and my cheeks hurt from grinning so much. No, this certainly did not feel like an interview. If I didn't know better, I'd say I was on a date with this very sexy man driving an equally sexy car, taking us to an undisclosed location that could have a very, very exciting conclusion.

He brought me back to reality in a hurry.

'Are you nervous?' he asked, above the wind that screamed into the car.

I was surprised at his question. I didn't think I was nervous now, although I had been earlier. But maybe he could sense something in me. Perhaps he was just that kind of guy, in tune with those around him. I wasn't ready to be completely honest with him. I could leave myself exposed – and vulnerable – if I revealed how I was feeling, so I did my best to hide any hint of it. I wasn't going to do anything that jeopardized my chances at this job. 'Should I be? I asked instead. 'Why do I need to know about Northbrook?'

'We're on our way to a meeting with them, and your test will take place there. Don't worry, I'm sure you'll do just fine. I'll be there to back you up, if necessary.'

I let my head fall back against the seat. I turned my face to the window, loving the breeze, and let it blow away my nerves. I closed my eyes and enjoyed the moment. I had a great sense of anticipation and, even though I had no idea what to expect, I would make it my chance to shine. Mr Tuesday was having an effect on me, too. I was unable to put my finger on how, I just knew that he was, but I didn't want to delve into the reason right now, or anytime soon, because of the meeting ahead. I needed to be on point. At the top of my game. So much was riding on it.

One thing I would admit: all the excitement was exhilarating. I liked it. The growing anticipation of the unknown, the mysteries that lay ahead. Every step I took kept me barreling forward in an almost reckless manner. This wasn't like me. All I could do was hang on for the ride and hope I didn't crash and burn. Could it be that I'd been so wrapped up in my revenge plot I'd lost sight of the world around me, forgotten to live, have fun? And that this thrill was the excitement I needed to shake me up and make me see what I'd been missing? Maybe, deep down inside, I wanted to live on the edge like this. I'd never been in this sort of situation before. It forced me to look at life from so many new and different angles.

I flipped open the file and studied it. It was hard to concentrate, but I had to. So much depended on my ability to grasp the situation, and so I drew on my research skills to find more information. I pulled out my phone and started doing some searches on Northbrook. I wanted to be fully prepared, just in case I got thrown a curve ball later. I found some very interesting press releases. One in particular caught my attention. Northbrook had developed a certain computer chip, and it was easy to guess that this was what Diamond wanted from the company. Northbrook claimed the chip would revolutionize the world of communications. I nearly snorted: a lot of inventions claimed to be revolutionary but not many were. I was leery. Diamond wasn't the only company mentioned as being interested in this new technology, and a comparison was made to a competitor with a similar chip. The information was rather vague in the press release and no amount of searching could turn up any more in-depth data. Even the best librarian couldn't make information magically appear. I'd have to fly by the seat of my pants on this one. I tucked the info away in my mind in case I needed it later. When I looked up, we were no longer in the city.

'Do you feel comfortable with the situation after reviewing the file?' Mr Tuesday asked.

'Yes, I think so.' I stretched a little on the seat to ease the crick that was beginning to settle in my neck. I turned my head and looked at him. I wondered why he had a frown on his face. Was it me who had put it there?

'It's not good enough to *think* you do. You have to *know*. Be absolutely *positive* you do. It's imperative that this deal goes through, and being well prepared will be critical in closing the deal. This is your test. So perhaps you should continue reviewing the document. There are at least another twenty minutes until we get there.'

Was he chastising me? I didn't like it, since I was doing my best to get a solid understanding of the details. Not easy to do when you're arriving late to the party. I sighed and opened the file on my knees to study it. Again.

I practically had the proposal memorized five minutes or so before we reached our destination. The background information gave me a good handle on Northbrook.

The supporting documents thoroughly showed the positive impact an acquisition of this nature would have on Diamond Enterprises. Even though it wasn't my area of expertise, I did have some background in negotiation. I'd worked in a male-oriented environment before, and I had learned to hold my own, especially around budget time. I wouldn't let a bunch of good old boys and their outdated ways be an obstacle in my path. I could be jumping to conclusions – maybe Northbrook's team wouldn't be a testosterone fest – but I wasn't going to bet on it. The corporate world was still very much a man's world. I closed the folder and looked out of the car window. We were way out of the city, God's land.

We drove along a beautiful country road, winding and hilly. I watched the scenery zip past and, when Mr Tuesday geared down, slowing the vehicle, I sat a little taller. We had to be almost there. He turned on to a tree-lined lane. The canopy over the pavement cast dappled golden light all around us. Neatly trimmed grass lay on either side, leading back up to the forest. I almost expected a deer to jump out, or a rabbit to scurry by. I sighed. I was glad when Mr Tuesday slowed down a little more and opened all the windows. The fresh air was rejuvenating. I began to feel more confident, even though I continued to be a tad nervous about what lay ahead.

We continued down the road, through the forest, for about a mile. On the left, a small driveway veered off to a parking lot, barely visible through the trees and full of cars. A lovely rustic building was a bustle of activity, golfers getting their bags of clubs ready and staff moving around in golf carts and strapping the bags into them. The car rounded more gentle curves and hills until we came into a clearing that stole my breath away. The rolling fairway sloped down toward a clear waters of the lake. Golfers were teeing off on the green we passed. I couldn't take it all in quickly enough. Then we drove over an arching, single-lane bridge with a low stone wall on either side, and under another canopy of trees, until we emerged at the beginning of a long drive that led up to the main clubhouse.

'My God! Look at it!' I said.

'Nice, huh.' Mr Tuesday looked around. 'Welcome to the Rockwood Country Club.'

'This is way more than nice.'

'We decided to hold the meeting here. We all felt it best to keep the negotiations quiet, away from Northbrook, to avoid starting any unnecessary rumors.'

I agreed. 'That makes sense. But what a place!'

'It sure is. We use it on and off for our executive retreats, employee workshops, or anything else that we feel the need to host away from any of our business offices. We even built a helipad here.'

His casual mention of the helipad brought last night's trip rushing back, but I refused to let my mind go down that rabbit hole.

I'd definitely been dropped into the jet-set lifestyle, what with the helicopter flights, fast cars and, most importantly to me, specially ordered coffee. A girl could get accustomed to this.

'Is it used often?'

'Actually, it is. For business lunches and dinners, and we host a charity golf tournament every year, among many other events.'

'I see. So it's kind of like a Diamond Enterprises exclusive venue.'

'I guess you could say that.' He paused. 'You do realize this is a very important acquisition for the company? Northbrook's ownership team seems to be waffling. A few are ready to sell, but more are hesitant about our offer. I think they want more money, but we've already gone as far as we want to. So that means you will have to be creative.'

'Well, if it's that important, why am I coming in to close the deal?'

'You're exactly what we need.'

I think my mouth must've dropped open. It was the first time he'd said anything that showed his faith in my ability.

He'd been casually supportive up until now, but to hear him clearly state his confidence in me was an added pressure, and it made me nervous. I had to believe I could do it, that I could gather up my courage and charge into this unknown world of helicopters, gourmet coffee and facing down an opposing negotiation team. *But what if I couldn't?* A seed of self-doubt took root. I shook my head slightly to push it away and prayed for the best. I glanced at Mr Tuesday and chewed my lip as we approached the clubhouse.

'I hope I can live up to both our expectations.' I shifted on the seat so I could look at him, and crossed my ankles. 'Since this is my responsibility, I will do my best to seal the deal.' My true reasons for excelling couldn't be mentioned and, damn it, each test was just one more barrier which, if I failed, would keep me from digging into Diamond's records. If I didn't succeed, I would be no closer to finding the documents I sought than I was months ago. Right now, I had six more chances – *opportunities* – to find the documentation I needed, opportunities I hadn't had before. 'It would help if I knew what Northbrook's biggest concern is.'

'They want money.'

'Did they give any reason for not being happy with this deal?' I was beginning to wonder if some important information was being left out. Perhaps to sabotage me. Or to make me work harder for a solution.

'Northbrook has been a family business for many, many years. They've grown too comfortable and arrogant. But they're under financial pressure now. So when they approached us, we jumped at the opportunity.'

'I see. But that should be in this file.' I tapped my finger on the cover of the folder. 'It's not. How am I supposed to do the best job possible with only limited information? Anything else I should know?'

'It says they are financially strapped in the file.'

'Yes, I saw the report, but a bit more detail would have been helpful.'

'They have always been proud to produce top-notch products, but they're unable to maintain that level of excellence in their current financial circumstances. Some of their products are failing quality-assurance tests. We've been back and forth a few times on the negotiations and have finally reached an agreement.' He pointed at the file. 'But we need their signatures to close the deal.'

I thought about it. 'That would be distressing, not being able to provide the service customers have come to expect. It puts both your reputation and your brand at risk.'

'Exactly why this acquisition is good for both parties. It helps us, as the new chip technology they've developed is what we need to take us to the next level in our business. Then we'll be ahead of the pack. We'll be at the leading edge, establishing the future positioning of Diamond in the world marketplace. For Northbrook, it helps replenish the family fortune without diminishing their reputation.'

I was wondering if that was really a major concern for anybody, the reputation angle. Scum of the earth as Diamond was, I'd met Mr King, and he'd given me every impression that he loved his company. I highly doubted he'd want anybody to come in and wrest it away from him, only to split it up and sell it off in parts. Nothing in the file had led me to believe that he'd do such a thing to someone else. There was more to this.

'It doesn't say anything in the file, so what does Diamond intend on doing with the company? Is the intention to keep the technology and sell off the rest of the assets?' Mr Tuesday's head snapped around to look at me. Had I hit on something?

'No, that's not the intention. It's a good, viable business. It just needs a helping hand, a general manager to oversee the daily operations, and an increased focus on research and development. If it can't do that, and there's no light at the end of the tunnel where our goals are concerned, then, yes, it is entirely possible that this business will be shut down and dismantled, but we won't know that until we're given an opportunity to turn it around. That's the challenge, and where you come in.'

'Challenge?'

'That's right. Even though we have the bones of an agreement struck, they're still a little antsy about the whole thing and we could walk away with nothing. Close this deal. This is what you need to accomplish today. Negotiate your heart out.' He gave me his smile again.

'How much room do I have for negotiation?'

'Let me put it this way: we want this company very badly, but they've pushed us close to the upper limit of our budget. There is still some room, though, and I'll be there to rein it back if it goes too high.'

That meant a blank check, in my opinion, but I didn't say anything further, deciding it was best to keep my thoughts to myself, even though they were flying around inside my brain like bats trying to get out of a cave. They were throwing me to the lions, I could see that. Would I survive? I opened the file again. Even though we had this meeting today and they'd made their final offer, I now understood what was at stake. I fingered the check stapled to the inside of the folder. I knew what it was for. It was to show good faith on our part. To come in with a $250,000 check, non-refundable to boot, showed how serious Diamond was about this purchase.

The inside of the country club was just as stunning as the outside. I stood in the grand foyer and took everything in.

Wood-clad walls rose to an open, second-story lounge, a railing running its length. There was a lovely restaurant and another lounge on the other side of a floor-to-ceiling stone fireplace. I could imagine cozy winter nights, cuddled up by the fire. 'Wow!'

'Do you like it?' Mr Tuesday asked, coming up behind me and resting his hand on my shoulder. I stiffened a tiny bit but forced myself to relax.

'I do. I don't think I've ever been anywhere so beautiful.'

Behind the fireplace, pillars that appeared to be made from actual tree trunks soared to the vaulted ceiling and let the wonderful light from the high windows pour in. Plants added peaceful greenery to the rustic room. Beyond the flagstone patio outside was a series of docks with speedboats and pontoon boats moored in them. There were even two float planes tied up.

'People actually fly in here?'

'They certainly do.'

'This place is a gold mine.'

'You're right, but we need to get going now. I did make reservations to grab a bite to eat after our meeting.'

He seemed pleased with himself after relaying that bit of news. As was I. I wanted more than anything to spend a few hours here.

'Well, since you know the way, please lead, and I'll follow. How about we get this meeting behind us?' My nerves spiked as I followed him to the conference rooms. It held the same ambience as the lobby and the restaurant. I truly loved this place.

Five men waited by the coffee bar that had been set up near the window in the room that had been booked for our meeting. They appeared very intense, and my heart filled with dread. When they saw me, a couple of them looked surprised. I wondered if I would be taken seriously. I had to step up my game from the minute I entered the room. It was important that these men respected me, considered me an equal. So I walked around the table, pulling from my memory the photographs I had studied in the file, matching names to faces.

'Good morning, gentlemen. As I'm sure you've been told, I'm Tess Canyon.' I held my hand out and walked up to the first man, who I knew was the patriarch of the family. 'Mr North, it's a pleasure to meet you.' He took my hand, shaking it firmly. 'Thank you so much for coming to this meeting with us.' I greeted the rest of the men in a similar way, and instantly knew that I had gained at least a small measure of respect. It was a start.

I chose to sit with my back to the window. Mr Tuesday took a seat beside me. The five men sat across from us. This positioning allowed me to see their faces very clearly. The outside light came in through the window and cast Mr Tuesday and me into shadow, giving us the slight advantage of being able to see their facial expressions better than they could see ours. I put the folder on the table but didn't open it.

'I see we are very close to an agreement, and I'm very confident that we will be able to finalize a deal today.' I decided to take the direct approach and not allow them the opportunity to back out. I needed to address them on a personal level, not proceed aggressively, which was what I felt most men did.

Fingers crossed it would work.

'I'd like to assure you that Diamond Enterprises is very excited about this acquisition.'

Then Mr Tuesday surprised me by barging in on the conversation. 'Gentlemen,' he said.

I'd thought he was leaving this to me. I glanced at him, and he gave an imperceptible shake of his head. So I sat back in my seat and waited to see what was coming next. Had I done something wrong? I'd barely gotten started.

I was surprised by his businesslike attitude. It was a complete contrast to his manner of a happy, carefree man he had shown me earlier. 'It's time we come to a final agreement. We've been back and forth on this often enough. The deal should be signed today.'

I was a little shocked by his harsh opening words. I flicked a gaze at the men at the other end of the table and saw them bristle. I hoped he knew what he was doing. The expression on the faces of the men across from me told me all I needed to know. They weren't happy. I looked at Mr Tuesday to see if he saw it as well. If he did, though, he gave no indication.

'I'm not sure I like your tone.' Mr North sat up taller in his chair. He looked as if he was ready to stare Mr Tuesday down.

'I'm sorry about that, Mr North, but we've been here before. This is the last time. We both know that you need this deal.' I understood the veiled threat Mr Tuesday was making: he was referring to the financial instability of the company.

Mr North stood up. He had a cane, and stamped it on the ground. For just a moment, he reminded me of Mr King in his wheelchair. I gritted my teeth and glanced at Mr Tuesday. His lips were moving, but I wasn't hearing the words. Blood rushed through my ears, drowning everything out. How could he be so callous? And why was he following these tactics? It could be a big, irreversible mistake. And I was supposed to be the one doing the negotiations. I looked back at the men. They were getting restless. I sensed that they were about to leave. I had to do something and, when they all began to rise, I knew it was now or never.

I put my hand on Mr Tuesday's forearm and squeezed. I shushed him, but so that only he could hear.

I spoke loudly. 'Please, Mr North. Have a seat.' I kept my voice firm and made it clear there was no room for argument.

'Give me an opportunity to talk to you.' The old man looked at me. I think he was taken aback by the tone in my voice, and it gave me the confidence I needed. I had him now. When I indicated his seat with my hand, he sat down.

'Thank you,' I said to him. 'I'm unsure why you're hesitant about this deal. After all, it was you who approached us. We are offering a good price for your company, and it is money we both know you need.' I barreled on, giving no opportunity for any interruption. 'I want you to realize just how important it is that you sign the paperwork today.'

The men were silent, and watched me, skepticism written all over their faces.

'We need to get this deal closed today. Both of us do.' I carried on: 'Northbrook will become a subsidiary of Diamond Enterprises. Diamond Enterprises will be recognized as the new owner of Northbrook. We have a deadline of midnight tonight for all the appropriate papers to be filed. If you fail to sign the agreement by that time, we will withdraw the substantial offer we have made. Are you prepared to go back to your board and explain that?'

The men looked at each other, then leaned together, whispering. Mr North gave a slight tip of his head, which I matched with a very small smile to myself. We might just have hit the nail on the head.

I pulled out the check and laid it on the table. 'This is to show that Diamond Enterprises is acting in good faith, and to sweeten the pot. We are ready to move forward with this agreement.' I slid the check across the table, and it grabbed the men's attention. The sum of $250,000 was nothing to scoff at.

'Should Diamond Enterprises choose to back out at any point, you can keep the money,' I said. The men looked at Mr Tuesday, and I felt him stiffen slightly beside me. He'd been quiet as soon as I'd started talking. I looked at him to see what he was going to do. Was he going to assume control? I waited.

He leaned forward and put his hands on the table. I was excited, and trembled inside. If he agreed with me, then I had a gut feeling the deal would be done. I had to hand it to him, Mr Tuesday exuded power, and I realized in that moment how attractive power was. I watched him, my breath shallow as I became turned on by his mannerisms and by his appearance. I held my breath, waiting to see what he was going to say. He laid his palms flat.

'I'm in full support of Ms Canyon,' Mr Tuesday said. It was as if the men across the table exhaled collectively.

I let out a breath. Mr Tuesday looked at me, and I saw a mischievous glint in his brown eyes. I blinked and furrowed my brows, not having expected to see that look in his eyes. Had he set this up to see how I would handle it?

I turned my attention back to the men at the other end of the table. 'Do we have a deal?'

Mr North spoke. 'Ms Canyon, we appreciate your candor.'

'Mr North.' I looked at the older man. 'You are the founding father, and I can certainly understand any concerns you may have about your brand. As such, we'd be delighted to have a family member sit on the board. But I do need to ask: do we have a deal?'

The room fell silent, everyone waiting for Mr North to give his answer.

'No, Ms Canyon, we don't.'

Quick. Think. 'I'm sorry, Mr North. I don't understand.' I kept my voice a monotone.

Mr North's son leaned across the table, pinned the check with his finger and slid it toward him. I nearly leapt across the table to retrieve it. The man gave me a very satisfied sneer. It was then that I realized I'd misjudged this group of men. They were money hungry.

'It's simple, Ms Canyon. We feel our company is worth more than the offer on the table.'

I felt myself getting angry. They were playing games. Suddenly, it dawned on me what they were gunning for. I smiled to myself.

'Mr North, the negotiations have gone along fairly smoothly. We agreed on a fair market value, and this is specified in the contract.' I tapped the folder in front of me. 'Not to mention the added bonus that your son has had no hesitation in taking.'

'We know the company's value. We employ top-notch scientists in demand around the world, creating cutting-edge technology. Their knowledge is a first-rate commodity. Our commodity.'

'If you are in demand worldwide, then why are you sitting here with us?' I asked. 'And haggling over a price? If there were other interested parties, we would be in a bidding war.'

I thought I heard Mr Tuesday make a sound. Maybe of surprise. To heck with him right now, I thought. He'd chosen not to inform me of the basis for this contract. I'd had to find it out on my own – and lucky that I had.

I stood and rested my hands on the table, leaning over, hoping to achieve some element of intimidation. 'This is unacceptable. We are fully aware of the technology Northbrook brings to the table. And of one product in particular.' I wasn't going to mention the chip outright. The men across the table turned ashen. *Bingo.*

I would not let the men intimidate me. So I stood back and walked around the table. My knees felt weak, but I ignored that as I reached over Mr North's son and picked up the check. 'This was given in good faith by us. I'm very aware that this new technology which you claim will be revolutionary is as yet unproven. I also know that your competitor EGL Communications has similar technology. Perhaps Diamond Enterprises should see if they'd be more willing to cooperate.'

'You can't take that!' Mr North's son exclaimed.

I held it up and gave him the iciest smile I could muster. 'I just did.' I went back to my side of the table, put the check back in the folder, and closed it. I remained standing. Let them digest that!

The men looked at each other, and I thought I might have seen looks of concern on their faces. I let them stew before I said anything else.

'Now, a fair deal has been struck.' I pointed to the folder. 'That check is still in play, just so you know, providing the contract is signed off today. But before you say anything, there is a condition.' I was wading into unfamiliar territory here.

'What is it?' Mr North asked.

'We want your lead researcher and executive team to remain on board for the transition.' I knew that people were the core of any organization and that to have these key members remain was essential. I knew it was somewhat unconventional to be buying employees along with the technology, but if I could pull this off it would be a huge coup.

'Then, to be blunt, Ms Canyon, you need to add to that check in the folder. If you do, I will close the deal now.'

'I'll be blunt right back, Mr North. No. We will not add anything. The amount is finalized. You are getting above market value for your company and we are assuming the company's debt. You have no other offers on the table. Our offer stays as it is, or we will call it off and go with EGL.'

'A moment,' Mr North Jr said.

The men stood up, walked to the far end of the room, and conferred. I was holding my breath, and did not look at Mr Tuesday. I didn't need to see any sort of disapproval on his face. My task was to close the deal, and that's what I was trying to do.

The men came back, and Mr North stepped forward. 'You are tough, Ms Canyon, but you have a deal. Show me where I have to sign – and I'll be taking that check back.'

I was flying higher than a kite. Northbrook's team signed the contract, we exchanged the required paperwork, and they marched off. I caught an odd look passing between them, but I chose to ignore it and focused instead on my sense of triumph. I'd done it!

I nearly jumped out of my skin when Mr Tuesday boomed, 'That was impressive.'

'Thank you. I'm relieved it worked out. For a moment there, I thought they were going to walk out and leave.'

'I did, too. But you handled it pretty well.'

'Did I?' I pinned a look on him. 'I picked up on your vibe – that you supported me – and I took a risk.'

'A great risk, too. You got more for us in the deal – the researcher and the executive team. I'm impressed. I didn't even mind that you put your hand on my arm to shut me up.' He gave me that big, wide smile I'd come to expect from him, and I felt all the anxiety that had been building up in me over the last few hours slip away.

'I'm glad you didn't mind. I felt that it was starting to go off the rails, and I had to go with my gut.'

'I'm glad you did.'

'We should be heading back into the city now and get these papers to Legal before the clock strikes twelve. I don't want these yahoos to play any more games. So I'm afraid we're going to have to cancel our reservations.'

I agreed. 'That's disappointing, but I understand. Maybe another time. I'm so relieved that things worked out.' I was proud of myself, and of how I handled a situation that was clearly going downhill fast.

I followed him from the conference room and through the building. I was sad I couldn't stay here a little longer, but I understood the need to get those papers back and finalized. I wanted to make sure they were filed before end of business – forget midnight – and the best way to do that was to hand them in myself. Once they were given to Legal, they would ensure that there was no reneging on Northbrook's part. I was concerned that, if there was another company interested, as they had stated, there could be complications. I'd seen a supposedly done deal go south before, when an exploration company had made a handshake deal with one of my old company's engineers. When the exploration company backed out of the deal, he'd nearly lost his job over it. They'd gone to a competitor, and our company had lost hundreds of thousands – if not millions – of dollars in that debacle. I wasn't about to let something like that happen on my watch.

We walked down a private path, away from any curious eyes. I figured it was to stop any potential wagging tongues. Someone might see us and the Northbrook men leave and put two and two together.

I took in a big breath, loving the scent of the forest.

'I think I can manage things from here.'

A deep and oh-so-familiar voice came from behind us. I nearly stumbled, and a shiver rippled through me. I looked over my shoulder. It was Mr Monday. My heart beat rapidly.

Mr Tuesday glanced at me, and then behind him. 'Hey there. I wasn't sure if we'd be seeing you today. I was told you might not be able to make it out here.'

'And yet here I am,' said Mr Monday, his ice-blue eyes on

me. I searched for any kind of expression in them. Disapproval was the first thing I looked for, but I didn't see any inkling of it. I was relieved. Did he know about the deal I'd struck? Would he be pleased or annoyed?

He checked his phone.

'You're always looking at your phone,' I stated, and cringed a little when 'phone' came out harshly. Damn Mr Monday for showing up and tipping my world further off its axis.

'This time, I'm checking to see how late we are and if we can make up any time. There is a deadline for the paperwork, no?'

'It's still hours away.' I wavered a bit, the emotion of the day and now seeing him so unexpectedly overwhelmed me, and I reached to steady myself. Mr Monday shot his arm out and snaked it around my waist. Mr Tuesday reached to help at the same time. He hesitated when he saw I was already in good hands. I raised my fingers and patted my cheek.

Mr Monday assisted me to the valet parking. 'I can walk,' I told him.

'I'm sure you can, but you're taking too long.' I hmphed and stopped resisting. I kinda liked his arm around me. This was the closest I'd been to him, and I was enjoying his muscled hardness. I glanced up, and he was looking over at Mr Tuesday, who was calling for his car from the valet.

Mr Tuesday walked back to us. 'So what's the plan now?'

Mr Monday looked at me. 'You have a choice.'

'I do?'

He nodded. 'Yes, you do. You can either ride back with him, or you can come with me.'

'Why?'

'You know how long it'll take in the car. But I have another mode of transportation that is much quicker. The business day is not over yet. And as you know, time is of the essence.'

I was confused for a moment. 'I know that. But how can we get back to the city more quickly? We'd have to grow wings and fly.' I giggled at my sense of humor. Also, I was feeling a bit punchy after my victory.

'Exactly. I have wings.' He pointed his thumb in Mr Tuesday's direction. 'He only has wheels.'

My heart dropped. 'Do I have to go on another helicopter ride?'

'That's up to you. But you have to make a decision fast.'

I looked at Mr Tuesday, and then at Mr Monday. One had a fabulous car and the other a scary helicopter which I absolutely hated. I pressed my lips together and looked from one man to the other. I knew exactly who I was going to go with.

Time flew, literally, in the helicopter. I couldn't believe I'd chosen it over the car – it wasn't as if I'd gotten over my fear of plummeting to my death since the night before. After making a quick stop to file the papers, we were back in the limo.

'Sounds like you had an interesting morning.'

How I loved hearing his voice.

'Yes, it was interesting.' I relaxed back into the seat, drew in a long breath, then sighed.

'You did well.' He reached over and put his hand on mine, resting on the seat between us. His touch scorched me, and I wanted to be scalded by him. Through and through. I didn't know why, but something inside me wanted so much more from him. I glanced at him and it took everything I had not to crawl across the seat into his lap.

I curled my fingers around his. He tightened his on mine, and it thrilled me. We looked into each other's eyes and I wasn't entirely sure what I saw there. For now, I was content with his look of admiration.

He looked out of the window as the car slowed to a halt.

'We're here. Your apartment. I know it's only mid-afternoon now. You accomplished your test in good time, so you're done for the day.' He reached into his pocket with his other hand and pulled out a card. I took it.

'For tomorrow,' he told me.

The card in my hand was the second key I'd been given.

'I passed the test?'

'With flying colors,' he said. 'Your confidence won the day.'

Two down and only five more to go.

MR WEDNESDAY

This was the second morning in a row that Mr Monday had picked me up. I really could get used to this: limo rides, excellent coffee and a basketful of New York bagels. Not to mention being enclosed on a luxurious back seat with the sexiest, most handsome man I'd ever laid eyes upon. He'd opened up a tiny bit yesterday when we'd talked about our childhood. He had been hesitant to say too much, and it made me wonder why. I wanted to know more about him.

Just like yesterday, he got out of the limo and held the door open for me. We made eye contact, and I smiled. He did, too, and I moved past him, more closely than was appropriate. My dreams last night had all been about him. They were hot and heavy, full of passion and breathless moans, our bodies slick with sweat as we moved together. Him on top of me, in me, bringing me to heights I'd never before experienced. I'd woken up exhausted, as if I really had spent the night making love. Now, I looked at him with an even greater sense of desire.

There was no denying I was attracted to him. And now he

had infiltrated my dreams as well, taking my interest in him to a whole new level. I had the urge to step into him, put my arms around him and pull his head down so I could trace my tongue along his scar, before finding his mouth and making him kiss me. I bit back a moan when desire, so powerful, nearly made me stumble. I must have wobbled because he caught me around the waist, just as he had yesterday at the country club. I didn't resist, but turned in his arms so we faced each other.

'And here we are,' I said to him, in a low voice which I hoped held a seductive allure.

'Here we are,' he answered, his voice deep and quiet and oh so sexy that a delightful shiver rippled through me. He didn't move either. In fact, I think he held me a bit tighter, until we were flush. The air between us seemed to sizzle and grow hotter. I felt it as plainly as I felt his arm around me. Time slowed down, until it was just him and me. The world around us passed in a blinding blur and the only thing I saw clearly was him.

His heavy-lidded gaze told me all I needed to know. He wanted me. I drew in a breath, satisfied and smiling. I loved the way his energy and presence wrapped around me like a layer of passion. To get in the limo meant I had to step out of his arms and I wasn't ready for that, but we couldn't stand like this all day. Reluctantly, I shifted away, pressing my hands against the hard, muscular planes of his chest that no suit fabric could ever conceal. It was hard to leave his personal space, the energy that ringed us, but I forced myself. When he released me I let my fingers deliberately trail down his arm as I got into the limousine.

It was all about touching him. Being close to him. Remembering how good my dream was and the ache to bring it to real life. The connection we'd somehow developed made me crave this, even if it was terribly wrong.

I held the fabric of my circa 1940s wide-legged pants so I

didn't catch the heel of my mules on the hem. I sat down and smoothed the burnt-orange-and-black polka-dot fabric over my thighs. I loved these pants as much as I did the white silk sleeveless blouse with a touch of lace at the edge which I had chosen to wear today. It was form-fitting and my breasts felt full, as if they were aware of his nearness and wanted his attention. My body was developing a mind of its own, an addiction, where he was concerned. My heart raced and, no matter how hard I tried, I couldn't make it calm, so my blood pulsed thick and slow through my veins to settle in a glorious aching need between my thighs.

How easily this man could distract me from my goal. How quickly I responded to him. I glanced at him, feeling closer to him today than I had yesterday, having shared those snippets of our childhood.

'It's nice that you escort me to the office. You don't have to, you know. I can find my own way.'

He glanced at me, and my jaw nearly dropped open when he reached over and touched my hand, much like he had yesterday, only this time he didn't hold it. 'I don't mind.'

I smiled at the few words. I was getting used to his taciturn nature. 'I'm glad.'

We watched each other, and I felt a subtle shift. Had we made a step somewhere that had taken our relationship to a different status? What was it? Maybe it was simply a new awareness of each other as a man and a woman, not merely interviewer and interviewee. He was so excruciatingly gorgeous, not to mention mysterious, our sexual chemistry was off the charts. Could there ever be more than that? Even though he didn't speak much, I was intrigued by the glimpses I was seeing of who he was. I let out a breath as I settled into the seat and crossed my ankles.

Mr Monday shifted beside me, closer than yesterday. I liked that. So I moved a tiny bit, too, decreasing the distance between us. The urge to snuggle up to him was almost unbearable and it took all my will to stay where I was.

'Coffee?' His deep voice reminded me how he had spoken to me in my dream: sexily, whispering naughty words into my ear.

'Of course.' My voice sounded breathy. 'Was it flown in this morning like yesterday?'

'Possibly. Just remember, though, a treat isn't special if it's indulged in all the time. But the bagels are fresh today.' He turned and gave me the biggest smile I'd seen yet from him. The corners of his eyes crinkled nicely and he had lovely dimples. He was simply perfection. I could look at him all day. I found myself tongue-tied, close to swooning.

'Oh – yes, um, well, I would hope that the bagels are fresh each day.' I blinked, realizing how stupid I sounded, and cursed myself silently. He didn't seem to notice, and went about fixing our coffees as if it were something that happened every day. I took the cup from him, and our fingers brushed. I didn't move away, and neither did he. We froze, looking into each other's eyes. I wish I knew what he was thinking; if he knew what I was thinking, we might just never make it to the office.

My blush heated me and I took my cup of coffee from him, holding it in both hands, and looked out the window. I needed to take a breath, to collect my thoughts and keep my face from giving away my emotions. He was getting under my skin in the most delicious way. I couldn't deny that, but I also had to remember the complications that would no doubt ensue. I couldn't be drawn to him. I had to remain steadfast. I needed to get through all these tests and dig up information to pursue my plan of revenge. Why did I have to meet someone like Mr

Monday now? Why couldn't it have waited until all this drama was over? He was different, and so appealing. I'd never been interested in being in a committed relationship before, but now that Mr Monday had come into my life so unexpectedly I realized that not only did I want to sleep with him, I also wanted to date him. I wanted to peel off the layers and see the real man underneath his sexy surface. I turned back to look at him and realized that I wanted to know him better. He seemed so attentive to me, unlike any other man I'd known. I liked that, even if the situation we found ourselves in was very strange.

Suddenly, I felt overwhelmed. Could I do this? The last day and a half, since meeting Mr King and Mr Monday, had been rather surreal and somewhat trying, but nothing compared to the death of my father and my mother's decision to move back to England. But I couldn't deny it had been unexpectedly exhilarating, too. I took a sip and welcomed the creamy richness of my coffee. Then I turned to look at Mr Monday. I'm not sure what was reflected in my eyes, but I was thinking, *Yes, I can do this*. His eyebrows raised and he sat back in the seat. Was he assessing me? I wondered if he'd seen something in my expression. At my old job, we'd had monthly poker games in the archives. My co-workers used to tell me my face was an open book, my every thought plain to see. I'd lost miserably until I'd learned to develop a poker-face. Those nights of cards, chips and beer were my only real social events in those days, and I missed them a great deal, but sacrifices had to be made. I drew in a breath and realized I must have let my mask of stoicism slip. 'What's wrong?' he asked.

I shook my head. I mustn't show weakness. I was surprised he was so perceptive. How could I answer him without giving it all away?

'Oh, nothing. Just remembering something.'

'What? A memory from your childhood perhaps?'

I spun my head to face him, my body tensed like a coiled spring. How could he know? He had come uncomfortably close to reading my mind. I searched his face for any indication that he was aware of the truth. If he knew the real reason I was here . . . but I couldn't detect anything, and I slowly relaxed.

'I was thinking about my dad.' Then I held my breath to see what he would say next. I was pretty sure they had researched me, and this might show me just how deeply they had gone.

But he didn't get the chance to ask any further questions because his phone chimed. I reached forward to put some salmon and lox on my bagel while he dealt with the call. So far this morning I was in a complete chaos of emotions. The pace, and all the uncertainty revolving around these tests, was beginning to get to me.

What was today going to bring? Yesterday had been enormously stressful but also extremely thrilling. Being able to hold my own against the men around the conference table and close the deal had been great for my ego. Maybe I did have what it took to be CEO. I was smart. I could be tough. But I was wondering how ruthless I could be. The compassionate side of me hadn't been touched yet. What would happen when it was?

The trip in the limo ended far too quickly. I could easily have sat next to Mr Monday and simply driven around all day. This time, the doorman was right there to open the limo door, and I got out, waiting for Mr Monday to round the back of the car and come to my side. He placed his hand at the small of my back. I didn't hold back my delicate shiver and looked up at him with a smile. He glanced down at me, and I loved the expression on his face. His features had softened so much he looked like a different man. This is what he might look like after making love, I thought. I could almost imagine lying next to him, wrapped in his powerful arms, watching him as I ran my fingers over his bare chest, teasing his nipples until they hardened, before following what I fully expected would be a tempting trail of dark hair that led down his belly and then disappeared beneath the sheet casually tossed across his hips to explore the prize that lay below. I almost moaned. The more time I spent with this man, the more I wanted him.

Holy shit, I'd just turned myself on with my vivid imagination. I stepped into him a tiny bit, hoping he wouldn't move away from me. If he didn't, that meant there were possibilities. If he did, well, then I'd have to be content with my fantasies.

He didn't move away. I let out a soft sigh. Yes, there was potential here. We looked at each other, as if we were waiting for something to happen. I jumped when the doorman slammed the limo door, snapping me out of my daydream. Mr Monday blinked, and what looked like a momentary flash of disappointment shadowed his eyes. That moment, whatever it had been, was lost, but I hoped we'd be able to rekindle it again at some point.

Inside the lobby, the security guard stood up behind his station.

'Stanley, good morning,' I greeted him, and signed the register.

He gave me a wide smile. He seemed pleased that I remembered his name. 'Ms Canyon, good morning.' He lifted his gaze to Mr Monday and acknowledged him.

I turned to Mr Monday and asked him, 'What are the plans for today?'

We had moved away from Stanley now, and Mr Monday and I were alone near the banks of elevators.

He looked down at me. 'Today, you're going to the twenty-fifth floor.'

'And that's all? No other instructions, except to go to the twenty-fifth floor?'

'That's right.' He smiled, and I nearly melted under the sizzle I saw in his gaze. 'You catch on quickly, yes? Mr King wants to see just how quickly.'

'Well, then, I guess I should be on my way.' I hesitated in front of him for the briefest moment, not ready to leave his side. I had to force myself to step away and up to the elevators. I turned and asked him, 'Will I see you again today?' My voice failed me and I sounded breathy again, almost seductive, and that wasn't how I wanted to sound at all. *Or was it?* His eyebrows rose imperceptibly, so he had obviously heard it in my voice, too.

'We'll see, Ms Canyon. Take it one step at a time. And don't forget to listen.'

'A cryptic statement. Sort of expected that.' Then I stepped into the elevator, pausing to take a quick look to see if he was still standing there. He was, and a thrill raced through me. I'd caught him looking at me, and I wanted to run back to him, but I didn't. His chin lowered and he watched me from under his dark brows. I could feel the intensity of his stare. Then the elevator doors shut, breaking our connection. I let out a shaky breath and tried to calm my rapid heartbeat. I needed to get my Zen back. This man kept me off-kilter and, surprisingly, I liked it. He frustrated and intrigued me. I still didn't know his exact role in this game we were playing, but I sensed it was an important one.

I almost forgot to punch the number for the elevator floor. Nothing happened when I did. I sighed.

I took the new card out of my purse and looked at it. It appeared to be no different from yesterday's card. I slid it into the slot at the bottom of the sensor. I pressed twenty-five again and, sure enough, it lit up. I felt the elevator move quietly, stealthily, and stared at the floor indicator as the numbers climbed to where I was to get off. I couldn't get my mind off Mr Monday. What did he do all day? What *was* his role here at Diamond? What would happen when this was all over? A sharp pain stabbed me in the heart at the thought that we might never see each other again if I didn't get the job. Surely I'd see him if I was successful. My stomach clenched when I realized that, in reality, I knew nothing about him at all. He was as much a mystery as everything else that was happening around me.

The elevator door opened. No receptionist was there waiting for me. I walked to the nearest door and slid my card through the reader. Then I pushed the door open and walked through. The space on the other side was typical of a bustling office, with lots of staff doing their thing. Whatever that might be. It was an open-concept area, much like yesterday's floor, except, here, there was no subdued lighting. This place was hopping.

Offices were lined along the windows on the far wall, and what was cool about them were the interior glass walls. It allowed the view outside to be seen by those working in the pods placed in a tight grid between where I stood and those far offices. I had no idea what the employees on this floor were responsible for. I guessed I would find out soon enough.

First on the order of business was finding the manager. I made my way to the offices on the other side of the floor. Surely someone had to be in charge. I wandered among the desks, and whenever anybody looked up I smiled. Some acknowledged me and others didn't, focusing on their work. I slowly walked past the offices – it appeared that only management was entitled to a door – looking in each one until what I saw in the end corner office halted me in my tracks. A man sat in a leather chair, his back to me. He had a phone to his ear, his elbow held high.

What struck me was the color of his hair. Flaming red. Like mine, until I'd dyed it. His was wild, like a lion's mane, completely unexpected for a management type. He had tipped the chair back and was resting his booted feet on the ledge of the low wall that ran under the windows. His wide shoulders rose above the seat back.

Oh boy, he was definitely a hunk of a man. My mouth dried up, and I moistened my lips. I could almost feel his presence radiating through the glass wall. I couldn't pull my gaze from him. Didn't want to. He dropped his feet to the ground and swiveled the chair round. He looked directly at me and I sucked in a startled breath. Had he heard me? Sensed me? I'd never know; all I knew was that he caught me staring at him.

'Excuse me, miss.' I dragged my gaze from him and turned to the woman sitting at the desk by the next office who had spoken. 'Are you Ms Canyon?'

I nodded. 'Yes, I am. I hope I've come to the right place?'

She smiled and answered, 'You have. I'm sure he'll be ready for you in a minute.' With the end of her pen, she indicated a few chairs in a cozy little grouping with a coffee table centered among them. 'Have a seat.'

I was about to walk over and sit, but first I took another look at the man through the glass wall. He was still watching me, and I was rooted to the spot. He kept me pinned me with those intense eyes. My heart didn't know what to do with itself as it hammered behind my breasts, which suddenly felt needy, as if they were desperate for some TLC of the male variety. *Must be carry-over from my dreams last night and the sensual ride in the limo.*

His coloring was one of the rarest combinations: red hair and blue eyes. Again, like me, until I'd dyed my hair dark. I stared at him, trying to digest the feelings this man had roaring around inside me. He waved for me to come in, then turned around. I felt a keen sense of loss, almost as if he had dismissed me. I didn't want this man not to notice me.

I turned to the woman. 'I think he wants me to go in,' I stated. She looked up very briefly, smiled, then went back to her work. I opened the door and hesitated a fraction of a moment just inside the threshold. He looked over his shoulder and our gazes met again. My heart stopped and I couldn't breathe. This man was ah-mazing. I even found his deep red beard attractive. He mouthed to me, 'Close the door,' then gave me a slow grin. He raked me with a stare that I swear seared the clothes right off my body. I drew in a short gasp at the – yes – *spark*. A very big spark that made every nerve and muscle twitch. He was saucy and unbelievably sexy and reminded me of a brawny Scottish Highlander, just like Jamie Fraser. If he stood up, I wouldn't be the least bit surprised to find him wearing a kilt. I was a huge *Outlander* fan. I had read all the books, watched every episode and absolutely lusted after Jamie Fraser. And now here he was, sitting in the chair in front of me. Well, his twin, anyway.

He nodded his head in the direction of the chair, the movement making his hair flop down over his forehead. He ran thick fingers through it, pushing it back where it belonged, only for it to disobey him and tumble around his face again. Mmhm, yes, big hands, muscled body . . . my mind was going exactly where it shouldn't.

He held up one finger, and I knew he wanted me to give him a minute, then he turned back to the window. I couldn't look away from him, so I felt my way to the chair, dropping into it rather ungracefully. Thank God he was looking the other way and missed my clumsiness. I quickly sorted myself out, and was in the middle of fixing the shoulder strap of my Victoria's

Secret bra, which had slipped a wee bit, when he suddenly spun the chair and caught me mid-fix. He looked at my hand, fingers curled around the burnt-orange – yes, I'd matched it to my pants – bra strap, then back at my face.

'Having a touch of wardrobe malfunction?' His voice was magic. There was not a trace of a Scottish accent, but it still did all the right things to me in places that hadn't seen any sort of sexual magic in far too long.

'Pardon? Um, yes. Well, no.' I shook my head to clear the lusty fog he was responsible for creating. 'I'm good.'

I sat there like a lump, unable to focus on anything except him. I crossed my legs and rested my hands atop each other on my knee, doing my best not to let my fingers tremble. His phone buzzed again and I was relieved for the reprieve from his scrutiny. I did my best to tune him out as he spoke, and gazed out of the window to the cityscape beyond. I had learned to be patient, but it was hard for me to restrain myself at the feel of the sizzle that seemed to fill this office. I concentrated on slowing my breath, which I hoped would have the same effect on my pounding heart.

'Yep. Ping me for the next conference call.' He tossed his phone on the desk and swiveled again in his chair. 'Tess! I've been waiting for you. Welcome to Diamond Enterprises.'

I was about to stand and reach out to shake his hand, but he didn't rise from his chair. So I didn't get up either, taking his lead. I was glad I didn't have to try out my suddenly untrustworthy legs. 'I'm glad I found you, too. With no instruction—'

'It's fine, fine.' His phone rang, and he sighed and picked it up. He listened to whoever it was and his eyebrows pulled together. He frowned and stood up. 'I'll be right there.'

Now that he was standing, I stood up as well. He wasn't as tall as Mr Monday, or Mr Tuesday, but he was compact: just under six foot, I reckoned, and heavily muscled. I could see it clearly under his suit. My heart wouldn't do as it was told and danced in my chest. He was extremely attractive. His wild, untamed and unpredictable aura wrapped itself around me like a Scottish mist. I was done for. Truly. Then a vision of another man rose up in my mind. A dark, amazingly sexy man who was my morning wake-up call.

What was it with all these men? One for each day of the week. Mr Tuesday yesterday. Now for hump day was this drop-dead-sexy redhead, Mr Wednesday, who happened to be very humpable, I might add. And the first was my sexy Mr Monday. I didn't stand a chance. I was in danger of becoming a lust-struck fool. I refused to let myself fall prey to a pretty face and a few hard muscles. I couldn't let these Mr Days-of-the-Week steer me from my ultimate goal. Revenge. Mr Wednesday's voice called me back from my musings.

'I'm really sorry. Something's come up.' He pointed to the phone. 'I have to go right now. Please make yourself at home here, and I'll be back as quickly as I can.'

I watched him leave the office, his powerful legs carrying him with a purposeful, even stride. He was gone before I could even blink. I stood in the doorway and looked around. What the hell had just happened? I glanced at the secretary. She was watching me. I raised my eyebrows and shrugged my shoulders.

'He does have a way about him that keeps you on your toes. It's like the air energizes when he's around – turbulent, wild – and when he leaves everything is calm,' she said, as if she could read my mind. She shook her head and gave me a sympathetic smile before turning back to her computer. I wandered back into the office and sat in a chair, drumming my fingers on the armrest, thinking about Mr Wednesday and his secretary. I looked through the glass wall to the door he had vanished through. I didn't even know the man yet I had the oddest sensation of loss, loss of something I hadn't even wanted.

Ten minutes went by, and frustration welled inside me. Sitting here like this was a colossal waste of time. But I was hesitant to leave his office and go off in search of something else to do. What if he came back and began my test and I was somewhere else? So I forced myself to be patient again. I looked behind me and saw some magazines on a table. I grabbed one, flipping through it without really seeing what was inside.

'I'm so sorry.' He'd entered the office and filled it with his energy, scaring the crap out of me. This time he dropped into the chair beside me.

'Everything okay?' I asked him. Not that I really had a right to ask, but he looked a little agitated.

He waved his hand as if to dismiss whatever it was that had called him away. 'It's fine. Everything will be fine.' For some reason, I wasn't convinced. The look of unease in his eyes was completely different from the look in them only a few minutes ago. He was concerned about something, worried, and it made *me* worry.

'Now then, where were we?' He looked at his desk as if trying to refresh his memory. 'Yes. Paperwork.'

I tipped my head to the side and looked at him. 'Paperwork?'

'Yep, just general employee information, nothing too in-depth. Name, address, emergency contact.'

'I don't have an emergency contact.' A beat of anger flared in my chest, because the blame for that could be squarely aimed at Diamond. If they hadn't fired my dad, he probably wouldn't have died so young and then my mother would still be in the

States. I felt a slight flicker of resentment toward Mom for leaving me here alone, but I squashed it down.

'Take a couple of days then. No rush,' he said. He stood and leaned over the desk, riffling through a pile of folders. I couldn't look away – nope – as his clothes stretched over his body, tightening across his back, and around his very well-shaped ass. I licked my lips and blinked rapidly, unable to believe he was so innocently putting on a show worthy of the Chippendales.

'Here we are.' He selected a folder and dropped it on the edge of the desk before sitting back into the chair beside me with a big sigh. He pointed at it. 'It's all in there. The form's in there. Fill it out, and leave it with Wendy when it's complete.'

'Thank you.' I reached out and slid the folder toward me, leaving it on the edge of his desk. He must be the director of Human Resources, or at least upper management. Maybe he'd been called away moments ago to a staffing crisis. I'd learned not to judge a book by its cover a long time ago, but apparently I'd just done that where he was concerned. It had never crossed my mind that he'd be high up in HR until now. Was he a kind and compassionate HR person, or was he a total company man? I took the file to distract myself.

His phone buzzed again, but he swiped the screen, sending the call to voicemail. He was a busy man. It struck me that buzzing phones were commonplace with these Diamond men. Even so, this man seemed to have a million things going on at once. It made me wonder how he managed to stay on top of it all without, presumably, letting anything slide. Was he a tyrant? I glanced at the staff beyond the glass wall. It seemed pretty quiet; nobody was moving around or chatting. Everyone seemed very efficient. There was no way for me to get the real picture, though, except by speaking to the employees. Was all of this part of the test? Or was I simply here to sign papers?

'Okay. There, that's all settled.'

'Problems?' I asked him. Why not ask him outright? See what he said. I needed to know for my own sake, and for my revenge. And I still had to figure out how to try to find the company's financial statements. Now, this unexpected meeting with Mr Wednesday made me think that employee files might also be key. I looked at him and my heart did a little pitter-patter as he gazed back.

He tipped his head to the side. 'Well, actually. Hmm, maybe . . . yes.' He was thinking out loud, talking to himself. It was so close to how I handled things at times, it was scary. 'Yes, it ties into . . . okay. I had a job lined up for you, and this will fit in perfectly.'

I leaned forward. 'Yes?' I knew that the previous tests were about bravery and confidence. I was eager to see what today's would be.

'I'd like you to put together a plan for employee engagement.'

'Oh?' That was a surprise. It seemed so . . . ordinary after the life-changing tests of the last couple of days.

'Yes, it's no secret that the country has had a number of tough years, and I'm seeing a drop in morale here at Diamond. Not necessarily any fault of ours, just the current environment. So much negativity in the world can't help but affect one's mental well-being.'

'And how does this tie into why you were called away?' I was intrigued. This was very interesting, even though it was out of my realm of expertise. However, a CEO did need to be aware of the states of mind of his employees.

'We've noticed an increase in sick days and leaves of absence, and, obviously, it has a direct impact on productivity. You can use the office next to mine.' He indicated it with his thumb.

'There's a computer, and you will have access to the HR shared drive.'

'Perfect.' I tried to contain my excitement. If I had access to the shared drive, I wondered how much information I'd be able to access. I assumed there would be some restricted areas for now, but if I became CEO then I would have full access to everything, right? Today it wouldn't be financial records, but it might be the next best thing.

'This is a busy floor.' I waved my hand, indicating the office pods behind me.

He leaned back in the chair. He seemed entirely confident as the chair groaned under him. So far, all the men that I'd met here had been heart-stoppingly gorgeous. I was eager to see what the remaining Mr Days-of-the-Week were like. If I hadn't had an agenda – and the tests to perform – then I might have felt freer to explore this smorgasbord of men. I had to stop thinking about them, and focus on my goal. I was now in my second day and so far had been unable to take advantage of being inside Diamond.

I lowered my head and looked at him from under my eyebrows, the bangs of my new short hair swinging down over my forehead, allowing me to watch him from behind the strands.

Mr Wednesday's phone buzzed yet again. I sighed when he grabbed it, swiped the face with his thumb and put it to his ear. *Would that thing ever shut up?* Clearly, I wasn't as important as what was on the other end of his phone this time. That relieved me in a way. I had to believe I'd just been assigned the test.

'Yeah?' He answered the phone.

I watched and listened. I'd learned that being a good listener was just as valuable as having patience. You never know what kind of important information you can pick up and tuck away for a later date. I picked up the magazine to keep me busy while he was talking.

He flickered his eyes at me and said into the phone, 'Yes, she's here.' I froze and looked at him, remaining silent. He was quiet also; it appeared to be a bit of a one-sided conversation. I tried to sit as quietly as I could so that maybe I'd be able to hear a bit of the convo on the other end. After all, they were talking about me. 'Hmm. Mmhm. Yup. Will do.' Then he shoved the phone into his pocket.

I cocked my head to the side. 'To do with me?'

He smiled, and I could've swooned. What a gorgeous smile. 'Yup. To do with you.'

'Anything I need to know? Any concerns?'

He shook his head and pressed his lips together in an upside-down frown. 'Nope, no concerns.'

That made me angry, and I had to squash it or I'd have blurted out something I knew I would regret. He stood and quickly organized his desk, stacking the few papers that were scattered to the side, lining his pens neatly to the right of his laptop. Once he'd finished, he swept the palm of his hand across the surface of his desk. I realized he was a neat freak. 'Another meeting calls. So make yourself comfortable in the office next door.' He indicated it with his thumb again.

'Thanks. Any suggestions or tips?' I stood and picked up the folder, waiting for a little more insight. He gave me a look I couldn't quite read. I furrowed my brows at his assessing gaze.

'Nope. You've got your instructions.' He hesitated, looking me up and down. It both gave me tingles and unnerved me. 'Nice outfit,' he said. I was shocked and thrown off balance by his observation. 'Looks vintage.'

You could have knocked me over with a feather.

'It is, actually.' I had no idea what else to say. A man noticing vintage clothes was a rarity indeed. 'I'm rather surprised you would recognize vintage clothing.'

'My sister. She's a freak for all that stuff.'

Could this man get any more attractive? He had a sister with the same love of fashion as me. But what was even more compelling was that he could recognize vintage clothing.

'I am truly astounded. It's not often a man notices.'

He bobbed his head, making his wild hair even more untamed. 'How could I not? It was all she talked about as a teenager. She made me drive her to all the shops and help her lug bags and bags of stuff home.'

I laughed. 'Same with me. I loved the old movies, and they were my escape during some . . . er, well, I fell in love with the clothes and style and started collecting. I would love to meet your sister one day.'

'Maybe you shall.' He winked, and goosebumps rippled down my arms.

'What a small world. She really isn't a freak, you know. That's rather harsh,' I gently scolded him. I know I wouldn't want to be painted with that brush. 'There's something so romantic and classic about vintage clothing and furniture. I just adore it.'

'That's what my sister says, too. She's so into it she has her own store. She's always hunting for things, and constantly at garage and estate sales, wherever.' I sucked in a breath. I needed to know this woman. 'She has her own store? I must visit. Is it in the city?'

He shook his head and my heart dropped. 'No, it's not. But she would like to open one here. I keep telling her it'd be a waste of money and time.'

Nooo, it wouldn't. 'Good stores are hard to find. What's hers called?'

He drew in a breath and glanced up the ceiling.

'I can't believe you don't know the name of your sister's store!' Another scolding.

'Give me a minute. I think – yeah, I think she called it Morningstar.'

'I know that store, it's fabulous! And don't you go and discourage her from opening up a shop in the city. There's certainly a market for it, you know.'

He pinned his gaze on me and smiled. 'Bet you like antiques as well.'

'I do. They are a key to our past. Our history. And yes, I love them.' I liked our banter. It was easy. He was fun, and laid back.

He laughed and put up his hand. 'Okay, okay, I give. I get the same thing from Shari.'

He was cute, I had to say that. And the fondness he evidently had for his sister made him all the more endearing, more human somehow. Not just a very sexy man who ran a very important department of Diamond Enterprises. I saw how his face softened when he spoke about her. As an only child, I envied that sibling connection. I bet Shari was his emergency contact.

'Good, at least we got that settled.' I left the office, and he followed. 'Okay,' I added. 'I'll find my way around. No need to babysit me.'

'Excellent, I knew you'd be self-sufficient. I'll be gone for a few hours. In the meantime, you can start working on what we discussed.'

He walked me to the office door and opened it. There was definitely a gentleman hiding away beneath all his brawn.

'Here you go.'

I stepped past him as he held the door open for me. I glanced up as I passed. He watched me, and my step hesitated, not wanting this sultry little encounter to end too quickly. But then I was in the office and he was walking away. I let my gaze linger on him, liking the way his body moved. His suit fit so well, I could have drooled. I sighed and turned around to check out the office. It was pretty barren, and I assumed it was a spare one.

I left the door open and went around the desk to sit in the chair. Pulling the drawer open beside me, I looked for stationery supplies. It was nicely stocked and I took out a black pen and scribbled on a Post-It pad until the ink started to run. Not only was I a vintage lover, I also got a kick out of office supplies. I'd hit the jackpot with this drawer.

I wiggled the mouse to wake up the computer. The desktop flashed up in front of me, but a log-in window halted me in my tracks. Nobody had given me any log-in information, so how was I going to access anything? I pulled over the folder Mr Wednesday had given me and flipped it open, quickly reading the questions inside. I decided to ignore the paperwork. I wasn't very eager to give Diamond any personal information they might be able to use to unmask me. I shut the folder and pushed it to the side. There was nothing in it to help me with my log-in. I sat back and chewed my lip. What could it be? I clicked on the screen to see if it might prompt me. It did.

Please enter your numeric password.

What numeric password? I clicked the password help icon, hoping for further instruction. A new window popped up.

This is your first log-in. Enter the four numbers you've been provided with. You will be prompted to enter a new password. You will have no further grace log-ins.

I sat back and muttered, 'What four numbers?' I quickly ran through everything that had happened since my interview. I hadn't been given any numbers. I closed my eyes, tried to relax my brain, hoping it would settle down and let me focus. What could there be that might have numbers on it?

'A-ha!' I blurted. *Maybe ...* I dug in my purse for the key card Mr Monday had given me the night before. That would make sense. The key cards acted as gateways, each one allowing me to progress further along my journey to the CEO chair – and my revenge. Peering at the card closely, I smiled. There, on the bottom, were four pale silver numbers.

I typed them in and – *boom* – the screen flashed and I was staring at the desktop. A number of icons ran down the left-hand side. Many were familiar, but there were a few others I didn't know, probably for internal programs.

I got busy, eager to familiarize myself with as much of this computer system as I possibly could before I tackled 'employee engagement'. I had no idea really how much time I'd be allowed here, so I had to make the most of every second. I clicked and launched the employee portal. It was well thought out and I was impressed. My first visit was to the social section, which housed a bulletin board; a bunch of items for sale was listed. Also, upcoming events, including a company picnic, planned for a few weeks away. Having investigated that, I pulled up Google and started digging.

I focused on the assignment Mr Wednesday had given me. The sooner I could get it done, the sooner I could start snooping around. My librarian background helped and, within an hour, I had enough info to prepare a report. I mapped the printer, then sent the relevant info to print. I pulled out the Post-It notes and started sorting. Soon I had the details categorized and had outlined a rough draft. Half an hour later the printer was chugging out a report. I found some binding spines in the supply room and swiftly had the report nicely ready for presentation.

'There. A good job, if I do say so myself.' Now I had time to investigate the rest of the floor.

I was about to head down the hall when a security guard rounded the corner. I looked for somewhere to hide and ducked into the bathroom. Logically, it made sense that they would be keeping track of me, but I didn't fancy the idea of making small talk with a security guard while I was snooping around. I was surprised at how nice the ladies' room was. It wasn't your typical bathroom, with only stalls and sinks, it had soft lighting, a vanity with lights, a small area with a couple of wing chairs, much like the kind I'd seen in the elevator lobby, and there was an array of lotions, soaps and feminine products on a long counter. Hmm, nice. Everything about Diamond seemed over the top, but all the little touches were nice. This was good for employee morale. I had to wonder if the employees appreciated these extras. If they didn't, they should.

I heard voices drifting toward the ladies' room, so I quickly entered a stall. They sounded excited so I decided to wait a couple of minutes before trying to leave. I felt a bit guilty for eavesdropping, but maybe I could learn something. One woman seemed to be crying. I tilted my head sideways so I could hear a little better.

'I don't know if I can do this.' She sniffled and then blew her nose.

The other woman sounded slightly older. 'We all do it, honey. Moms have a big cross to bear.'

This was interesting. Unhappy employees. Now I felt a tiny bit better for listening in. I almost rubbed my hands together in anticipation. Any dirt I could dig up would help me in my quest for revenge.

The older-sounding woman spoke again. 'It's only been a week. You have to give it time. Your baby will be fine.'

'Have you not heard of all those horrible things that happen in daycare? Sexual assault, children getting left alone, abuse. It's eating me up!'

The woman sounded distraught, and I felt bad for her. I couldn't imagine what it would be like to leave your children behind to go out to work. I pursed my lips, angry at the position mothers with young children are put in when they have to return to their jobs. I had no idea how hard it might be to leave a crying baby in daycare. I imagined a hysterical child clinging to my leg, pleading in a small voice for me not to go. I think I would die.

'There, there, Jenny. You mustn't let your mind run away with you. You're jumping to conclusions. And I know how well you researched your daycare options. You'd know which one was a good place – you have your degree in child psychology, right?'

'Yes, but working in child psychology doesn't pay as well as here. My husband is giving me a hard time, too. He wants me to work, because we need the money, but he can't stand how upset I am at leaving Jason in daycare, and then all the baby does is cry all night long. He's starting to get sick, too.'

The older woman's voice was calm, and I admired her for being so supportive. 'He's only been there a week. How quickly could he get sick?'

'Well, you know what I mean. If only there were a suitable daycare center closer to work, then it wouldn't be so bad, but I have to get the baby up at five o'clock in the morning. How can that be the right thing to do? It's not normal for anybody to get up at that time of morning, let alone a contentedly sleeping baby.'

'Are you sure there's not something closer to work?'

'I looked. The places nearby are only feasible if I want to pay more for daycare than I'm earning. But then what's the point in working at all?'

I felt that I had eavesdropped long enough. So I moved my feet and began to make some noise to let them know I was in the stall. I didn't want to barge in on them in the middle of a conversation without giving them a chance to stop talking. They were in the sitting area on the other side of the wall from the sink and the counter. Without missing a beat, they kept on talking, which told me that they didn't care if I overheard.

After I'd washed my hands and rounded the corner, I hesitated but then went to speak to the women. 'I didn't mean to listen in, but I have to give you credit. Working with a baby is not easy, I'm sure. Good for you to be giving it a try.'

The younger girl, Jenny, nodded, grabbed more tissues from the box on the table and blew her nose. 'I don't know if I can carry on. I don't feel productive or anything any more. I'm constantly worried about my baby.'

'I understand,' I told her. But how could I possibly understand? I wasn't in her shoes. I didn't have a child. And I felt rather ashamed all of a sudden. My purpose was to destroy or, at the very least, humiliate, this company. If I did that, then her job, and everyone else's, would be in jeopardy. I sighed, conflicted. I was here to take revenge for what had happened to my father, but I hadn't really thought about the ramifications. Looking at this young mother and her co-worker, it could be their jobs, pensions and benefits on the line. I hadn't thought about the people factor before.

Hearing this woman's tale of woe only drove it all home. It made me aware that there were people out there suffering, much like I had, some a whole lot more than I ever did. Maybe there was another angle I could approach my revenge from? I'd have to think about it. It's one thing to plot out revenge coldly on paper, but now, seeing the human element made me think again.

'Is there anything I can do to help you?' I asked her. Not that I had the slightest idea how I could.

She looked at me and wiped her swollen eyes. 'That's so nice of you to offer. But I don't know how, unless you can miraculously create a daycare center on site here.' I smiled. *Funny you should say that*, I thought to myself, an idea suddenly forming.

The other lady spoke. 'I haven't seen you around before. I'm Carol.'

'It's my second day.' Obviously, I had to keep where I'd been yesterday out of the conversation. I looked at my watch to buy myself a minute to think.

'Oh my gosh, that is an absolutely beautiful watch!' Carol exclaimed. 'It's not often you see somebody wear such an exquisite piece of jewelry. And your nails. What a lovely shade of polish.'

'Thank you. It's a more subdued color than I usually wear. I like to have fun with my nails and polish, but I've kept it rather conservative this week. The watch was my mother's. My father gave it to her on their wedding day, and she gave it to me before she moved back to England.' I touched the face, loving the feel of the glass and diamonds under my fingertips.

Jenny leaned over to look at it and sighed. 'It's so beautiful. Oh, you come from England! Why did she go back? Oh, excuse me,' she said. 'It's none of my business, I'm sorry for asking.'

'No, it's okay. Mom never did adjust to life in the States. She is British to the bone and was forever complaining about living here. So it made sense for her to go back. She's much happier.' I wasn't about to go into why she left, or that the reason my parents' marriage had broken down was that she didn't want to deal with the bad memories. She had believed that Dad was guilty, whereas I was convinced he was innocent. I clenched my teeth and pushed the angry thoughts away.

'That must be hard for you. Do you visit her much?'

I shook my head and felt sad. I missed her, but then she was very preoccupied with her own life there. I didn't fit into it any more. My fear of flying didn't help matters either. 'Not as much as I would like. It's been a few years since I was over.'

'That's very sad. I'm so sorry,' Carol said, her voice holding emotion that clutched at my heart.

'Thank you.' I didn't really want to talk about my mom any more, so I turned to Jenny. 'That's the closest I can come to understanding having someone you love out of reach.' She frowned, and I saw the tears well up again. 'I'm sorry, please don't cry.'

'I might have to quit.'

Carol and I blurted out at the same time, 'Don't do that!' Then we both looked at each other and laughed. Thankfully, Jenny did, too.

Carol said, 'Great minds think alike.'

I countered with, 'Or fools seldom differ.' We both laughed again, as did Jenny, and I was glad of the lighter mood. 'That's one of my mom's favorite sayings. Jenny, are you free to have a coffee? Carol, you, too? I'd really like to get to know you guys better. I was about to have one myself.'

'Yes, I have a few more minutes of my break left,' Jenny answered.

'Me, too,' Carol said. 'I'll show you the kitchen and lounge – it's just on the other side of the wall.' She pointed in the direction of the wing chairs and then pulled open the restroom door, holding it so Jenny and I could walk through. 'We can go and sit in the lounge by the window. Have you been in there before?'

'No, I'm just getting to know the building. I move to a different location every day.'

Carol asked, 'So you're not working in HR?'

'Nope. They're moving me around to see where I fit best.'

Jenny pointed to the chairs by the windows. There were hibiscus trees situated right in front of the glass. It was nice, although I'd rather not have been that close to the edge and reminded of how high up we were. So I turned my back on the glass, and was amazed at the array of coffee machines, and the baskets and glass-fronted cupboards showing a host of treats tucked in them. It was better stocked than my little kitchen!

'There's more in the fridge. Fruit, cheese, hard-boiled eggs, hummus. You name it, it's in there.' Jenny walked over and opened the door.

'Wow, they really take care of you here.' I was impressed. I turned to Carol and Jenny. 'Can I make you something?'

'I think I should be getting back, actually,' Jenny told me, glancing up at the wall clock. 'I don't want to be late.' She faced Carol. 'Thanks for being my ear.'

'It's no problem, hun. We'll talk more later.'

I didn't want her to leave just yet. 'Jenny, have you been working here long?'

She shook her head. 'No, only a few years before I went on maternity leave. I'm sorry, I really have to go. It was nice meeting you.'

'Bye, Jenny, nice to meet you, too.'

I watched her walk away and turned to Carol. She spoke before I said a word.

'I've been here twenty-five years. So I've seen a lot,' she told me.

This could be a handy relationship to develop if I stayed at Diamond. She might have heard of my dad and what had happened back then.

'Wow, that's a long time.'

'It is, yes. There really wasn't a Human Resources depart-ment back then, so things weren't as tightly run as they are now. There was a transition over to HR practices about sixteen, seventeen years ago.'

Right about the time my father was fired.

'Really? That's so interesting. How did you ever keep track of everybody? Without a dedicated HR department, it must have been difficult.'

'Well, it's not like we were in the Dark Ages. Things were computerized. Although not as efficiently as they are now.'

I agreed. 'Just imagine all the paperwork before that.'

'I know. Some of our files have been transferred over. Orig-inally, it was a mindless scanning job for a summer student, but then the new privacy laws went into effect and the lawyers put the kibosh on that. So we still have lots of old files and boxes piled up in storage.'

'I know from my previous job that there are some very rep-utable secure storage facilities. Does Diamond use one?' I hope she didn't think I was getting too nosey, asking all these ques-tions out of the blue. I was hoping to learn the location of the older files and maybe find my dad's.

'No, we don't. There's secure storage here on site.'

'Oh, really. This building must have lots of spare room. It's huge.'

Excitement grew inside me. If I could get access to the per-sonnel files that were stored away somewhere . . .

Carol and I looked at each other, and I sensed she was about to leave. I wanted her to stay a little longer so we could continue talking. 'I'm dying for a cappuccino,' I said, 'and I was a barista extraordinaire once upon a time. Sure I can't make you one?'

'Oh hell, twist my arm. I'll just say I was helping the new girl out.' Carol laughed and leaned her hip on the counter as I went about getting what I needed. I hoped to discover more, but I was worried I was being too obvious. I didn't have much time to find out the information I needed. I also wanted to ask her something else before she rushed back to work.

'Tell me, has anybody ever raised the idea of having daycare on site?'

Carol shook her head. 'No, I don't recall it ever being brought up.'

'Are there enough staff to make it viable?'

She thought for a moment. 'Yes, I think there could be.' She gave me a slow smile. 'What are you thinking?'

'I've always thought that happy employees are productive employees. And when employees are treated poorly, it can have devastating and long-lasting results.' I frowned, remembering how distraught my dad had been after they fired him. I had to stick to my resolve and get the information I needed to exact my revenge, but I was starting to feel there were two sides to this company. Meeting and talking with these two women had given me something else to think about. Now, I needed to be snooping around through the computer system, but I did want to talk to Carol again. I drew in a breath and finished off a cappuccino, making just the right amount of foam. I even drew a little decoration on the top. 'Here you go.'

I handed her the cup, and she smiled with delight. A swelling of emotion filled me, completely catching me off guard. I made one for myself next.

'You are good,' Carol said.

'It was how I put myself through school. Typical student jobs. Plus, I won a few scholarships.' I looked for some raw cane sugar in the cupboards, figuring that there would be some here, given everything else that was available. 'Ah, here we go.

Have you tried it with this on the foam?' I ripped open the package and sprinkled it on top. 'This is the best part. I crunch my way through the foam.'

'Here, I'll give it a try.' She held her hand out and I emptied a package into it.

We sipped in silence a few moments and Carol bobbed her head in approval. I wondered what her role here was.

She walked over to the chairs by the window and sat in the one closest to the glass. I chose the couch farthest away, facing the interior of the building.

'Don't like heights?' Carol asked.

I shook my head. 'No, not in the least.'

'Everyone has their thing. I have a really hard time riding the elevator. Claustrophobia.' She looked at me and widened her eyes until I thought they were going to pop out of her head.

I laughed. 'It's funny, really, these little fears we have, but they're not so funny when you're living with them.' I shrugged.

'Nope. I just look at my feet in the elevator.'

Taking another sip of my drink, I decided to bring up the subject of daycare again. Even though I'd asked earlier, I hoped Carol might have a bit more information.

'I had no idea about the complications around childcare, but seeing how upset Jenny was made me realize how significant the problem is. Funny that Diamond has never considered it a possibility.'

'I suppose, like most organizations, they don't really worry about it. It's not their problem, it's the employees'.'

I shook my head. 'Companies should be more forward-thinking.'

I wondered if Carol read my mind, because her next words really hit home. 'Well, if you think about it, it would be a great employee benefit.'

'It certainly would. Even if a company subsidized only part of the cost of the daycare as a benefit, it would lower the expense for their employees.'

'Exactly. Companies are stupid if they don't think about things like this. Just imagine how happy the parents would be. Oh, goodness! I really should be going. Where did the time go?' Carol put her cup in the dishwasher. 'I am so happy to have met you. I hope you find the right place for you in Diamond.'

'Thank you. I enjoyed talking with you as well. Hopefully, we'll cross paths again.'

I wandered around the lounge, sipping my now cooling coffee. My mind was racing like a chicken with its head cut off. I debated whether to toss out my original research from this morning about employee engagement and pursue this idea instead.

It wasn't until I'd come to the conclusion that I was going to take up this battle that I realized where I was standing. Alarm barreled up my spine as I wavered, thankful for the thick pane of glass in front of me. I pressed my fingertips to the window to steady myself and did my best to fight my building panic at standing so close to the window. Damn my fear of heights. I had to get over it. I had to try, so I forced myself to stare down to the street below.

When I couldn't stand it any longer, I stepped away and took a few deep breaths to help calm my pounding heart. I didn't know if I'd ever get over my fear, but this was the longest I had ever managed to stay on such a precipice. I backed up and turned with a sigh of relief. I headed back to my temporary office. I had work to do. Daycare-center work to do.

I was ridiculously excited about doing research about daycare. I felt strongly that it would help people, and it was something Diamond hadn't thought about before, at least from what Carol had said. I nodded. Yes, this was much more important than a report simply on employee engagement.

A few hours later I had compiled a fair bit of information and bound it into a presentable report.

I hadn't realized the passage of time. I checked my watch and realized it was past five o'clock. I glanced across at the office floor. I hadn't even noticed the staff leaving, I'd been so absorbed. I got up, grabbed the two reports from the edge of the desk, and went to see if Mr Wednesday had returned. I peeked around the wall into his office. He was sitting at his desk, busy on his laptop. I watched him for a few minutes.

He looked up, then back down at the keyboard. 'Tess, you've emerged.'

'I have. I didn't know you had come back.'

'Yep, couple of hours ago. But you seemed very focused on your work.'

I raise my eyebrows and nodded. 'Yes, I was.'

'How did you get on?'

I put the project report on his desk. 'Here is your report.'

'Thank you. Hopefully, we have a winner.'

'I'm confident that it is thorough and that it will give the executive team something to consider.'

'I see you have something else in your hand.' He raised his eyebrows and lifted his chin, indicating the other report, which remained clutched in my fingers.

I cleared my throat. 'Yes, well. It's an addition to the employee-engagement report. Something came to my attention earlier today, and I felt it was worthy enough to do some research. My findings are very interesting.'

He sat back in his chair and laced his fingers over his muscled chest. Even such a simple move as that was enticing. 'Tell me about it.'

I pulled the chair up to the edge of his desk and sat down, setting the bound report in front of me.

He leaned forward with interest.

I pushed the report toward him, then spun it so he didn't have to read upside down. 'Proposal for a daycare center on site.'

He looked at me and his eyebrows shot up. 'A daycare center?'

I smiled, happy with myself. 'Mmhm, yes, a daycare center. I think there is a huge need for one here at Diamond Enterprises.'

'Is that right? And where did you get this idea from?' He picked up the report and flipped it open.

'Earlier today I overheard a couple of the staff members talking. I asked a few questions, did a bit of research, and here we are.' I watched nervously as he leafed through the pages of my report. I hadn't realized how until now how invested I was in this proposal. Talking to Jenny had opened my eyes to how important an issue it was.

Mr Wednesday lingered for a moment over a pie chart before meeting my gaze, a pleased expression on his face. 'I must say I'm a little astonished by this. I figured you would have your hands full with the employee-engagement report.'

'You never know where inspiration will come from. I had completed the initial task and was moved by a young mother's story.'

He dropped the report on to the desk and tapped the cover. 'Rather than me having to read the whole proposal, give me a one-paragraph pitch.'

I threw my head back and laughed. 'You want me to do in one paragraph what took me all afternoon to put in that report?' I pointed at it.

His blue eyes sparkled, crinkling slightly at the corners as he smiled. 'I certainly do.'

'Did your mom work?' I asked him.

'She did.' He crossed his arms over his chest as he waited to see where I was going with this.

'Did you go to daycare?'

He shook his head. 'No, although my mom worked a couple of days through the week, and two nights when my dad was home to watch us.'

'Have you ever wondered what it would've been like?'

He frowned and thought for a few seconds. 'No, I haven't. But my aunt was a single mom and I remember my cousins had to go. I don't think they liked it much.'

'How did your aunt react, do you remember?' I think he was starting to understand the impact daycare could have on a family. Maybe, in his experience, it was negative. He slanted his head to the side and thought about it. 'She did seem stressed a lot of the time.'

'So, if you remember that, and how it made your aunt feel, think about the staff here. Imagine the relief they would experience, knowing their children were safe and close by. At a place they can afford. Imagine the loyalty they would feel to Diamond. There's no reason why daycare can't be a positive experience for the family. It just takes a bit of thought and dedication from everyone to launch a caring, educational and nurturing facility.'

He was nodding, and I could see he was thinking about it. Maybe something would come of this. I was amazed at the excitement I felt for this project. It hadn't been on my radar before today, and now suddenly it was a dream I wanted to see come true.

'So what do you think? Is this something that Diamond Enterprises will do?' I rushed on, not wanting him to interrupt with a big fat no. 'You do realize how well this will be received by all the working mothers and fathers? It's a great way to show compassion toward employees. Build loyalty . . . and employee engagement.'

He chuckled and put up his hand. I stopped and sat back in the chair, holding my breath, anxious to know what he was going to say. 'You've sold me. Well done. I have a management meeting coming up and I'll present your proposal then.'

I clapped my hands, unbelievably excited that he liked my idea. 'That's wonderful.'

'Would you be willing to oversee it?'

'Of course.'

'Now, now. Don't get ahead of yourself. It still has to pass through the proper channels.'

My mind raced furiously, thinking about what I could do to make this happen. I was beginning to believe I had the ability to do this. If a girl like me, a not-so-meek librarian, could stand up and gain the respect of engineers, people with PhDs and metallurgists in a very male-dominated mining industry, I could do this! All I had to make sure of now was that I got hired, because, as CEO, I could implement the new daycare project right away. Then I was brought back down to earth really quickly. The excitement of the daycare idea vanished when I remembered the real reason I was here. Here I was thinking about making the workplace better for families, but I'd also be destroying their livelihoods if I continued with my revenge plot. Maybe I needed to come at this from a different angle. As CEO, I could affect change from within. By making new policies and bringing to light questionable financial practices, I could be truly making a difference for the better. Come to think of it, I couldn't believe that I hadn't thought about my revenge for my father at all during my research this afternoon. The daycare idea had consumed all my thoughts, not leaving me any room to think of anything else. I really hated to admit it to myself, but that was refreshing. I'd spent most of my adult life consumed with the idea of bringing down Diamond, forgoing a social life and other normal pursuits to concentrate on my goal. Mr Monday popped into my head, making me think I was ready to make up for lost time.

'Are you hungry?' Mr Wednesday asked me.

'I am, actually.' I hadn't eaten anything since the bagel in the limo this morning with Mr Monday, aside from a quick snack from the vending machine. Thinking of Mr Monday made my heart tumble over a little. I needed to get my feelings in check. Because whenever he crossed my mind, my body refused to behave. My breathing was affected and a flush raced through me, only to settle in a sweet ache between my thighs that begged for release. To my horror, I felt my nipples harden, so I crossed my arms, hoping my arousal for the man in my thoughts wouldn't be evident to Mr Wednesday. Being surrounded by sexy men made it hard for a girl to keep it together. I'd never been around so much male perfection before.

Last night, Mr Monday had come to collect me from Mr Tuesday. Would he show up again today? I looked at the red-headed hunk in front of me and tried to figure out how I was feeling. Was he just good to look at, or was there something more to him? What would I do if Mr Monday walked in right now?

'How about we go and get a bite to eat, then?'

'Just us? Well, what I mean is, you and I alone?' Shit, that still didn't sound any better. 'What I mean is—'

'I know what you mean.' His voice was low and sounded terribly intimate. 'Yes, just us. If that is okay with you?'

Was it okay? Was there something more happening here? I didn't know what to do. Be brave, I guess. Take a leap.

'Of course it is. I would love to go for something to eat.'

'I completely understand if you're not comfortable with the idea. Don't feel you have to, please, but it would be nice to whisk you away from here, away from the stresses of work.'

That made me feel a little better, and I relaxed.

'Plus, I'd like to get to know you better.' He smiled, and my anxiety eased further.

'And where do you have in mind?'

'Well, there's a quiet little place I know nearby . . .'

The thought of having some private time with him made my heart beat a little faster. 'I like that idea.' I was picking up sexual tension from him, and I shivered. 'Excellent. Then what do you say we blow this pop stand?'

'Yes, let's.'

My nerves were on edge. I was picking up his signals loud and clear, and I was pretty sure I was sending some as well. So far, there was no sign of Mr Monday, and it was late in the day. If he was coming to get me, he would have arrived by now. That left me free and clear to explore this connection I could have with Mr Wednesday. Anticipation mixed with trepidation inside me. When Mr Monday's face ghosted in my mind I wasn't entirely sure exploring the connection was what I wanted to do.

In the elevator, Mr Wednesday stood back, and I reached into my purse for the key card. I slipped it into the slot and the light panel illuminated. I turned to him, and he was looking at his phone. Stepping closer to my side, he leaned down. My heart jumped.

'Look at what my sister sent me.' He held out his phone so I could see it. I glanced at the screen but was unable to focus, as the sensation of him next to me was so completely overwhelming. His energy came off in waves and rippled all around me. I drew in a soft breath and hoped he didn't notice how he was affecting me. I looked up at him, and he was smiling down at his phone. It gave me the opportunity to look at him more closely. I had the urge to reach out and feel his beard, run my fingers through it and into his shaggy hair. Then he turned, and our eyes met. My hand was halfway up to touch him and I curled my fingers into a fist before pressing my knuckles tight to my chest. He lowered his head a little. *Was he going to kiss me?* My breathing became shallower. I leaned into him, needing to see how he would make me feel.

'You are an intriguing woman.' His words were low and soft, tender, and his blue eyes were full of a new emotion. Passion.

I trembled, not bothering to hide it. His arm curled around my waist, pulling me closer until my shoulder was tucked into his chest. I immediately compared his embrace to Mr Monday's. How I felt now compared to how I'd felt when I'd stumbled yesterday and he'd caught me. Was it different? Less or more electric?

I searched my feelings, needing my reactions to one man to be different to those to the other. I didn't get any answers. My body reacted to them equally powerfully. My brain wasn't cooperating and, for the time being, I decided to let it shut itself down. I needed to live in the moment. I almost didn't know what to feel or how I'd respond. In the space of two days, I'd met a number of sexy men and been in the arms of two.

'I shouldn't be doing this with you. I know better. And I'm sure you know better, too,' he murmured, and lowered his head toward mine.

I was unable to form words, so I didn't even bother to try. The elevator slowed as it arrived at the ground floor. He stepped away from me and I didn't want him to let me go, which surprised me. Then he pulled me back and I was flush against his chest. He dipped his head and I tipped my face up. Our lips met. It was tentative, until he deepened the kiss. I accepted him, needing this affirmation. There had to be something, some spark, but there was nothing. Granted, we'd been apart for most of the day but, in this case, absence hadn't made the heart grow fonder. I was both hugely disappointed and unbelievably relieved. The decision had been made. The elevator door opened and I hesitated for the briefest moment. I kept my eyes closed and kissed him back, just to be sure, my hands resting on his shoulders.

I heard the elevator door try to close. It made a jarring sound, as if the door had banged on something. I opened my eyes and looked. I let out a yelp and leapt out of Mr Wednesday's arms as if he'd exploded into flames. My stomach rioted when I met Mr Monday's icy gaze.

His face shuttered quickly, but not before I saw a thunderous expression slide away to reveal an impassive one. He turned his attention to Mr Wednesday, who seemed perfectly calm, despite the awkward situation.

I was horrified.

Mr Wednesday took my elbow and began to lead me from the elevator. I followed, unsure what to do. Once we were in the lobby, Mr Monday spoke.

'Thank you for your attention to Ms Canyon. I'll take things from here.'

Mr Wednesday halted and turned slowly to Mr Monday. I looked from one man to the other, breathless. The silence drew out painfully and I was about to explode when Mr Wednesday let me go.

'Tess, it's been a pleasure. Good luck with your endeavors.' The look on Mr Wednesday's face made me sad, but I had experienced a moment of clarity the minute I saw Mr Monday. If I was going to be kissing anyone, it should be him.

'Thank you. I've enjoyed my day.'

'Don't worry. This doesn't change anything regarding your proposal. I really hope your daycare idea is approved.' He cast a look at Mr Monday, then back to me. 'It shows compassion. And that is an important quality, which, sometimes, is sorely lacking here. We could use some compassion in this company.' Then he turned and walked away.

I couldn't be more shocked by that revelation, and that he'd pretty much pointed a finger at Mr Monday. What had all that been about? Had he just told me something about the inner workings of Diamond? No compassion? Not people-oriented? I was definitely looking forward to some quiet time to sort everything that I'd learned today out in my head.

I glanced up at Mr Monday, fully expecting him to be watching Mr Wednesday march off, but he was looking at me. He held out his hand, and I glanced down. Another key card. So I had succeeded today, even if his face did have an angry expression on it. I was at a loss for words, but took the card and shoved it into my purse.

'Let's go. You haven't eaten anything all day.'

I furrowed my brows. 'Are you spying on me? How do you know I haven't eaten?'

'Do you really think we wouldn't know your every move?' His words were sharp and cut deep. He was mad at me. What did that mean? He'd caught me kissing Mr Wednesday, and now he was being an asshole. Was he jealous? I eyed him to see if that was a possibility. No indication whatsoever of how he felt. Well, if he'd made a move first, then maybe I wouldn't have kissed another man.

I didn't want to be mad at him, but now I was. Nor did I

want him to think he owned me. More than that, though, I had to decide if I was more upset that my desire for him might now never be satisfied, now that he'd caught me kissing another man, or at the fact that my every move was being monitored. He looked at me and I shivered under his glowering stare. I wasn't sure what to say. Suddenly, I felt very uncomfortable. How stupid I was to think they wouldn't be keeping tabs on me! That meant I'd have to be extra careful. But did I even know what I wanted to do any more? I knew the man I wanted, but the direction my future was going to take looked a lot less clear.

MR THURSDAY

I hovered in the vestibule of my apartment building, peering through the torrential rain outside, waiting for Mr Monday to arrive. Clearly, I'd become used to our morning ritual. I frowned, getting worried. He should have arrived by now. I checked my watch. It was five after seven, and the first time he'd been late. For someone so annoyingly punctual, this was very out of character. The weather *was* horrid, close to hurricane conditions, and the traffic was sure to be hellish, too. But what if something had happened to him? My belly flipped over. I didn't like that thought one little bit. *Why?* I pondered it for a few minutes as I watched the rainwater skate down the street. I wasn't sure I was ready for the *why*. It opened up a whole new emotional frontier.

Was I falling for him? Could it be possible after such a short time? We had only had a few morning and evening encounters, one tender hand-holding, some sultry looks and flirtatious banter . . . all things that, under normal circumstances, might lead to more after time. Was this 'more' something that was even possible? I sighed when my body reacted once again to the mere thought of Mr Monday. Yes, I looked forward to our mornings together. Yes, I was becoming increasingly receptive to the idea of 'more' with him. Yes, I was attracted to him, more than any other man I'd ever been with, but, no, we hadn't even come close to a kiss. How could this feel so powerful when, in reality, nothing had really happened?

Had I totally screwed things up by impulsively kissing Mr Wednesday in the elevator and letting Mr Monday catch us? Was that why he was late? Maybe he wasn't late at all, maybe he was no longer coming. 'Oh God,' I moaned when I remembered the look on his face last night. 'Why was I so stupid?' Would he report back to Mr King that I'd been fraternizing with an employee? Been unprofessional and behaved in a manner unsuitable for a potential CEO? What if I had fucked things up? And all because of a kiss.

My belly clenched and I felt sick. I fretted and waited another ten minutes, chewing on my fingernail. Finally, I accepted that he wasn't coming. That hurt more than I cared to admit and, damn, if tears didn't prick at my eyes. Shit, shit, shit. I didn't like how upset I was feeling right now. I needed to pull myself together. I rubbed my eyes and looked through the window, out at the rain-soaked street.

I'd better try to get a taxi. Whatever the reason behind Mr Monday's absence, I still had to go to Diamond Enterprises. Until I knew for sure that I'd failed, I had to keep going. There was too much at stake to get disqualified through sheer accident.

One of my neighbors came down the stairs and paused by the door.

'Now, that's a downpour,' she said.

'I know. I'm waiting for the courage to run out and find a cab.' I hope she hadn't heard me whining to myself a moment ago.

'Are you going downtown? We could share one if you like?'

'Yes, I am.' It would be nice to have a bit of company.

We watched through the door for a cab. I still couldn't shake the feeling of unease, and I felt even more upset. Finally, a taxi came down the street.

'There,' I said, and pulled the hood of my sunshine-yellow raincoat – a find dating back to the sixties – over my head and ran out, my neighbor hot on my heels. Thankfully, the cab stopped and we climbed inside, out of the rain. I could have been a whole lot wetter if I hadn't worn my 'hippie' raincoat and wellingtons – as my mom called them. She'd been shopping with me when I'd found them, shortly before she'd moved back to her hometown of Eastbourne, England. Suddenly, I had a pang of missing Mom. She had stayed in the States until I went to college; then, there was no point lingering any longer, she'd said. I was an adult, and she wanted to go home. The melancholy settled in as the rainy day reinforced my dreary mood.

'I like your rain gear,' my neighbor said. 'Oh, and I'm Mia. I've seen you around, but we've never officially met.'

'Hi, Mia, I'm Tess. Good to finally meet you.'

'Yes, I hope we have the chance to meet again.'

'That would be nice.' I really meant it. Meeting her had made me realize how friendless I was, and I blamed that completely on my obsession with getting my revenge on Diamond.

We chatted during the drive, and I was glad for the distraction.

'We should go out sometime. I'm in 101 – just come and holler for me any time.'

'I will for sure. Things are really crazy right now. How about we chat when the dust settles?'

'Perfect. I look forward to it. Here.' Mia handed me some money and opened the cab door at her stop. 'Thanks for sharing the cab.'

Then she was gone. Loneliness swamped me again. As I rode the rest of the way to the office, the world a streaky blur through the windows, I thought about how hazy my future was. Then moved on to how my brief conversation with Mia had served only to highlight how much I'd sacrificed for my revenge. Friendships. Life. Enjoying the world around me. And Mr Monday's absence made things worse. While he didn't give me much help about what to expect from each day, the tidbits of information he did dispense usually had me heading in the right direction. I missed him. There was no flirtatious hello, no Costa Rican coffee or New York bagels, no casual touches. Most importantly, there was no him.

The cab arrived at Diamond Enterprises and the doorman waited patiently while I paid the cabbie. I was truly thankful for the covered driveway. Thunder crashed; it seemed to shake the foundations of the building. Spray from the deluge of rain misted around me as I dashed through the doors into the lobby. I hoped the growing storm wouldn't be an omen for how the day was going to go. Stomping my feet to get rid of any extra rain water on my wellies, not wanting to slide and potentially fall, probably very ungracefully, on the highly polished marble floor, I walked to the reception desk.

I smiled when Stanley stood up. 'Good morning, Stanley,' I said. 'How are you?'

'I'm fine, Ms Canyon. Welcome back for another day.'

'Thank you. I'm still here – it's a miracle.'

I pointed toward the driveway. Have you seen Mr—?' I trailed off, because I still didn't know his real name and referring to him as Mr Monday to Stanley seemed rather ridiculous.

Stanley shook his head. 'No, I'm sorry. I can't tell you where he is.' He looked down as if checking something and shook his head again.

'No worries. Have a great day.'

He clearly didn't buy my forced cheerfulness, but he was kind enough to let me maintain my pretense. I turned to face the elevator bank, my heart sinking again. I toyed with the key card in my pocket, flicking my thumb on the corner. Mr Monday usually told me which floor the day's test was going to take place on. Without him, I'd have to resort to inserting the card and pushing all the buttons until I found the one that worked. Great.

'Wait, Ms Canyon. I have a letter here for you.'

Stanley held out an envelope, which I took. It was of very high-quality paper and had a little seal in the top-left corner. It was a fancy K in an elegant font. My heart leapt. This would be the first communication I'd had from Mr King since Monday night.

I glanced up at Stanley. 'Thank you.'

I turned the envelope over in my hand, carefully slipping my finger underneath the sealed flap and working it open, trying not to ruin the envelope. I headed toward the elevator bank. The envelope open, I hesitated before pulling out the single sheet of paper inside. I called for the elevator. Once I was inside, I pushed in the key card and played the guess-the-floor-game. Finally, the button for the seventieth floor lit up.

'Going up in the world, I see,' I murmured to the empty elevator. I slid the letter out of the envelope and held it, dying to read the letter but also dreading it. What if it told me I had failed the last test? That I was finished, that it was time to leave? But then Stanley would have been given some kind of instructions to not let me in. Based on that, I decided I wasn't out on my ear yet.

Gently, I unfolded the paper, which was also high-quality, and had an embossed letterhead, and read the letter.

Ms Canyon, this is your fourth test. That means you are doing well. Of course, I'm not surprised by that. You wouldn't have made it to the first interview had you not been capable. Congratulations. Presuming you continue to do well, I will be seeing you in a few days. Regards, King

Well, that was a whole lot of nothing, I thought, but at least now I knew one thing to expect over the next few days. I stepped out on to the seventieth floor and was immediately struck by the beauty of the decor. It was almost like the floor on which I had had my initial interview, but much more over the top.

Unlike yesterday, there was a receptionist, and she was clearly expecting me.

'Good morning, Ms Canyon.'

I smiled, and had to stop myself from rolling my eyes. I'd gotten used to the fact that everybody knew me before I even got a chance to learn their name.

'Good morning.' I knew better than to ask what was on this floor or what I'd be expected to do today. Even if the receptionist did have the clearance to know about this crazy interview, she still wouldn' t tell me anything.

With a polite smile, the woman pointed at a door to the right. 'Through there, please.' I heard a click and realized she had unlocked the door from behind her desk. I wasn't surprised. The security in this building was tighter than in Fort Knox. I thanked her before slipping through the door.

I was rather startled by the offices lining both sides of the hall. It was busy, chaotic, with lots of people bustling around.

One office was a disaster, with bankers boxes and loose files stacked impossibly high. The only clear spot was a path for the office's occupant to walk from his desk, barricaded by a mess of clutter, to the door. I was horrified. How could anyone work like that? I lingered a beat too long in my horror and the guy looked up at me. I smiled and nodded, but he ignored me and went back to his work. *Hmm, rude – much? But who can blame him when he works in a pit?* I carried on, and it became clear that I had come to the worker-bee area. No other office was as bad as that first one, but there was a feeling of neglect and unkemptness across the whole floor. It did not match the glossy veneer of the public areas of the Diamond.

I continued to wander down the hall, peering into offices as I went. There was nothing to tell me what they did up here on the seventieth, but I was sure I would find out soon enough. I figured somebody would find me and take me to where I needed to be, or I would stumble across it. That's how things seemed to be working in general.

The hallway turned sharply. A conference room on one side ran along the windows, with more offices on the other. I looked into the conference room and noted that there were a few people huddled around the table, laptops and manila folders scattered across it. A man looked up from his position at the head of the table, a very good-looking, impressively built man. I immediately knew this was where I was meant to be. I walked in, absolutely confident the man was Mr Thursday.

'Good morning,' I greeted everyone. Four pairs of eyes looked up at me. It was hard not to feel intimidated, but I did my best to keep cool. I closed the door, took my raincoat off and hung it on the coat tree. Then I drew in a quiet breath as I slipped out of my wellies and put on my indoor shoes, a pair of nice ballet flats that fit well with the slim black slacks I was wearing that ended just above my ankles. I smoothed down the three-quarter-length sleeves of my power red blouse, pleased at the way in which my nail polish matched my top. I turned and found myself a spot at the table.

Everyone watched me, and no one appeared the least bit surprised at my having come in, which confirmed that I was in the right place.

Mr Thursday crossed his arms, sitting back in his chair and watched me with a look that made my belly flutter. He was handsome, I'd give him that. His grey suit fit him to perfection and complemented his eyes, which were multiple shades of gray. The only thing that was a little chilling was that they held no emotion. I glanced around the table, quickly assessing the two other men and one woman as they gazed back at me, all with similarly closed and almost judging expressions.

'Ms Canyon, good of you to join us,' said Mr Thursday. His voice was smooth as silk and a little tingle ran down my arms, but his tone inferred that I was late. At least, that's how I perceived it. I glanced at my watch, hoping he'd notice and realize that I wasn't all that late. Eight o'clock was the time Mr Monday and I usually arrived at the office, and I wasn't too far off that. I carefully kept my face expressionless when I remembered him, then returned my attention to Mr Thursday.

'I'm glad to be here. What are you working on?' I slid my chair forward and clasped my hands on the table, looking at each person in turn, then settling my gaze on Mr Thursday.

He watched me back and I thought I saw a flicker of respect – or *some*thing – I wasn't entirely sure, flash in his gaze. I had to concentrate on keeping my hands from trembling and my breathing even, so I tightened my fingers. Until I knew my test and could focus on it, I'd be on edge. I'd discovered that about myself over the past couple of days. Once I knew the task at hand, I was relentless until it was completed. It had been hard not being in control and I was surprised at how well I'd adjusted to these on-the-fly tests. I hadn't really expected to be faced with the human element of a corporation either. It had been an eye opener and, even though I still wanted revenge for my dad, I was beginning to wonder if it was worth the price of destroying so many other lives. I looked around the table and tried to wait patiently to see what drama would unfold today.

'Cathy, please give a file to Ms Canyon.'

The dark-haired woman sitting across from me selected a folder and pushed it over to me. I opened it, and my eyes nearly bugged out. It was the legal paperwork for the Northbrook deal. I glanced up at Mr Thursday.

'Is there a problem with this?'

'To keep this meeting brief and on point, I'll give you a quick overview.' He stood up. I couldn't help checking him out as he turned and faced the windows. He put his hands on his hips, pushing the tails of his suit jacket back, and giving me a very fine view of his very shapely and muscled behind. His blond hair was neatly trimmed across the back of his neck and over his ears, short on top. He was tailored in every way. I bet he even had his nails manicured. I drew in a breath. These last few days had been exceptional in the visual department where men were concerned.

When he turned back to us I glanced at his hands. Yep, either he was very good at doing his own nails or he had them done. They even had a fine sheen to them. Looking at them, his long fingers splayed over his hips, drew my attention to the front of his slacks. Right where I shouldn't be looking. Thankfully, there was no significant telltale bulge to get me flustered any more. I dropped my gaze. While he was a very fine specimen of a man, he only succeeded in reminding me of Mr

Monday, and I felt another pang in my heart, wondering why he hadn't shown up.

'I am impressed with the negotiations you did with Northbrook on Tuesday,' he said, taking his place back at the table. 'We've filed the papers, and I did put in a clause about the effectiveness of the microchip.'

'Is there an issue? We went into the deal knowing the chip was still unproven,' I asked. A sick feeling that, somehow, I'd screwed up started to grow.

He waved his hand as if dismissing my concern. 'No, nothing to do with Northbrook. Look at the next document.'

I flipped the stapled Northbrook papers over. I had no idea what to expect. There were outlines of two separate companies. Intrigued, I read through the documents quickly. It appeared there was an option to buy one of two businesses. I checked the names. That of Rockwood Country Club stunned me. I smiled.

'What do you find humorous, Ms Canyon?' Mr Thursday asked, and I glanced up at him. The smile ran away from my face at his no-nonsense expression.

'The Rockwood Country Club is a fabulous place. I love it, and to see that Diamond wants to finally buy it is great.'

'What do you mean by finally?'

'Well, I was told on Tuesday that it had been put on the list of potential businesses and land purchases for Diamond to acquire a while ago. It just never happened.' I shrugged my shoulders. 'Now it might.'

'Yes, indeed.' He pointed to the file. 'Look at the other one.'

I flipped the papers over and furrowed my brows. It was a company I hadn't heard of.

'Who are they?' I scanned the pages, looking for a description of their business.

'A fiber-optics provider.'

'Really? And the reason for considering them?'

A man to Cathy's left spoke up, and I looked at him. 'With the acquisition of Northbrook, having our own fiber-optics supplier will significantly reduce the costs of outsourcing some materials and labor.'

I nodded. 'Makes sense. And I assume you have a job for me?' I looked at Mr Thursday.

He smiled for the first time, and I was enchanted. I came *this close* to telling him he should smile more often. 'Yes, I do. You have developed a bit of a reputation for digging up information. We need to know everything there is to know about these two companies in order to be able to make the right decision.'

I nodded. 'Right up my alley. But what do you mean, I've "developed a bit of a reputation"?'

He lifted a shoulder. 'Simply that. You've impressed the company over the previous few days, and we need your skills.'

'But you have an army of staff.' I indicated behind me with my thumb.

'Perhaps, but this is a task best suited to you.' He rested his fingers on his cell phone, which sat on the desk, then pulled it toward him. He glanced down at the time. 'You have until the end of the day, and then we will reconvene.'

One day! To do in-depth research on two different organizations? It was impossible. I wasn't about to voice that, though. 'Right, then. Is there a computer and an office available to me?'

Mr Thursday swept up his phone and a few of the folders and stood up. 'Follow me.'

I did, and we walked out of the office, back into the hive of activity and along down the hall, before stopping in front of the office of the man with a million boxes.

Mr Thursday stood in the doorway and I stepped in closer

to him so I could also see through the door. The man looked up. He appeared none too pleased by the interruption.

'George, I'd like you to meet Tess Canyon. She's going to be with us today, in the office across the hall from you. Tess, if you have any questions, George is your man.'

I made eye contact with him and tried not to be intimidated by his irritated expression. 'Hi, George. It's nice to meet you.'

He pushed his wild, Einstein-like hair back and narrowed his eyes, as if he could see right inside me. I swallowed and stood my ground, even though this man had me almost quaking in my ballet flats. He was a severe-looking guy.

'Tess, good to meet you. If you need something or have a question, just pop on over.' His voice was pleasant; his demeanor had belied his manner.

I was surprised. I hadn't expected him to be so cordial. I'd half expected his nature to be just as gruff as his appearance, but his cranky personality seemed to fade away at his words. I relaxed and let out a soft breath.

'Thanks, George, I appreciate the offer. I'll try not to bother you.'

'No problem at all. Anytime, like I said. I have a long memory.' He smiled, and the bridge of his nose crinkled.

George dropped his attention back to his work, and I backed up as Mr Thursday turned around and indicated the office across the hall. I went inside, and wasn't surprised when it turned out to be just as barren as the office I'd been allocated yesterday.

'Okay,' Mr Thursday said. 'You're all set, then. I'll check in on you later.'

I felt the time-crunch sit with the weight of an elephant on my chest. 'Will do. See you then.' I pulled the files he'd dropped on the desk in front of me and flipped the top one open as I spun in the chair to fire up the computer. I logged in, now becoming quite the pro at maneuvering around the system. My brain was flying as I clicked and opened a bunch of windows. I appreciated the dual monitors in this office. I dived into my normal research routine, finessing tidbits of useful data from internet trash, and then my mind began to wander as I thought about Mr Thursday. He was clearly one of the top lawyers for Diamond, if not the lead counsel, so I considered trying to pump him for info.

All of the previous Mr Days-of-the-Week had held a certain attraction for me, and there was a bit of a spark with Mr Thursday, but he was no Mr Monday. Mr Thursday's good looks were overshadowed by his abrupt mannerisms. He was a no-nonsense, get-the-job-done kinda guy. I suppose Mr Thursday resembled Benedict Cumberbatch a bit, in a disheveled, sexy way. I was reminded of a GIF I'd seen on Facebook which Cumberbatch had posted on International Kissing Day. It was one of the sexiest kissing GIFs I'd ever seen and I got warm thinking about it. I'd watched that clip over and over and over, wishing I was that girl he was so deliciously kissing. I pictured Mr Thursday's face in place of Benedict's, but it soon morphed into Mr Monday's. I sighed, dropped my chin into my hand and played the scene over in my head yet again. I was snapped out of my moment by a bunch of people rushing past my office door, loudly arguing.

Back to work.

Now that I had at least an outline of the initial points for my research, I read the files more thoroughly. I wanted to understand them completely. Legalese was not my forte, but I was able to make sense of most of it. I made some notes on a legal pad, concentrating more on the fiber-optics company than on the country club. Mr Tuesday hadn't said anything about this when we drove out to the club, so I had no idea if it had already been extensively researched, but I would do my own due diligence.

There was one point about KevOptics that leapt out at me. It could have been easily missed, but I found it. The name of the owner seemed to be cleverly hidden, and it was only through a chance search that I found it. When I ran a search on the name Kevin Lyle, not much came up in the results but, interestingly enough, Diamond's website topped the list. Could there be some kind of connection between Diamond and Kevin? Could he have been a former employee?

Hmn, I thought. I wondered why he had left, how he had left, and if there was an ulterior motive behind the proposed deal. Was Kevin Lyle trying to set something up? My natural curiosity needed to be sated, and I knew exactly who to talk to. I gathered up my papers, putting them back in one of the folders, closed it and placed it on my seat so no one would disturb the order of the pages. I made sure I had yesterday's key card, because I needed to go and visit Carol. Inside the elevator, I inserted the card and pressed the floor for HR. I breathed a sigh of relief. I was right in thinking that the old key card would work. I rode down to Human Resources, not feeling out of place this time. Once through the outer door, I scanned the floor, looking for Carol. I wandered between the desks and finally found her. She had an office of her own, a good one with a great view. I realized then that she had to be management.

'Knock knock,' I said, rapping my knuckles on the doorjamb. She looked up and seemed genuinely happy to see me.

'Tess! What a nice surprise.'

'Carol, hi. I hope you don't mind me popping in on you?'

'Of course not. What are you doing here?' She beckoned me forward, and I stepped inside the office.

'I need a moment of your time, if you're free?'

I looked around to see if anybody was close enough to eavesdrop. What I was about to ask Carol to do would be breaking company rules. Closing the door with a firm click, I sat in the chair across from her desk.

'Oh, seems like you're on a mission,' she said, and her eyes widened.

'Kind of. I need a favor.'

Carol leaned back in her chair, toying absently with a pen. 'How can I help you?'

'Well, I've been given a project and, during my research, I've come across an oddity, and I thought you might be able to help clear it up.' I leaned forward. 'You have access to the records for previous employees, yes?'

'Of course.' She indicated the computer with the tip of her pen.

'Okay, great. I'm looking for information on a former employee by the name of Kevin Lyle. Does that ring a bell? Can you help?'

Carol looked at me thoughtfully, now tapping the pen on the desk, before dropping it and steepling her fingers. 'Kevin Lyle. I don't recall that name. But still, there's something niggling in the back of my brain. Give me a minute.' She turned to her computer, and her fingers flew over the keyboard. After a couple of minutes, she said, 'That's curious.'

If I leaned any further forward, I would be sprawled across her desk. 'What is?'

'There's no Kevin Lyle listed as an employee. But a *Robert* Lyle did work for us.'

'Are there any further details? What was his position? Why did he leave? Was he fired?'

'Whoa! Whoa!' Carol cried out, laughing. 'You're firing

questions at me more quickly than I can give you the answers. Hold your horses, and let me find out.' She sobered and caught me with a look. A very determined one. 'You know what you're asking me to do is a violation of confidentiality. If I get caught, I could lose my job over this.'

I fidgeted in my seat. Carol would be putting it all on the line for me, a stranger, but I had to believe I could protect her if it came down to it. As CEO, I'd have access to all this information anyway. 'I know. I wouldn't ask if it wasn't important, to me and to Diamond. Your name will never come up.'

'You know, it's hard not to trust you. Perhaps it's foolish of me, but you were so kind to Jenny yesterday I believe you have good intentions.'

My heart swelled. It had been a long time since anyone had said anything nice to me. 'Aw, thank you. You don't know how much that means to me.'

Carol nodded and smiled. It was an almost motherly smile, which made me feel a bit sentimental about my own mom.

She turned back to the computer and navigated through the personnel system. 'Okay, it seems he left about ten years ago. He was a Research and Development guy. Hmmm, there's not a whole lot of information here. Let me see if I can pull up a performance review.'

I tried not to feel anxious about what she might find. Everything to do with Diamond had layers upon layers. It was never straightforward, just a mess of secrets and concealment. I got drawn into this mess because my father had been falsely accused, and now here was another former employee hiding something from the company. Though these tests kept me too busy to look for the documents I needed for my revenge, I felt as if I were on a precipice, as if taking one step forward would change everything.

'So here we go. His last appraisal gave him a glowing report. The only negative was that he overstepped boundaries.' Carol looked at me and raised her eyebrows. 'Some companies would consider that a good thing. Innovative. Forward-thinking. Pushing the envelope. Not here at Diamond. You either conform or you're out. My guess is that he didn't conform and chose to leave.'

'But why?' I mused out loud. 'Do you think he's the same guy as Kevin Lyle, just under a new name?'

'I don't know. There's nothing to indicate they are one and the same man.' Carolyn leaned forward and concentrated, tapping on the keyboard, her brow furrowed. 'Hang on!'

'What?' I sat up, hoping for a grand piece of information.

'Look at this,' Carol said. 'He had a brother listed on his employee paperwork as his emergency contact, a K. Lyle.'

'Seriously?' I sat back, and thought about it. Carol was quiet, too. Then I looked up at her. 'What are the odds that Kevin Lyle and K. Lyle are the same person?'

'Well, I don't know what you found to make you think Kevin Lyle worked for us in the first place, but it seems reasonable to believe that he and Robert are connected.'

'I think so, too. Can you print out the records?'

Carol sighed, leaned back in her chair again and shook her head. 'No. I don't dare. You know they can trace print-outs and emails. The system logs everything. So, here –' she pushed a pad of paper and a pen over to me – 'I can read out the information and you can take notes.'

'Okay.' I grabbed the pad and rested it on my knee. 'Ready.'

For the next couple minutes I frantically scribbled down what Carol said. Most of what she told me was minutiae, but there were a few pieces of information I could use to dig up more dirt on the internet. You'd be surprised what you can find when armed with your target's personal email address and current hometown. A few minutes later, I ripped my notes out of the pad and put it back on her desk, dropping the pen on top. With swift fingers, she exited the program and both of us sat back in our chairs, giving a big sigh of relief. I know I felt like a conspirator, and I wondered if she did as well. Hopefully, we'd get away with this illicit search.

'Thank you,' I said to her.

'No problem. That's the most fun I've had in a while. But just remember what I said.' She was still smiling.

'Absolutely! I have your back.'

I heard a sound and nearly swallowed my tongue when I saw Mr Wednesday in the office doorway. 'Tess, what are you doing here?'

Carol and I jumped, as if we were guilty of the vilest sin, and looked at him. I hoped the flush I felt race across my cheeks wasn't too evident. My heart leapt into double time and I was worried that if I spoke I would stammer and make a fool of myself. I was still a bit unnerved after our kiss in the elevator.

'Oh, hi.' I pushed the folded sheets of paper under my thigh. 'I was just visiting Carol. We met yesterday and I had a moment so I decided to come down and say hi to her again. How are you?'

He was quiet, and I knew full well what was going through his mind. Our kiss. Mr Monday seeing it. His sarcastic remark. I felt bad, and wondered if I had led him on. I hoped not.

'I see.' Yes, he was reserved. All business. Gone was his sexy manner from yesterday and in its place was a chilly attitude. I'd hurt him and I felt terrible. 'I thought you weren't on this floor today.'

So the Mr Days-of-the-Week knew what I was up to each day. I looked at Carol, and smiled. 'It was good chatting with you. I guess I should get back up to the office I'm camped out in today.' I stood and scrunched the papers into my hand.

She seemed to understand that I was sending her a silent message. She put on a good poker-face and remained just as businesslike as Mr Wednesday. 'Thanks so much for coming down to visit. We'll have to get together for another one of those cappuccinos you're so good at making.'

'It's a deal. Any time.' I stood and walked to the door.

Mr Wednesday blocked my way, I wasn't sure if it was intentional or not, but his nearness flustered me a little. I lifted my hand and touched my lips, the lips he'd kissed less than twenty-four hours ago. It hadn't been Mr Wednesday's kiss I really wanted. I felt uncomfortable near him, but I hoped there'd be no long-term repercussions. As I walked past Mr Wednesday, I flicked up a glance and gave him an uncertain smile. 'I guess I'll see you later.'

He looked down at me and nodded. 'Yes, I think you probably will.'

I dashed to the elevator. I thought about what he said as I rode up to the Legal department. Had he meant anything by his comment? Chills ran down my spine. Did he know something I didn't? It was highly likely, and no real surprise, because everyone knew more than me.

All the thoughts galloping around in my head muddled up the rest of my emotions. I was on such high alert for any possible thing that could go wrong, I'm pretty sure I was close to thinking it was all a conspiracy. I needed to get a grip and stop reading things into words that were probably nothing to be concerned about. Of course he'd see me later. He was the head of HR and I was having a week-long interview.

Once the elevator door opened, I shoved all unsettling thoughts away. I had a job to do, and that had to be my main focus. All my plans depended on it. Back in my temporary office, I shut the door and spread out the papers with my scribbled notes. Carefully, I smoothed out the crinkles so I could concentrate on organizing the information.

I was convinced there was a relationship between Robert and Kevin Lyle. Now that I had additional information about Robert, I did another search and found his obituary. It didn't list a cause of death, but it asked that donations be made to a cancer charity in lieu of flowers. A few clicks later and I'd found a memorial webpage.

Robert was an electrical engineer, a graduate of MIT. From what I could find, he'd developed some kind of communication optic before he passed away. I was impressed. This man was no slouch. So did he voluntarily leave Diamond because he was sick, or did the company force him out?

I decided to research Kevin's education to see if he had a similar background, but I found that he had done an arts degree. There was nothing in his history to suggest a familiarity with technology or business. So how did he end up running KevOptics? How could he run the organization and sell fiber optics if he knew nothing about the product? Maybe Kevin had been trained by his brother before Robert died, but that seemed a bit of a stretch.

So I looked for investor-relations information about the company. There wasn't anything of substance, because it had never gone public. All I had was the limited information on KevOptics' website. It confirmed that Kevin was CEO, and there was a brief paragraph about the background of the company that said a whole lot of nothing; no mention of Robert at all. My instincts told me that something was going on here. Where were the glossy sales brochures? The testimonials from satisfied clients? Why were there no interviews with Kevin, or profiles of the company, in trade publications? I needed something to prove whether KevOptics was a legit company, or not. It was time to break out the really big research voodoo.

After some time, I sat back and blew out a puff of air, now firmly convinced that KevOptics didn't really exist. On a hunch, I had done a search through Legal's files, reasoning that if Robert had been let go because of his cancer, the company would've checked with Legal first. I found that he hadn't been fired so much as put on long-term disability at a reduced salary, after having exhausted his sick days. If he'd recovered, he could've returned to work but, in the meantime, he'd been stuck, paying a good portion of the cost of his health insurance out of his own pocket. Between that and his medical bills, Robert had blown his savings. The only thing of value he had to leave his brother was a patent on a new type of fiber-optic cable.

Kevin had basically built a shell of a company around the patent, banking on Diamond investigating the technology and not looking too closely at the company. My guess was that he thought he could get more money for a company, rather than just a patent. The deal was a farce. Kevin wanted money and revenge for his brother. I surged to my feet, alarmed. The chair flew back into the wall with a crash, and the noise brought George to my doorway.

'What's happened?' He looked concerned, and I stared at him, unsure how much to tell him. So I decided to play it down.

'Oh, nothing. I just tripped over the chair when I stood up.' I waved my hand and gave a little laugh, which I hoped didn't sound too fake.

'You're sure?' he pressed, and I answered with a bright smile. I couldn't very well tell him that I'd discovered someone hatching a revenge plot against Diamond. George stared at me as if he were trying to read my mind. I concentrated on righting the chair, giving it a little spin as I tried to collect my thoughts.

'Yes, absolutely. It's all good. Thank you for asking.' I glanced at my watch, and sat down again in the chair. 'I'm sorry, but I really do need to finish this.'

He nodded again and shuffled across the hall to his chaotic office. I turned my attention back to my dilemma. What should I do? I could tell Mr Thursday that the only thing of value at KevOptics was the patent and that Diamond could withdraw or change their initial offer. I could say nothing and recommend the country club as a better choice. Or . . . I could say nothing and recommend KevOptics. I could let Kevin achieve his revenge, as I so badly wanted to achieve mine.

But at what cost? What would happen if the sale went through and Diamond discovered they'd paid an exorbitant sum just for a patent? It would be years before they recouped their money, if ever. Still, Diamond was such a huge company, surely the money would just be a drop in the ocean for them. Yet what about Mr Thursday? Would he get in trouble for not having worked out that the deal was fraudulent?

A part of me – a large part – wanted to help Kevin. Diamond had abandoned his brother in his time of need, just like they'd screwed over my father. The rest of me, though, knew this was wrong. My plan of releasing the executive expenses reports to the media might be considered theft of proprietary information, but I wouldn't be benefiting from it personally. Kevin stood to walk away with millions of dollars.

I was still wrestling with my moral dilemma when a voice startled me.

'So how's it going?' Mr Thursday stood framed in the doorway, one hand on the jamb, as he leaned slightly into the office.

'Pretty good.' I had a burning urgency to blurt everything out, and I barely managed to contain myself.

'Well, it's well past lunch, and I think it's time for a break.'

I glanced at my watch. Wow, I'd had no idea the time had flown by like that. 'Yes, we're almost at the end of the work day. Do you want to know my findings?'

'All in due time. Are you hungry?' he asked.

I gave him a smile and turned my head to the side coquettishly. Anything to distract him from the fact that I had no bloody clue what I wanted to do with the information I had. 'Are you inviting me out for a late lunch?'

He gave me a slight smile. 'Yes. If you would like to look at it like that. I am inviting you to lunch.'

I stood up and smoothed down the top of my pants. Nothing like having lunch with a hot guy to keep the mind from imploding over an ethical dilemma. I'm glad I managed not to say the words out loud, because they wouldn't have gone over all that well. He was a rather forceful sort of man.

'Where? Is it still raining?'

'It's fine. Come on. I like to get out of the office at lunch.'

That surprised me. He seemed so much the company man, I thought he'd have his nose to the grindstone all day.

'Oh, okay. Let me go and get my coat and boots. It was pouring the last time I checked.'

'The sun is out, but the weather reports say there's more rain coming. It cut the heat a bit so, if we go now, we'll be fine before the rain comes back again.'

'My mom always watched the weather. She would report to us all the time so we were prepared.'

'It doesn't hurt to know what Mother Nature has in store. Trust me.' He looked at me, and I was curious, because there seemed like there was a story there.

'Why, did you get caught out in a particularly bad storm?'

I saw a muscle in his jaw twitch. 'You could say that.' But he didn't elaborate further and hustled me out the office.

'What happened?' I asked him when we were in the elevator.

'I grew up in Florida. Hurricanes like to visit.'

'Oh, yes.' I looked at him from the corner of my eye. I was dying to ask him more about what that was like but thought better of it.

'What's with George? His office is crazy. It can't be healthy, or even safe. What if there was a fire? It's a rabbit warren.'

He looked at me coolly, and I realized then that, while he might be handsome, he wasn't my type at all. Mr Monday never made me feel bad for asking questions.

'He's our longest-serving on-staff lawyer. Been around here since dirt was born.' I smiled at his comment; I hadn't thought he had it in him to have a sense of humor. 'He's a conspiracy theorist and *trusts no one.* So he refuses to have anything put into corporate storage. All his old files are in his office and it's locked up tighter than a drum whenever he leaves.'

'What an odd man,' I mused. 'That's interesting.'

Could that debacle of an office contain some documentation on my dad? If it did, how would I ever find it in there? Plus, if George was as suspicious as Mr Thursday said, it wasn't as if I could snoop around in there.

'Doesn't he have to have all those papers scanned into the digital repository? For security purposes, or in case there's a fire?'

The elevator door opened and Mr Thursday stood aside, his hand in front of the door so I could pass.

'It took him a while to come on board with digital archiving. Once we managed to convince him it was necessary, he started scanning stuff during his spare time and, sometimes, he'll let people he trusts scan things as well. It's been a long process, and he's gotten about halfway there, but he still refuses to give up the hard copies. He's due to retire next year. Then we'll be able to get all the scanning done and finally shred everything without him hovering about like a mother hen.'

I felt Mr Thursday's presence as he walked behind me. Any initial attraction I had for him had long since faded and, in truth, it hadn't been all that powerful to begin with. Mr Monday flashed through my mind again. What had happened to him? The fact that I didn't even know his real name meant I couldn't even ask anybody. So I was left in this state of limbo and concern, desperate to know why he hadn't shown up today.

I wondered where Mr Thursday was taking me for lunch. There were restaurants and cafés everywhere in New York City.

'What are we going to eat?' I realized I was starving.

'My favorite.'

'Which is?'

'Hot dogs.'

I laughed out loud. 'Seriously? Hot dogs?'

He gave the most genuine smile I'd seen since I first laid eyes on him this morning. 'Yep. There's a great hot dog cart just around the corner.'

I wasn't sure if I was disappointed to be having a street dog. 'It's been a long time since I've had one of those,' I said.

I looked for Stanley as we passed the Security station, but he wasn't there. There was another man instead, and I wasn't surprised to see that he was also very muscled and impressive-looking. We left the building and walked out on to the street. It was cooler, clouds blocking the relentless summer sun, but it was still very humid.

'I thought you said it was sunny,' I challenged Mr Thursday, before admitting, 'I do like days like this, cloudy, with an almost sultry feel to the air.' The only downfall of being in the city was the persistent summer smell of damp garbage and hot sewage. I would have much preferred to be back at the country club.

'It was sunny when I last checked.'

I looked up between the towering skyscrapers. 'I can't see any sign of sun. My mom used to say that if there was enough blue sky to patch a sailor's pants, it was going to be a nice day.' I turned to him and smiled. 'She's English.'

'Well, I guess those sailors are going to have a lot of holes in their pants today.' He smiled back.

Mr Thursday touched my elbow and led me through the crowds on the street. It was as if everybody had spilled out of the buildings when the rain let up, and the streets were packed. It was nice of him to take me to lunch, even if it was just for a hot dog, but I couldn't help wishing Mr Monday were here instead.

There was a line at the hot dog vendor's, but I didn't mind. It was nice to be outside and to be standing next to a good-looking man. I noticed the looks of the other ladies close by as they gave him the once-over and then threw an almost snarly look at me. They thought we were a couple. I didn't mind that, but little did they know that the guy who was working his way into my heart was even more gorgeous than Mr Thursday.

'So tell me, what have you found? Give me a quick overview.'

This was it. I had to make a decision right now. Did I side with Diamond and warn them, or did I help Kevin achieve his revenge? In the end, I had to do what I believed to be right.

'Well, I found out some very interesting information. So my recommendation is to be very wary of KevOptics.'

He shot me a look and raised his eyebrows. 'Really? What makes you say that?'

'I believe the company is not what it appears to be.'

We were at the front of the line now, and he ordered for us without asking me my preference. As he reached into his pocket for some money, I quietly asked the vendor for onions on my hot dog and a bottle of lemonade. Mr Monday would've made sure I got exactly I wanted. I watched Mr Thursday peel a twenty from a wad of cash and hand it to the vendor.

He shook his head when the man offered him change back, and took the hot dogs, handing me mine. I added a little bit of ketchup and mustard, juggling the hot dog and the bottle of lemonade. His hot dog was fully loaded, and he added on every condiment possible.

I took a bite and closed my eyes with delight. After my first chew and swallow I said, 'There certainly isn't anything like a street dog.'

'You got that right,' he answered, then took a bite of his. He lifted it and nodded his head in approval.

'I know.' I raised mine and we did a 'cheers' with our food. I was waiting for him to ask more about my research, almost hoping he wouldn't. I decided that eating my hot dog was the best course of action.

The fact that we were on the street eating a hot dog, not upstairs in a posh dining room, plus the fact that he'd given the vendor a hefty tip, told me a little more about him. I was used to lawyers always being worried about having the best of the best, or about being seen wearing the latest status symbols. Mr Thursday had a very expensive, well-tailored suit on, but now I could also easily see him in Tommy Bahamas clothing, with bare feet, just chilling with a beer on a beach-side patio.

We ate in silence. He finished much more quickly than I did, and he drained the last of his can of soda before putting his garbage in the appropriate recycling bins. That also spoke volumes to me.

'Hurry up and finish so we can get back. I want to hear what you've discovered.'

Now he was rushing me. Contrarily, I made sure to nibble slowly at the last bite of my hot dog, and then I sauntered over to the bins to dispose of my garbage, sipping at the dregs of my lemonade. After delicately wiping my face with a napkin, I tossed it, too, and walked back to Mr Thursday.

'I have a few hours left on my deadline. While I'm confident of my assessment about KevOptics, I still have to do some digging on the country club.' He placed his hand on the small of my back and guided me back through the crowd of lunch-goers. Just before we got into the underground driveway, the skies opened up, and we ran the last little bit. I laughed, and he did, too.

'That was perfect timing, if I do say so myself.' Thunder rumbled and lightning flashed as we ducked inside the lobby. Stanley still wasn't back, and I frowned. I couldn't help but feel that his absence and Mr Monday's were connected. I thought about it as we rode the elevator up. Mr Thursday's phone had chimed just as we got in, and he was dealing with whatever text had been sent to him. I hadn't checked my phone in ages, so I pulled it out and was pleased to see a text from Mom.

All is good here. How are you darling? Xoxo

I typed back: *Fine here. Will give you a call next week. Xoxo*

I didn't want to have to explain why I'd quit my job so I could participate in a crazy interview process for a CEO job in order to pull off a revenge scheme I was no longer entirely sure I wanted to carry out. I don't think Mom would have understood.

I brought my thoughts back to the present and my concerns about KevOptics.

'What are your reservations about the company?' he asked me. 'Because I have some as well.'

This was interesting. Perhaps whatever he had to say would give me another thread to tug at.

'First, what are *your* concerns about them? It might help me with further research.'

'Well, the opportunity seemed to come out of the blue, and I'm not sure exactly how our acquisitions team discovered it. That's what bothers me.'

I nodded. 'That *is* odd. Do you have a preference between the two companies?'

We stepped out of the elevator, and he looked down at me. He had a big presence and it filled the reception area. I didn't look at the woman behind the desk, as I was caught up in his powerful aura. The glimmer of the laid-back man chomping on a hot dog was gone. In its place was the formidable man who had unnerved me when I'd first arrived this morning, now edged with a subtle difference I couldn't quite place.

'Personally, it doesn't matter to me which company Diamond purchases. That's not my area. It's about the legal actions we could be exposing ourselves to if we make either purchase that I'm more concerned about.'

'I understand. Well, as you must know, I'm not a lawyer, nor am I a financial expert. I'm basically a librarian and researcher. So what I can do is get the information for you to pass along to the acquisitions team.'

His next words put the weight of the world on my shoulders.

'You do realize that we are expecting you to make the decision.' It wasn't a question, it was a statement. 'With your research and the information you find, it's you that has to recommend the right company for Diamond to purchase.'

I drew in a ragged breath. *Pressure – much?*

We parted ways at my temporary office and I settled back in the chair, knowing I had only a little while longer to finish.

I had all I needed on KevOptics, so I turned my attention to the country club. There were no surprises there. I prepared my report and glanced at my watch. I was ready.

'Ms Canyon?' A woman I hadn't seen before stood in the doorway.

'Yes?'

'If you could come with me, please.' She turned before I could ask any questions, so I hurriedly gathered my report and followed her. We went through another door into a very posh section of the Legal department, very unlike the rest of it.

She stopped by an open office door, and I looked in. Mr Thursday sat behind a big desk.

'We'll talk in here,' was all he said.

His office was so much more opulent than those of the previous Mr's. I suppose that was par for the course.

I sat down in a butter-soft leather chair. 'Nice digs,' I said to him.

He came around and sat in the chair beside me.

'Speak to me,' he said. He was the most upfront and abrupt of all the men I'd met here so far. This Mr Day-of-the-Week took the cake.

'In a nutshell? Ditch KevOptics and buy the country club.' He didn't want the niceties so I felt there was no point in mincing words.

I had to fight back a smile at my perverse sense of satisfaction at seeing the shocked expression on Mr Thursday's face. I suppose he had been expecting me to waffle a bit. It was the strongest emotion I'd seen on him today. I liked that I was able to pull it out of him, now knowing that he still had some feelings buried inside. How deeply hidden were they?

'So, no fiber-optics company. Maybe you can explain that a little?'

'I'd be happy to.' I handed him the folder, and he opened it. His eyebrows rose on seeing the papers inside. Of course, my report was expertly compiled and organized and, with the contents page on top, he'd have no trouble finding any information he wanted. He glanced at me and gave me an upside-down smile of approval. I took that to mean he was impressed with my work. I had assembled legal information as part of my research in the past. Not a lot, but enough to help me with this test.

We were quiet for a few minutes as he scanned the file, flipping through the papers, nodding his head, raising his eyebrows, giving me quick looks. Then, finally, he closed the folder. He rose and walked around to sit in the chair behind his desk. It was a dark oak desk with a leather blotter, and his chair was equally dark and upholstered in shiny leather. All very impressive. Clearly, no expense was spared in his office. Even the artwork on his wall was recognizable; it was all by well-known modern artists.

'Right then, based on your research, you are claiming that KevOptics is attempting to defraud us.'

'Yes. The owner of KevOptics, Kevin Lyle, had a brother who used to work at Diamond, Robert Lyle. Robert became ill with cancer and Diamond put him on reduced salary leave, effectively casting him aside. I believe Kevin wants revenge.'

Now I really had Mr Thursday's attention. 'Revenge? Isn't that a little melodramatic?'

I shrugged. 'Kevin's not stupid enough to announce that he's coming after Diamond on social media, but it's a reasonable assumption to make. Without a paycheck, Robert became bankrupt, and died shortly afterwards. Kevin is using his brother's invention as bait, but there's no evidence that this particular cable works, or even exists.'

'You're right.' He picked up a pen, and I watched his fingers play with it. He leaned back, and the chair creaked. 'Regardless of what happened with Robert, the fact is that KevOptics' only true value is the patent, and that's the only relevant fact at this time.'

'I agree.' I crossed my legs, and his eyes dropped to watch the move. My breath hitched at his male interest, but when he met my gaze again I saw no more emotion in his eyes than before. 'The country club is solid?'

'Yes. I have found nothing to be concerned about. The attendance is a little low at the restaurant and conference bookings are down, but that's nothing that can't be turned around. The pro shop and golf bring in the most profit. In addition, since the club is Diamond's preferred venue for charity and corporate events, the company will save money by owning the property outright.'

'If we move forward with the purchase of the country club, would you be able to make recommendations on the budget?'

I'd already admitted I wasn't a financial expert, so what did I have to lose?

'I would do my best. I'm sure it wouldn't be that hard,' I said – and waited for my nose to grow. 'Okay, then. It's settled.' He stood, and I got the impression that our meeting was over.

He tapped the folder on his desk with one of his long, elegant fingers. 'You've done well. I'm pleased with your research and your report. You're very thorough, and you would make a great addition to our team.'

'Thank you.' I stood, and waited for the next step.

He pressed a button on his desk, and the woman from a little while ago appeared at the door. Mr Thursday held the file out. 'Please give this to the acquisitions team.'

'Yes, sir.' She left.

I stood there, feeling awkward. *What now?*

'There will be a ride for you downstairs.'

'Oh?'

Could Mr Monday be waiting for me? I was suddenly very ready to leave.

'Yes.' He looked at me, and I at him. 'You did well. I will make sure to note that in my report.'

So they are making reports on me. That makes sense.

'Thank you,' I said, and straightened my back. 'Since I've passed another test, I'll be leaving for the day.'

He was looking at his desk, but glanced up at me. 'Of course. It was good to meet you, Tess. I'm sure we'll be seeing each other again.' I felt dismissed.

I left and found my way back to the elevator. I wasn't happy with Mr Thursday. It felt as if he saw me as a tool he could use, rather than as a person. However, once I was in the elevator, I began to get excited as I reflected on my day. I'd passed another test! Plus, I was thrilled about the acquisition of the country club. There were so many possibilities for its use. When – if – I became CEO, I would definitely make the most of it.

The only fly in the ointment was my plan for revenge. I'd felt that I had to tell Mr Thursday about Kevin's plans, but what did that mean for my own plot? Kevin's revenge would've cost the company some money, but mine could have a severe impact on the stock, and possibly also lead to the company downsizing. It could affect people's lives. Maybe it was time to put aside my desire for revenge and concentrate on the good I could do as CEO.

As I rode down, I kind of got lost in a daydream, thinking about what the future could hold for me. Mr Monday played a rather prominent role. I arrived at the lobby and stepped out of the elevator, looking at the ground, lost in thought, not paying attention to where I was going. I smashed right into somebody.

'Oh! I'm sorry.' A familiar scent whirled around me and I reached out to steady myself. My hand fell against a hardened, muscly chest. Could it be?

I shot my gaze up and, sure enough, it was him. I couldn't help the smile that broke across my face and the excitement inside me at seeing him. He looked down with his usual somber and intense appearance, but there was something different about him today.

'Is everything okay?' I didn't lower my hand from his chest, and pressed more closely into him.

He sighed and took my hand in his. 'Let's get going. I hear you had a good day again.'

That meant he'd spoken to Mr Thursday. But the compliment felt wonderful coming from him.

It felt even better having him next to me. The dull ache of missing him was soothed by his presence and being back in his company. As we went through the doors, his hand at the small of my back, I understood now just how important he had become to my day. He was the highlight. Mr Monday seemed to have taken up residence deep inside me, unlike anyone else had ever done before. He dropped his hand from my back, taking my hand again, as if it were the most normal thing to do. My heart swelled when his fingers curled around mine. We walked in silence, and I was completely focused on our connection. Our physical connection, however innocent it was right now, foretold just how hot it could be later. He helped me into the limo and followed in behind. I didn't slide right over to the corner, staying closer to the middle, and he settled beside me.

This time, he put his arm around my shoulders and pulled me in tight. I twisted so I was facing him a little more, and he tucked me under his arm. I didn't know what to do with my hands because of the position I was in. I rested one in my lap, but I wanted to touch him. So I put my other hand on his thigh.

I felt him tense, and the power of his muscles played under my fingers. I was dying to see him stripped down and in his full, naked glory. I needed to make that happen. He sighed and leaned his head back, stretching his feet out as he gazed at the limo ceiling. I watched him. Something had happened today. I could sense it, but I wasn't about to ask again. If he wanted to tell me, he would. I'd learned that much about him over the week.

When he spoke a few minutes later, his deep voice filled the back of the limo. There was a different tone in it today, a tired and almost despairing sound.

'I'm glad the day went well for you. You're almost there.'

I was concerned. I couldn't help myself. 'You seem upset. Do you want to talk about it?'

He turned his head and gazed at me, then closed his eyes. I wondered if he would say anything more.

'I've had better days.'

'I thought something had happened to you this morning, when you didn't come.'

He nodded. 'Yes, I had something to take care of. I'm lucky I was able to get away now to get you.'

'Is there anything I can do to help?' I asked him, my voice quiet and soft. He opened his eyes and looked at me, and my heart tumbled over. His smile was sad and I wondered just how bad his day had been.

He pulled me tighter and pressed a kiss against my temple. Arousal shot through me at his tender kiss, mixing with the concern for him that welled up inside my heart. The combination was staggering. I twisted further in the seat and took my hand from his thigh to hug him.

I squeezed my arm around him, and he clutched me tight. I remained silent, waiting for him to open up.

'No, not right now. Just having you beside me is comforting.'

I lifted my face up to him and stared into his eyes. I could see pain in their depths, and I grew alarmed for him.

'Something bad happened today?'

He nodded. 'Yes, something did.'

'Are you sure you don't want to talk about it?'

He shook his head. 'I'm not ready.'

He raked his fingers through his hair and twisted on the seat before placing his hands either side of my face. I was captured by him, not only by his intense scrutiny, but by the tender hold he had on my cheeks. His face tilted and lowered. I held my breath. His lips touched mine and my eyelids fluttered closed. The tenderness of his lips quickly changed to demanding passion. His fingers tightened on me, and his tongue lit a fire in me as he sought mine. I opened for him. He pulled me even tighter. I lifted my hands to his neck, my fingers tickling in his hair. He moved and pushed me back so I was almost lying down under him. I let him, thrilled finally to be with this man in the way I'd been longing for.

I was enclosed in his presence, his wonderful scent, his power. I drew in a breath, breathing him in and feeling his aura touch every part of me, but it was his passion that had me spellbound. I had instinctively known we were so right for each other. It felt foreign to me, this body-rocking sensation he roused in me. I'd never been so swept away. I felt as if he were giving me life itself, as if I'd been walking around half dead and only now was I coming to life. It was an affirmation. We were together.

I curled my arm around his neck, and one hand shifted from the side of my face around to my back. I arched until we were flush together. Wherever we touched, even through our clothes, was electrifying. I pressed into him, wanting him to know just how much I needed him. Longed for him. Craved him. I felt every inch of him next to me and, when he shifted further, his erection thrilled me as it pressed into me. Heat flared deep inside me and I felt myself grow ready for him. If he had torn my clothes off, I wouldn't have resisted. I would have welcomed him and lost myself in him as we made love in the back of the limousine.

He knew the art of kissing, and I didn't want to know where or how he'd learned. I pushed away the twinge of jealousy, not wanting it to color our passion. Never had I been so aroused by a kiss. His kiss was anything but simple. It was complex in so many ways, and I didn't want to try to work it out now. There would be time for that later. All I wanted at this moment was to *feel*, to be his vessel, a safe harbor in the storm he was experiencing today. Whatever had happened to him, I longed to take away his pain. I was desperate to make him feel better. To make him forget whatever it was that had upset him so terribly.

I ran my tongue over his, and my fingers dug into his back, sweeping up and down. I wanted to imprint him, map him. I hooked my leg over his and raised my hips as he shifted between my thighs. He groaned into my mouth and I took the sound deep inside me. Our breath mingled and grew ragged, its sound filling the back of the limo. Vaguely, I wondered if the driver could see us through the closed glass divider.

Somehow, Mr Monday had worked his way into my heart. Even with our limited time together and his reserved nature, there was a powerful connection developing between us.

He encircled me in his arms. His muscles, strong and tight, held me firmly as he pressed me into the seat of the limo. His weight on me was heavy, but I didn't want him ever to get off. I wanted to stay that way with him for eternity. He tightened his hold and his kiss grew more heated. I lost my sense of time and place, overwhelmed by his touch, his mouth on mine, his hands moving over me. It wasn't until the phone in his pocket buzzed between us that I was brought back to startled awareness. He lifted his head from me and looked into my eyes. His smoldering look seared me and I moaned, lifting myself up to him and trying to capture his lips again. He dropped a heart-wrenchingly gentle kiss on my lips. I gazed at him through the passion that clouded my vision. He was glorious.

'You are definitely a surprise, Ms Canyon.'

'As are you,' I murmured.

He gave me a smile. I was quickly accepting the impact he had on me. I reached up to curl my fingers around his neck, under his hair, and my heart fell when his phone buzzed again. I knew it was going to steal him away from me.

'Can you come up?' I asked, before he could see the new demand on his phone. I took his face in my hands and claimed his lips, my tongue searching for his. He groaned into me, mingling with my own moan of delight. I reluctantly released him when he shifted to pull his phone from his pocket.

'I'd love to, but—' He looked at his phone and frowned. 'I really do need to take this.'

I nodded and pushed myself into a sitting position. My heart still raced painfully in my chest and the ache between my thighs would recognize no true release from him. I couldn't calm myself down and looked out of the window to see where we were while he took the call.

We were sitting by the curb outside my apartment. How long had we been here? I flushed a little, wondering if the driver knew we'd been making out. Then I realized I didn't really care. I was still basking in the glow of it. I looked at Mr Monday. His face was dark and his mouth pulled into a frown. He was nodding and listening to the person on the other end of the phone. My heart fell. I was right. He was going to be yanked away from me.

'Understood,' was all he said, before he put the phone down on the seat between us.

I looked at it with loathing. I wanted to pitch it out of the window.

'Are you sure you can't come up?' I asked him again, not doing a very good job at keeping the hopeful tone from my voice.

'As much as I'd really like to, I really can't. I have to go.'

He opened the door and stepped out, then turned and reached for me. I took his hand, loving how his fingers tightened possessively on mine. We stood, chest to hip in the dappled sun, under the canopy of trees lining my street. I placed my hands on his shoulders, he wrapped an arm around my waist and his other hand slipped behind my neck, his fingers pressing into me, and pulled me close. The breathless kiss we shared before he stepped away was powerful. I trembled and couldn't control the desire I felt. He gave me a hug and I walked up to my door. I was thrilled when he followed me.

We stood quietly, gazing at each other on the doorstep. If my thoughts were racing in chaos, surely his were as well.

'Okay. Take care, and I'll see you tomorrow.' I could only manage a shaky whisper.

He nodded and brushed a kiss on my cheek before turning away. I watched him walk back to the limo. Even his walk was arousing. Once inside the car, Mr Monday leaned out to grab the door handle and glanced back at me. He smiled and raised his hand before closing the door. I stood there for a few minutes, watching, as the limo wove its way down the street. I sighed and pushed the door open, shocked to find myself fighting back tears. What was wrong with me? That kiss between us had changed everything.

I trudged up the stairs and unlocked the door to my apartment, letting out a sigh of despair. I was staggered by the wave of loneliness that swept over me, and it made me tremble even more. I collapsed into the chair and was overcome. Tears streamed down my face. I cried for everything I'd held in for so long. Losing my dad. Wondering if he really had done what he was accused of and, for the first time, unsure about it. My mom leaving me to go home to England. Investing so much time into my revenge, I had sacrificed my life to it.

This past week had made me realize I was alive. I was a woman. I had needs, desires to fulfill. Meeting Mr Monday had made me recognize how much I'd given up. I wanted what he had given me a glimpse of tonight. But could I leave behind my past to reach for the future he offered?

MR FRIDAY

I hadn't yet come down from my emotional high. After I'd had my pity party and a good cry, I'd gotten over my maudlin moment and bucked myself up by reliving last night's make-out session with Mr Monday, which had me soaring. I was still breathless whenever I thought about how we had steamed up the back of the limo. I regretted that we hadn't actually made love, and that he'd had to leave in such a hurry. In truth, though, having sex with him in the back of a car wasn't what I wanted for our first time. The first time with him, I wanted it to be perfect, and the sooner the better.

Sleep hadn't come easily. All my thoughts were of him. His touch. His lips. And my body had been on fire all night, until I finally fell asleep, just before dawn. So needless to say, I was exhausted. Still, my belly fluttered whenever I thought of Mr Monday. I cursed whoever had called him and pulled him away from me. I knew we would have spent the night together if it hadn't been for the phone call. He was a mystery, and one that needed solving. As I was learning every day, there was so much more to him.

Now, I was standing out in the street, on a beautiful cool, sunny morning – yesterday's storm had really cut the heat – impatiently waiting for him to come to me. I looked up the street, and then at my watch. It was quarter to seven. I was out here far too early, but there was no way I would be able to wait for fifteen minutes in my apartment or in the vestibule this morning. I was too anxious to see him again. I paced the street and kept looking at my watch, glancing both ways to watch for him. But there was no sign of his car.

Oh God, what if he wasn't going to come? Like yesterday. I stamped down the panic that started to well up in my throat. *Calm yourself, girl. He'll be here.*

Sure enough, a couple of minutes later, ten minutes early for him, a silver sports car roared up the street. The rumble of the engine reached right inside me and revved me up. I was almost panting with excitement, and I heard the car switch gears, the throaty roar of the engine reminding me of Mr Monday's groans yesterday. It was all so terribly exciting, and very, very sexy. I saw him in the front seat as he pulled the car up to the curb, stopping abruptly, with a screech of tires. My heart leapt and I felt like a smiling fool as I watched him through the window. He'd come for me, and in his own car – and without the driver.

I was grinning madly, and I nearly bounced on my toes when he smiled back. I've no idea what make of car he was driving, but it was fabulous. I couldn't help but wonder, again, what his role with the company was. I wanted to know *him*. To find out every little bit of information about him that I could, both mentally and physically. I wanted to unwrap this man, to discover all his secrets, like how he got his scar or, oh, his *name*. I was obsessed. I tried to rein myself in by thinking about the day ahead. Another test lay before me, and maybe a chance finally to look for those financial documents. I was still conflicted about my plan, but I'd come too far just to give it all up now.

I ran around the front of the car. Mr Monday leaned over and flicked the door open. I jumped in and looked at him. I wasn't at all self-conscious about my wide smile or that we'd crawled all over each other yesterday. I wanted more of him, of us together, and I wanted to see exactly where our chemistry would lead. My heart nearly burst out of my chest when he leaned over. *A good-morning kiss.* I raised my hand and touched the side of his cheek.

'Good morning,' he murmured against my lips.

I was in heaven.

His lips sealed over mine, rendering me incapable of replying. I moaned into him and curled my hand around his neck, pushing my fingers into his hair. This good-morning kiss made the sun shine even brighter. The blossom smelled sweeter in the trees. My heart sang. We fell into each other, and it was last night all over again, only more. More intense. More passionate. More everything. God, there were moments when I wanted to believe this was love, but could I really love a man whose name I didn't even know? Surely it was just lust.

My body willed him to come closer. I ached to feel him next to me, but it was impossible with the console of the sports car between us. The deep bucket seats meant that we sat at an awkward angle and kept us maddeningly apart. His tongue swept along my lips and I opened for him, pressing my fingers a little more firmly into him, holding him to me. After a few moments he lifted his lips from mine, and I breathed out a sigh. He rested his forehead on mine, our noses touching, breath mingling.

Our eyes locked on each other. Then he closed his and inhaled deeply.

'Is everything okay today? Better than yesterday?' I asked.

Very, very slightly, he shook his head. My heart broke for him.

'Everything will be fine, though. Don't worry.' He sat back in his seat and kept his gaze pinned on me. I held my breath. 'I want you to know –' he hesitated, as if what he was going to say was difficult – 'you are making all the difference for me right now. Thank you. I'll be able to tell you more later. You understand?'

I nodded. I didn't really understand, but it was enough to know I was helping in some way. I was just glad that I could be a port in the storm for him. I held his hand, and he squeezed mine.

'If only I could do more for you,' I told him.

'You've done a lot.'

I didn't know what to say and glanced down at the console. I smiled when I noticed the two travel mugs.

'For us?' I asked, tapping the top of one.

'Yes, for us.'

His smile was warm, the most relaxed I'd seen from him. I loved his smile and wished he would do so more often. It broke the grim lines of his face and showed me his more passionate side. Like a little window into the mystery of the man.

'Costa Rican?' I asked.

'Clever girl,' he said flirtatiously, tucking a strand of hair behind my ear.

'Why, thank you. I agree.' He laughed, something else I wanted to experience more often.

I reached for the mugs and handed him one. 'Flown in this morning? I've been spoilt by the luxury of good coffee.'

I think he purposely touched my fingers when he took the

cup from me. The bolt of desire nearly polarized me, rushing right out to my fingers and toes. My whole body lit up for this man, and I didn't know how I'd get through the day on this knife edge of arousal he had me on. My lungs constricted and my heart beat frantically as he geared up the car and checked the traffic in the rear-view mirror. If he could do this to me with the barest of touches, I was both longing to see and frightened to know what he could do to me with a more prolonged touch. I calmed myself, breathing slowly, and then took a sip of the delicious coffee. Every day brought a new intensity, a deepening, to our relationship.

He was quiet for a few minutes as he drank some of his, before putting the cup back in the holder. He placed his hand on my knee. I nearly jumped out of my skin, and flushed hotly. Was he aware of the way he affected me? He seemed genuine, but my mind began overthinking things. For the first time, I wondered if he himself, and our attraction to each other, was part of a test. Could he be a temptation, something meant to throw me off track? I rested my head on the seat and turned to look at him. He was concentrating on the road. There was no expression on his face so I was unable to read him. I still felt him with every nerve in my body. *Did he feel the same way about me?*

I wanted us to become physical, but could I handle a one-night stand, if that's all it was for him? I'd have no choice, and I comforted myself knowing that I'd at least be able to get him out of my system if one night ended up being all there was to us. Yet I had hope. The twin connection of physical and emotional I felt with Mr Monday was growing far more quickly than I could ever have expected.

'Today is going to be a difficult day for you.'

'What?' I didn't grasp what he was saying at first. Brought

back to reality, I was reminded of the reason I was here with a resounding thud. Gone were all the warm and fuzzy feelings he gave me. I felt deflated.

'It's going to be a challenge.'

I snapped my head around to look at him. 'What do you mean?'

He raised his eyebrows but continued to concentrate on the road. Then he glanced at me quickly and I could see the concern on his face. I saw that not only was he concerned for me, there was something more going on. He was hurting inside and showing me only the surface of his pain.

What happened to him?

He shifted gears, expertly working his feet on the clutch and gas to zip in and out between a crush of traffic. I sucked in a breath and pushed my feet into the floorboard, bracing my head on the seat. I gripped my knees, then let out a sigh when he slowed down.

'I don't like shitty drivers,' he commented.

'So it seems,' I retorted. 'Where did you learn to drive like that?'

He lifted a shoulder and wove between cars at a much more sensible pace. 'I've done a turn or two on a track. No official racing or anything.' He looked at me. 'I like speed.'

My eyebrows shot up. 'No kidding, if that was any indication. Give me a moment while I peel my fingers out of my knees.'

He smiled and turned his attention back to the road. The buildings as we approached Diamond were becoming familiar. Our drive, just the two of us, would be over far too soon.

'I want you to be aware that today could be a little trickier than you expect. And that what you have accomplished to date has been noticed. You've done very well.'

What was going to happen? His words were slightly

alarming. He hadn't given me any help so far and now, today, he was giving me these cryptic warnings. For him to say anything, it must be pretty big.

'I'm sorry. I can't say any more. I just want you to do as well today as you have done in the last few days. Keep your head on your shoulders. Keep your eyes open.'

'You're scaring me,' I said to him, my heart beating faster. He put his hand on my knee and I covered it with mine.

He caressed my knee before turning his hand over and taking mine. He curled his fingers around mine, and I was immediately comforted. Even though I now knew that my test today would be like none I'd yet faced, his touch calmed me.

'There's nothing to be frightened of. Trust me. You just might find yourself outside your comfort zone.'

Squeezing his hand, my gaze traced his profile as he focused on the road. I loved the strength of his chin, the slope of his nose. Everything about him was chiseled and so unbelievably gorgeous. He was put together so perfectly I could never tire of looking at him.

'You do realize that I've been outside my comfort zone every day this week?' I saw the side of his mouth tip up before he turned to me.

'Has it mattered? You've triumphed in every test presented to you. You should be proud of yourself.' He paused and gazed at me long enough to warm me up all over again. 'It's not my intention to frighten you. I just want you to make it through to the end.'

'That's the closest you've ever come to giving me a hint that you do. Or telling me that you want me here.' I didn't want to say too much more and cause him to close up again.

'I think last night proved how much I want you.' His voice was like a caress, and he trailed his fingers over the back of my hand before reaching for his coffee. I watched him sip, his Adam's apple bobbing as he swallowed, and I tried desperately to regain the breath he'd just stolen from me.

We drove in silence then, and I tried to get my brain working. Should I respond to his flirtation? Ask him about yesterday morning? Would he share with me now? No, if he could admit that he wanted me sexually, he would also have shared his emotional pain with me if he wanted to. I shouldn't say anything. I glanced out of the window. We were nearly at Diamond Enterprises. Impulsively, I did what I'd just decided against doing.

'Why didn't you come yesterday?' I continued to look out of the window because I was afraid to see the expression on his face. If I'd made him angry, I didn't want to see the proof.

He was silent and didn't say anything for a few moments. I didn't repeat the question. Saying it once was enough.

'Personal reasons.'

I had assumed that, so this wasn't news, but his confirmation of my assumption was still a giant step forward. As much as I wanted to know more about Mr Monday as a person, I accepted my small victory and didn't push. I put my hand on his arm and rubbed it gently.

'I'm here if you need me.' I said no more than that. He frowned and very briefly nodded. I couldn't help but speculate about what could be causing him this deep pain. Had he lost someone he cared about? Had he suffered a traumatic event? All my guesses served only to highlight how much there still was to discover about him.

A comfortable silence fell between us as we traveled the last few blocks. Mr Monday drove into the driveway with an alarming screech of brakes, narrowly missing a cab that had just pulled away from the curb. I saw the doorman discreetly lean against a pillar, rubbing his chest, as if having palpitations.

Neither Mr Monday nor I felt the need to move, we just sat looking at each other.

'Are you coming in?'

He shook his head. 'No. Not today. I have a lot to do.' He reached into his pocket and pulled out a key card. *I'd almost forgotten about it.* He held it out to me and I took it. 'I didn't get to give this to you last night.'

I took it and slipped it into my purse. 'So, beware a difficult day? Any other advice you can give me?'

He shook his head. 'I'm sorry. I wish I could.'

'Can you at least tell me what floor I'm heading to, or should I just mash all the buttons in the elevator again?' I asked dryly.

He shook his head again, before curling his fingers around the back of my neck and pulling me to him. His kiss was full of fire and emotion. I was breathless as his mouth covered mine; he teased his tongue against my lips and I opened for him, welcoming him. I didn't want the kiss to end and was disappointed when he sat back. His breathing was heavy and ragged, as was mine.

'What you do to me,' I whispered.

He still had his hand around my neck, and pressed his fingers on my cheek and turned me to look at him. 'Never ever think that you don't affect me, too.'

All this, in just the space of a few moments. He dropped his hand and stared at me. His eyes nearly broke my heart. I was tempted to bail on the tests – the CEO job and my revenge be damned – just so I could stay with him. As if he knew what I was thinking, he shook his head once more. 'Go. Twenty-third floor. Kick today's ass.'

The door opened beside me and I let the doorman help me out. Thankfully, I had on a wide, flowing skirt. It made getting out of the low-slung sports car easy.

'I guess I'll see you later.' It wasn't really a question, so I didn't expect him to answer.

'Yes, we'll see each other again. Of that you can be sure.'

I smiled and reached in to grab my pink leather satchel; it was almost as big as me. I slipped the shoulder strap over my head and gave him one last look as I was leaning into the vehicle. It wasn't until his gaze slipped down to my chest that I realized my boat-necked top gaped, giving him a very fine view of my breasts. That wasn't intentional on my part, it was a completely innocent move, but the air turned scorching hot. The change of the expression on his face was wonderful. Desire filled his eyes. There wasn't even a tinge of embarrassment at the knowledge I had caught him staring at my boobs.

'Soon, Ms Canyon.' His words were laced with a delicious *double entendre* and I resisted the urge to fling myself back into the car. Instead, I hunched my shoulders forward, deliberately giving myself an amazing cleavage.

'Definitely,' I replied.

Then I gave him a wink and turned to walk through the doors, moving my hips with a little extra sway. I resisted the urge to look back, and there was a beat, two beats, before I heard his car roar away. Stanley was on duty and we exchanged pleasantries as I signed in. As I walked toward the elevator bank, I attempted to bring my raging emotions under control. If Mr Monday thought today would be particularly challenging for me, then I needed to be at my best.

Once the elevator doors opened on the twenty-third floor, I slipped the key card from its slot and into my satchel. Before me was an empty reception area, similar to all the other floors except for the Legal department. This should feel old hat now, as it was the fourth day I was heading into the unknown, where one misstep could cost me everything.

My arousal subsided as my anxiety levels crept higher. I picked a door at random and went through. On the other side lay a clone of the floors from the previous days. Office pods and people. Once again, I found myself wandering among the rows of desk, today crossly thinking that it wouldn't kill Diamond to have some hapless intern waiting to guide me. Still, I knew I was looking for a department so I headed for the corner offices. In the first one I tried was a stunningly handsome man who happened to be leaning over, looking at something in a book-case. I took a second to appreciate his spectacular ass, purely for aesthetic purposes, before knocking.

'Good morning,' I said.

The man stood and spun around. 'Ah, yes, good morning. Tess?'

I smiled politely. 'The one and only.'

'Excellent. I've prepared everything you should need. Just go to the office two doors down – I've left the files on the desk. You'll also have access to the relevant systems on the computer. You can get started right away, and we'll reconvene at the end of the day, yes?'

He wasn't particularly looking for a response, but he got one anyway. 'Wow, you guys all went to the same management school, didn't you?'

'Excuse me?' Mr Friday drew his brows together and frowned.

At this point, though, after nearly chucking it all away for Mr Monday, I wasn't overly concerned that perhaps I was step-ping out of line. I've done well so far, but all these cryptic directions and orders being given to me by these men were starting to grate on my nerves.

I readjusted my satchel on my shoulder. 'Every day has been the same. Everybody has been the same. I get files – no context given – instructed to familiarize myself with their contents, an empty office and an impossible deadline.' I sighed, ending my mini-rant. So much for a challenge. It was no different to the rest. Just another hot guy named after another day. I was about to head for the office he'd suggested when he called after me.

'Did you think the tests to become CEO would be easy? Diamond is a multibillion-dollar corporation, spanning a wide variety of industries. Its CEO has to be able to adapt easily to whatever problem they're facing that day. If you can't think quickly on your feet, if you find these tests too difficult to cope with, then perhaps it isn't the job for you.'

Panic shot through me when I realized I'd almost bitched myself into disqualification, but I was a little pissed at Mr Friday's tone. Maybe when Mr Monday warned me about facing a difficult day, he'd been referring to the man, not the test.

'I can do it, sir. Whatever the assignment is, I will complete it to the best of my ability.'

He crossed his arms, leaning back against his desk, staring at me. Under his unrelenting gaze I wanted badly to fidget, but I forced myself to show no weakness. After a few more uncomfortable moments, he said, 'Yesterday, you recommended that Diamond purchase a country club. Today, your assignment is to review its budget and come up with ways to increase cost efficiency. I was told that you didn't think you'd find that too hard.'

What had I been thinking when I said that? *A budget?* I could barely balance my bank book – how the hell was I supposed to come up with a budget for a substantial going concern? Something about this man was very domineering, and I felt it was wise to say as few words to him as possible. I just knew he'd use any slip-up against me. So I only replied, 'Yes, sir.'

I shifted on my feet and kept eye contact with him. His gaze was steady on me. I forced myself not to shiver under the power of his gaze. It was as if he could look right inside me and see my innermost secrets.

Mr Friday stood out from all the Mr Days-of-the-Week. He was aloof, blunt and to the point, which was both unnerving, intriguing and a little bit exciting. He looked every inch a CFO, with his perfectly tailored suit and his wire-rimmed glasses. There was an energy to him that seemed to boil underneath his calm exterior. To me, numbers were the unsexiest things around, and I hated maths with a passion. Yet this man had a strange allure, some kind of radiance that seemed to draw me in. At my small sign of insubordination, he had slapped me down verbally immediately, reminding me that I wasn't CEO yet. Could I warm this man up with a bit of conversation? I decided to try before I went to bury myself in the files. The thought of hours and hours with nothing but numbers in front of me made me groan inside.

'Have you been with Diamond long?' He didn't blink at the non-sequitur and I felt the urge to swallow, or fix my hair or something. He made me edgy and somewhat ill at ease, but I found that terribly exciting as well. I thought I'd take a chance and ask a few questions.

'Long enough.' I guess he wasn't about to give up much information. It was then that I noticed his jacket hanging neatly on the suit tree beside the wall. The white shirt he was wearing was crisp and perfectly pressed. While he stood there watching me, he ran his silk tie – in a perfect Windsor knot, by the way – through his fingers. I was rather mesmerized by that movement. Especially when he twirled the end up between his index and middle fingers.

I had a flash of an image in my head, of him using that tie for something other than wearing with his suit. I drew in a soft breath and imagined being bound by it, my hands helpless, my body splayed, defenseless ... I shot a look at his face. A mysterious smile curved on his lips, as if he knew exactly what I'd been thinking. Ah, no, it hadn't been Mr Friday leaning over me in my fantasy. Wanting to make a hasty retreat, I backed out of the office.

'I'll get on to the budget right away.'

I hurriedly found the empty office and dropped my satchel on the desk with a heavy thud that was nearly as loud as the pounding of my heart. I needed to pull myself together. Mr Monday may have been holding that tie in my imagination, but it was Mr Friday who had initially lit the fire of my arousal. He might not be much of a people person, but the man had a way about him that made you very aware of his presence and I couldn't help but respond to it. I opened the first file and stared blindly at the page in front of me. Mr Monday had warned me today would be difficult, and Mr Friday's reminder about what was at stake certainly echoed that, but my mind was still fixated on the imaginary feel of Mr Monday's hands on my body as I writhed against silken bonds.

I cleared my throat and turned to the computer, determined to concentrate. Quickly, I logged in to see what I had access to. A fair bit. I pulled up electronic files associated with the papers in the folder and was staggered by the numbers on the computer screen in front of me. Never had I seen so many zeros. I was blown away by the large amounts of money being tossed around. I was able to get through most of the online data, but it was a painful slog. I simply couldn't understand how people could stare at numbers all day. With me, they started to slide off the page, swirl around and become a jumble of nothing. Still, I guessed I'd have to get used to it if I became CEO.

After going through everything I had a list of areas of the

country-club business that needed to be addressed. Staffing was the biggest expense. If even I thought the figures were rather high, somebody much more number savvy would definitely be questioning the bottom line. I had a feeling the recommendation would be to lay people off. There were bound to be some redundancies. I could see it, but the last thing I wanted to suggest was that people lose their jobs. They would have families who depended on them. I remembered how great the impact on my family had been when my father was fired. Never mind the circumstances in which he was let go, the loss of his income had in itself been very stressful. I couldn't imagine inflicting that kind of pain on another family unless there was no other way. I shook my head in denial. I'd find another way.

All this reminded me of my revenge plot. These tests which Mr King had orchestrated for me encroached on any spare time for my own private research. And now I was here, with nearly unrestricted access to the company's financial records. I raised my head and looked around. Nobody was paying me any attention and I was in front of a computer from which, with only a few clicks, I could probably pull up all the information I needed. My hand hesitated on the mouse. What was happening to me? Why wasn't I clicking?

You gave up everything for this.

Before I could second-guess myself, I opened the company books and squinted at the screen. I had to force myself to read every line – all of the notations, everything – until I found what I was looking for. I could see there were discrepancies between the books and some of the executive expense reports. They didn't gel; the numbers were way off. I checked the dates, and they seemed to correspond with when my dad had worked here. I found his expense reports and fell silent. I hadn't been prepared to see images of his expense submissions. Seeing his flamboyant signature scrawled across the bottom of the report unexpectedly brought tears to my eyes. I forced myself not to get emotional.

There didn't seem to be anything out of the ordinary. Just typical expenses, which didn't seem to be overly inflated. I compared them to the company financial records, and everything was in order. How could they fire my dad over nothing? There had to be a reason. I dug deeper and then a name that rang a bell popped up. That of my dad's former boss: Grant Kennedy. I pulled up the scans again and picked a month, hoping I would see something in it. And I did.

The signature on a report approved by Grant Kennedy was not my father's. It had been forged. My heart pounded as I printed it off, and similar reports. Then I went back to my dad's earlier reports and printed a few with his real signature on them. I spread them on the desk in front of me and compared them. It was painfully obvious the signatures were not the same. Somebody had been claiming expenses under my dad's account code and falsifying his signature. To make matters worse – or better, depending on how you wanted to look at it – there were expenditures on products and services that were clearly for a woman.

This was it. This was a vindication of my father. Again, tears sprang to my eyes, and I had to swipe them away before they fell down my cheek. I couldn't wait to tell Mom. Dad hadn't been the one having an affair, it was his boss. The man had used Dad as cover so no one would find out, and it had cost my father everything. I sat there for a few minutes, stunned. I'd always known Dad was innocent and finally to be holding proof was overwhelming. Numbers don't lie, and these printouts showed the truth.

It occurred to me that if it had happened once, perhaps it had happened again. So I went through expense reports submitted by other people and found a few more which seemed fraudulent. I printed them out, too. Who knows how many I hadn't found? How many other people had got caught in the wake of this mess? Who knew about it? How high did it go? If I got the CEO job, I could order a full-on investigation. I could make things right, maybe even press charges. I wondered what the statute of limitations was for fraud.

For now, though, I had to concentrate on making it to the end of these tests. I found an envelope in the desk drawer and slid all the papers I'd printed out inside. I sealed it shut and breathed out a big sigh. Finding what I had set out to find felt both exciting and somewhat anticlimactic. Now, I had the ammunition; I just needed to decide when to release it.

After a quick glance at the clock, I redirected my attention to the country-club budget. There had to be other areas than staffing to save money. There simply had to be. What was it that I'd said to Mr Wednesday? A happy employee is a loyal employee, and productivity will be high. That could be applied here as well. Maybe if we looked for ways to make the staff more productive and customer-service oriented, the club's reputation would improve and we would attract more customers. In addition, we could offer a retirement incentive. Downsize by attrition.

I switched my focus to Operations. You never knew what was going on behind the scenes. There were all kinds of ways that money could disappear – supplies that were ordered and never received or food falling off the back of a delivery truck. While I was quite familiar with purchase orders from my last job, I was stunned at the costs of maintaining a golf course. Water, sod, fertilizer – the outlay was sky-high. I wondered if there was anywhere we could cut corners in that area.

I needed to understand fully – well, at least as well as I could from my 'armchair' standpoint, how to run a golf course. So I did what any librarian would do, and I researched it. I was flabbergasted by how much water it took to maintain a golf course and how many man-hours to keep everything pristine and perfect. Apparently, golfers didn't want to play eighteen holes on dying grass.

There had to be another way to maintain the golf course so, next, I looked at alternatives to watering systems and at natural fertilization. My head was spinning with all this new information and I took pages of notes. Clearly, the best way to keep costs down was to make sure the head groundskeeper knew everything there was to know about looking after a golf course. I came round to the idea of bringing in more business. Getting the country club's golf course to a higher standard could make it a destination for serious golfers, maybe even attract a professional tournament.

However, my test was to reduce the budget, not think of ways to increase revenue. No matter how hard I looked at the infinitely long pages of numbers, I still didn't really see where any significant cuts could be made. God, I hated numbers. The hours I spent looking at these ones were the longest of my life. Frustration welled inside me. I didn't know which direction to go and felt I was floundering.

'Tess, come with me.'

I nearly jumped out of my skin. Mr Friday stood in the doorway, leaning on the jamb, staring at me. The way he was posing, he could be the featured model in a male-fashion magazine spread. It was hard to believe he was the CFO. The office, which had felt spacious enough before, now felt too small as his presence took over the space. I don't know what it was about him, but he seemed to set me off kilter in a way I didn't understand. Despite his outwardly casual appearance, his body was tense. Controlled. His wire-rimmed glasses made him seem stern, and I wondered what he'd look like without them.

He pushed himself upright and left, presumably to head back to his office. I gathered that I was supposed to come trotting along behind him like a good little girl. I shoved the envelope of incriminating evidence I had compiled under the blotter on the desk and collected my notes and headed for his office. He was standing in his doorway now, waiting for me, no expression on his face. At my approach, he stepped back for me to enter, then pointed at a guest chair. 'Sit.'

Yes, he clearly saw me as a child or a puppy, and I was offended either way. This was a man who was used to being in charge. He had a demanding nature – a dominant nature, if you will. There really was a fine line between love and hate, though, because I slid right back into impure thoughts. I wondered idly if he was just as dominant sexually as he was in the office. I sat back in the chair and crossed my legs, smiling inwardly when his eyes flickered down at the movement.

For the first time, I looked around to see if it gave any inkling who this man was, beyond the numbers. I'd assumed he was a CFO, since all the other Mr Days-of-the-Week held leadership positions and I assumed were VPs. Outside of Diamond Enterprises, when he took off his CFO hat, who was he? I noticed the soft classical music that filled his office. This song, while soft and quiet in the beginning, built to a very insistent notes. I tilted my head to listen a little more closely.

'Is that *Boléro* I hear?'

Mr Friday was back behind his desk in his chair, and studying me thoughtfully. I thought I saw a hint of surprise in his reaction to my question. 'Yes, it is. Are you into classical music?'

The way he said *into* seemed to carry a very suggestive tone.

'Not really. Most of what I've heard is very whiny and hurts my ears. But this is nice. I've heard *Boléro* before.'

'I like classical music,' he told me. 'And anything with a deep, *pounding* beat.'

His eyes seemed to darken, and I held my breath. Suddenly, I had that feeling again, as if all my secrets lay exposed before him. It was unsettling, like being a timid mouse confronted with a starving dog. You weren't normally their preferred snack but, if they got hungry enough, they'd make an exception. My heart beat faster. I didn't know whether to feel flattered, exhilarated, terrified or turned on.

I needed to distract myself. 'Do you play any instruments?' I asked him, not really knowing what else to say. Except perhaps to keep talking about music. Didn't music and maths go together? I thought I'd read that somewhere.

He smiled, but it didn't seem to reach his eyes. It was as if he sensed that my conflicting emotions were battling for supremacy. 'I do, as a matter of fact.'

'What do you play?'

The small smile he gave me seemed to hold all kinds of meaning I could only guess at, and yet I felt as if I had accidentally intruded on to an area of his personal space. The question had seemed harmless enough.

'It's okay. You don't have to tell me if you don't want to.' I already had all the mystery I could handle with Mr Monday. I wasn't about to invest any time in yet another enigmatic man.

'I play a variety of instruments.' I couldn't help but notice the emphasis when he said *instruments* or *watch* the way his fingers handled the pencil he was holding. It rotated in tight, rhythmic circles that were oddly hypnotic. He let it fall to the desk and, the spell broken, I glanced up, my breath catching when I saw the way he was looking at me. Coupled with his suggestive answer to my question, my thoughts turned to instruments of pleasure. I wondered if he was into BDSM. Did he have a playroom? I shivered, thinking of him in such a room, lined with all sorts of toys and instruments, every manner of paraphernalia for pleasure and pain.

'Okay. Well, then. A status update. I don't have a formal report put together yet, but while the staff is the biggest expense, and I've red-flagged some of the purchase orders as hinky, I think our primary goal should be to raise revenue rather than slash the budget. Although I do recommend keeping a close eye on the maintenance costs of the golf course.'

I rested the file on his desk, leafing through my notes for any other points I should bring up. He stretched over, reaching for the file, and my eyes widened when I caught a glimpse of the tattoos that peeked from beneath the cuff of his shirt. My gaze shot up to his face and, in that moment, I knew my suspicions about him were correct.

He opened the file and looked over my notes. Nothing. He pursed his lips. His voice was low when he spoke. 'Was I perhaps somehow unclear when I outlined your assignment? You were to find ways to cut costs, not identify ways to spend *more* money.'

'I said that I wasn't a financial expert. And I only said that I would try if I was asked to make some recommendations for the budget.' I pointed to the file he had in his hands. 'And I tried.'

He gave a little smile. I wasn't quite sure what to make of it.

'I want to go out to the location today, do a quick inspection. Take a look at the environment, at some of the items you have identified here as potential problem areas.'

That surprised me a little. 'Makes sense,' I said. 'I think you'll like it there.'

'I've been many times,' he said. 'I know you were there on Tuesday.'

I was initially taken aback that he knew I'd been there already, but then I remembered that the Mr Days-of-the-Week seemed to like sitting around and gossiping about me. I preferred the image of them exchanging funny Tess stories to the reality that they were meeting to decide my fate.

'Oh,' I said weakly, feeling very much as if I had no private life when everything I did here was known about. I glanced at my watch. 'It's a bit of a drive, and there won't be a whole lot of time to have a proper tour.'

He glanced at me from above his glasses. 'We're not driving.' My heart sank. I knew exactly what that meant. 'But you are correct: we don't have much time.' He stepped around from behind his desk, holding my notes, and held his hand out towards the door. 'Shall we?'

What could I say? I had no choice but to do as he bid. I grabbed my satchel. I walked past him and, the closer I got to him, the more I sensed his energy. It grew stronger until I felt his powerful aura; it almost matched Mr Monday's. I heard his breathing, as if it were amplified. I dared not look up at him, because I was afraid of what I might see in his eyes. Goosebumps prickled along my arms and up the back of my neck. It was as if he were touching me with his gaze. I both heard and felt his presence behind me as we walked between the offices. Although I was intrigued by him, I knew he wasn't the one for me. Mr Monday had left too much of an imprint on me. If I was going to allow anyone to dominate me, it would be him.

We were silent during the elevator ride to the roof. My emotions were warring inside me. I glanced at him, but his attention was completely fixed on the file as he scrutinized my notes again. I could imagine what it would be like if he focused all that attention on a woman under his touch, and shivered slightly.

Here I was again. On the roof. Walking toward the waiting helicopter. Only this time it was daylight and the dark of the night was not there to help conceal how high up we were. I hesitated as I stepped on to the walkway, and Mr Friday was right behind me. I felt him with every nerve ending I was still balancing on the edge between feeling desired and feeling hunted.

I stepped carefully, my shoes totally inappropriate for the walk across the metal catwalk. The heels were delicate and could easily slip down into the holes of the grid. This didn't help my blossoming vertigo, and I grabbed the railing tightly, doing my best to find the courage to walk across it. Did Mr Friday know about my fear of heights too?

Then he placed his hand on my shoulder, startling me, and I nearly dropped to my knees in fright. 'It's okay,' he said. His grip was firm. I almost felt as though all my fear were being drawn out of me and into him through the connection of his fingers to my shoulder. I looked up at him, a little surprised at this new sensation. How did he do that? I couldn't quite place what I saw in his eyes, but it made me feel quite powerless. I let the sensation run over me before kicking myself out of the weird mood and gently moving my shoulder out from under his touch.

'I'm fine. Thank you.' I stepped much more confidently toward the waiting helicopter. While he had just provided me with a moment of comfort, he was still highly unnerving. I wasn't sure which bothered me the more, him or the helicopter.

I was glad of my skirt; as with the sports car, it made getting into the helicopter a whole lot easier. I settled in the same seat as the other night. Mr Friday sat where Mr Monday had, and I had an immediate negative reaction. It was as if Mr

Friday were intruding on sacred space, and I resented him for being where Mr Monday should be. These emotions, of course, were completely illogical, and I had no idea where they were coming from.

He leaned back as if he hadn't a care in the world. His confidence and powerful aura filled the helicopter. He was an imposing man, I'd give him that. My mind slid back to sex. I wondered if he was a Dom. I didn't know that world all that well. My only context was what I'd read in a few romantic novels or seen in movies. The lifestyle had never felt enticing until earlier today, when I'd imagined being bound to Mr Monday's bed. I tried to picture being naked in front of Mr Friday, and my arousal diminished. Trust definitely played a large part in my fantasies.

Light bondage was one thing, but I didn't think I'd be a good submissive – not a proper one. Letting go of all control wasn't something that appealed to me. I could understand why it was a turn-on for some women, letting a man make them feel fabulous, letting him take away all their stresses and worries. I definitely wanted a man who knew his way around the bedroom, but I wanted to be free to reciprocate. I wanted to drive him equally crazy with lust.

With my mind playing out all sorts of exciting scenarios of sexual adventures, I'd almost forgotten I was in the helicopter with Mr Friday. When he reached over and touched my knee, the ensuing flare of sexual heat that scorched through me pulled me out of my musings. I couldn't believe my reaction to it, and I told myself it was only because I had been thinking about Mr Monday.

'Oh! You startled me.'

'I know,' he said, his voice knowing. I did my best not to shiver. Mr Monday may have claimed my heart but, while I didn't think our kinks meshed, Mr Friday did have moments of pure sexiness.

'You have excellent notes here. Tell me your recommendations.'

The whomping of the helicopter blades increased, and I gripped my knees as it tilted in a banking turn. I didn't think I would ever get used to this.

'You're afraid of flying,' he said. I opened my eyes, realizing I had squeezed them shut. I looked at him in the dimly lit cabin. He was just a dark silhouette, back-lit by the bright sunlight behind him, and he seemed so imposing and huge. I was reminded of Mr Monday, which gave me the burning need to be back on the ground, not up here with this domineering man, and waiting for Mr Monday to arrive to take me home, as he had every night this week.

I wasn't going to admit to my fear – I had done enough of that these past few days – so I turned and looked at the window, trying not to close my eyes.

'It's nothing to be ashamed of. Everyone has fears. It's how you face them that matters.'

I just nodded in response.

'I can help you with your fear.'

Had I heard him properly? I knew exactly what he was saying. I turned my head slowly to face him. I knew he wasn't talking just about my fear of flying but also about something much deeper. A part of me was tempted to go down that rabbit hole with him, but the rest of me wasn't. He was no Mr Monday. It was easy to tell him no, easier than I thought it would be.

'Thank you for the offer. And no offense, but I do believe I will pass.' I held his gaze, wanting to give an illusion of strength I really wasn't feeling right now. I did feel intimidated by him, and to make things worse the damn helicopter shook slightly as we were buffeted by a strong wind.

He tipped his head to me and smiled. It was one of the first true smiles I'd seen him give all day. 'Just remember, the offer stands whenever you're ready.'

I had no words to respond to that at all. I just nodded my head and gazed out of the window again. This helicopter ride couldn't end quickly enough.

'I think we're nearing the country club now,' I said, pointing. I was feeling a little bit calmer. Maybe forcing myself to do things that scared the crap out of me was a way to get over my fear of heights. 'Wow! It looks really pretty from the air.'

'It does. I think it will be a good purchase. The cuts we'll make will help ensure the club becomes quite profitable.'

I turned to face him. 'What cuts?'

He looked at me, as if surprised I was asking. 'You know the answer to that. Your notes clearly identify areas that need culling.'

Oh my God, he meant the staff. He was going to cut the number of employees.

'I may have identified areas that needed attention. But I also gave solutions that would prevent the need to make lay-offs.' My fingers twisted together nervously as I tried to convince him.

'I saw that. But the quickest way, in my estimation, to relieve the strain on the finances is by reducing staff.' He dismissed my concerns with a nonchalant wave of his hand.

The helicopter tipped as it descended for landing. I sucked in a breath and balled my hands into fists, before forcing myself to relax. 'That may be true, but I think it would be a huge mistake. This is a service industry. You can't provide a top-notch service if the staff are stressed and overworked. It will roll over into the customers' experience.'

He held up his hand to halt me. I furrowed my brows. I did

not appreciate his lack of respect for my opinion. 'That may be so, Tess—'

'There are no buts. You can't just lay off staff. You may be able to try and reduce staff numbers by attrition, and perhaps offer a buy-out option to long-time employees. But I firmly believe that lay-offs aren't the way to go.'

I could tell he wasn't used to people disagreeing with him, but I wasn't about to back down. I'd seen the other day how unproductive unhappy staff could be, and I was ready to argue the point. Mr Friday regarded me thoughtfully for a moment as the helicopter bumped to a landing. Then he conceded, 'For the time being, then, we will try to avoid laying off any staff.'

Relief flooded through me. I didn't know how many jobs I might just have saved, but even saving just one would be an accomplishment. I watched Mr Friday jump out of the helicopter, and he reached inside for my hand. I looked at him and decided his gentlemanly behavior was some kind of olive branch so I accepted his assistance. I was relieved, though, when there were no more goosebumps rippling along my arms, or flares of desire.

'Lead the way, Ms Canyon.' I gave him a quizzical look for being so formal; he'd been calling me Tess all day. I shrugged my shoulders and took the path that I had walked on only a few days before.

'I've only been here once, so anything more in depth is something you'll have to do on your own.' Mr Friday checked the time. 'We have a few minutes before the meeting.'

'What meeting?' I asked, not having expected this turn of events. He was texting away, pretty much ignoring me, and I had to repeat my question before he answered it.

'A departmental management meeting,' he said absently.

'Why didn't you say so?'

'Not everything is told to you upfront. Hasn't that become clear by now?' Mr Friday said, pocketing his phone and looking around him.

I huffed out a breath, unimpressed, although he was speaking the truth. 'Still, it would've been nice of you to give me a heads up so that I could prepare.'

He held up the file. 'You already have. Now, I know there's a conference room here somewhere. Can you find that?'

God, could he be more condescending? 'Of course I can. It's this way.'

We walked through the impressive entryway doors, and I experienced that same sense of awe I had when I was here on Tuesday. I thought I'd fallen in love with this place. I led us to the same conference room as before and inside were half a dozen people, including, surprisingly, Mr Wednesday. My heart tumbled over in my chest. I was so shocked to see him here, I had no idea what to say. He tilted his head to me in greeting, and I smiled awkwardly back.

Seizing on an excuse to look away, I glanced around the table, trying to assess the other people; they must be the club's management team. All of them looked a little nervous, and I had the urge to comfort them, to tell them not to be afraid for their jobs. I glanced over at Mr Friday and narrowed my eyes. Would he stand by what he'd said in the helicopter? Then I glanced at Mr Wednesday and tried to gauge the expression on his face. Both men were unreadable.

I wasn't surprised when Mr Wednesday called the meeting to order. He handed out sheets of paper containing the items on the agenda. My gaze rushed over my copy, and I was relieved to see they had listed only the budget as an item, not any specifics. Maybe we would dodge the lay-off bullet after all.

'This meeting has been called out of respect for you and your employees.' Mr Wednesday moved back to the head of the table and sat down. He had a way of making everybody feel at ease, and I saw the tension on the managers' faces relax somewhat. I relaxed right along with them and grabbed a chair at the far end, waiting to see how this meeting would play out. Mr Wednesday continued, 'As you probably know by now, Diamond Enterprises is purchasing the country club. I'm sure you've heard rumors through the grapevine, so we're here to ease your mind.'

Mr Friday handed me back my notes and indicated that I should give them to Mr Wednesday. Another reason to wish I'd been given a heads-up about this meeting: I could've put together a proper report. I stood and walked around the table, and touched Mr Wednesday lightly on the shoulder, before putting the file down in front of him. I felt him stiffen under my fingers, and I was sad to realize I must have hurt his feelings the other night.

'Ms Canyon has done a financial analysis for us. Based on her research, she has identified problematic areas and suggested possible solutions.'

'Will you be laying off any staff?' The speaker was wearing a dark green polo shirt that bore the club's logo, and khakis. His casual, comfortable attire probably meant that he managed either the golf course or the maintenance crews.

Mr Wednesday glanced at me. 'Tess, would you take that one?'

I made direct eye contact with the speaker. 'I'm sorry, I don't know your name,' I said.

'Vincent.'

'Thank you, Vincent. No, at the present time, we will not be laying off staff.' I did my best not to look at Mr Friday with a smug expression. 'Obviously, we are still in the fact-finding phase and we will not make any decisions hastily. However, I can share with you – and this information stays in this room, because we're not ready to make any announcements to the rest of the staff – that we are discussing instituting new inventory controls, in addition to offering a retirement incentive.' I looked at Mr Wednesday and raised my eyebrows questioningly.

'Yes, Ms Canyon is right. Offering an incentive is something Diamond is looking into very seriously. Once we've integrated the club's employee records into our existing system, we will be able to identify those who qualify and discuss things further with them. In the meantime, we will go with the status quo, but make no mistake, changes will be coming. And one of the most important goals you will be given is to increase membership and boost revenue. Each of you will be tasked to determine ways in which your department can make this happen. So I suggest that you begin brainstorming and that we reconvene in a week.'

The meeting was over before I knew it, and right to the point. It felt rather anticlimactic after all the build-up. The speaker in the polo shirt departed rapidly, probably off to tell the rest of the staff the good news about there being no immediate plans for lay-offs. The others spoke to Mr Wednesday and Mr Friday, while I sat at the table, acutely uncomfortable that they were both in the same room. God help me if Mr Monday showed up – which was entirely possible. After a few more questions and a smattering of small talk the managers trickled out of the room and we were left alone, just the three of us.

'This is my first time up here. King always schedules those management retreats during HR's busiest time,' Mr Wednesday announced. He turned to Mr Friday. 'Your first time, too?'

He nodded. 'Yes. I was hoping Tess could take us for a tour, but apparently she didn't see much of it when she was here last.'

'Okay, so what are your actual plans for this country club?' I asked the men. They both looked rather surprised at the question. 'What? That's a fairly easy one to answer.'

Mr Friday crossed his arms over his chest. 'Rather than us telling you what we think the plans for this country club are, why don't you tell us what *you* think they should be?'

'Well, as you mentioned, Diamond was already booking a lot of events here. When the company owns the property, we'll save a lot of money by continuing to utilize the club as a venue for large events and retreats. In addition, I think it should be a perk for the staff.' I looked pointedly at Mr Wednesday. 'They could receive an employee discount on spa services or green fees. Freebies could also be given away periodically as a way to boost morale. But the biggest thing I think the company should consider is marketing the golf course more effectively. We could lobby to host a tournament or enter into a partnership with a local hotel, offer a package deal on lodging and tee time. In any case, with all of these ideas, staffing levels are important. You can't have quality events without quality staff.'

The men quizzed me for a few moments, then Mr Wednesday spoke.

'I'd still like to look around,' he said. He didn't ask me or Mr Friday to join him. He walked out the door of the conference room, leaving us alone in the room.

'Walk with me,' Mr Friday said, as he left the room, too. Once again, I had no choice but to trail along behind him as we wandered back into the main lobby.

'When I was here I was eager to see more of the grounds. There was no time for that, though,' I told him as we crossed the dining room.

'Well, no time like the present,' he said, and pushed open the door to the flagstone patio.

A beautiful breeze blew in off the lake. I took a deep breath and filled my lungs with the unpolluted air. 'I must say, I do love the country air.'

'I agree,' Mr Friday said, and we walked down the wide steps towards the waterfront.

There were only a couple of boats tied up at the docks. 'There were float planes here the other day,' I commented.

'I heard that planes flew in here. That's another amenity that could be used to attract high-end clientele.'

I turned to look behind me. The beauty of the nature here was astounding. I truly had fallen in love with the club and its surroundings, and I was hoping that I'd be able to spend a lot of time here when I was CEO. *Wow, listen to me. Already thinking of myself as CEO!*

Five days of passing tests seemed to have gone to my head. Who knows, though? Maybe I didn't pass today's test? There was no sign of Mr Monday, or a new key card. I looked around, hoping to see him here, disappointed that he wasn't here. However, since he had to make the time to drive me in this morning, given whatever personal crisis he was currently dealing with, I supposed there was no way he'd drive all the way up here to get me. I forced myself not to expect him. I made my way back up the steps toward the main clubhouse and wondered when we'd be heading back. Suddenly I was exhausted. It had been a crazy week and I was beyond drained. I could sleep for another five days after this. I reminded myself that if I passed today's test I still had two more days of tests to look forward to.

Inside the clubhouse, I was dying for a coffee, and I didn't want to wait for Mr Friday to catch up. He was a big boy and could take care of himself. I needed a moment on my own so I climbed on to a tall stool in the dining room. I readjusted my skirt and turned to look out through the floor-to-ceiling windows with the magnificent view of the lake. The waitress came to take my order and I found myself taking note of the way she served me. I was pleasantly surprised and very pleased by her graciousness and the quality of the attention she gave me. If she was any indication of the serving staff, we'd be doing just fine.

I had no idea how I was going to get back to the city. I could only assume we'd be flying back in the helicopter. I was enjoying my little break from the intensity of dealing with the 'days'. But I was sure Mr Friday would come to find me when it was time to leave. The coffee was good and I felt myself starting to unwind. I was glad Diamond were going to buy this property. I was also glad that I might have the chance to be able to oversee its development. For some reason, I felt a kinship to the country club.

I had a lovely time spinning castles in the air about what the future could hold for the club so I was a little disappointed when Mr Friday came to collect me. 'We're heading back,' he said.

I slid off the stool. 'Did you get your tour?'

'Yes, I did.'

'Well, are you happy with this acquisition?' I asked, and almost crossed my fingers as I waited for his answer.

'Yes. I'm satisfied with it.'

I shook my head and reminded myself he was the numbers man. Black and white. Adding and subtracting. But, after today, I knew there was a passion lurking deep inside him, something he hid very well behind his book-keeper's exterior.

As we settled into the helicopter, something crossed my mind. 'You want to know one way to save some money?'

I was buckling my seatbelt, as was he.

'Of course I want to know. What is your suggestion?'

'To quit flying around in this damn helicopter.'

For the first time today, he laughed. It was a nice laugh, deep and throaty. I smiled and relaxed back into my seat. He sure was an intriguing man. Just not intriguing enough for me.

It was then that I remembered I'd left the envelope of incriminating evidence – incriminating of me and Diamond Enterprises – at the office.

MR SATURDAY

I was dreaming. It had to be a dream, because everything was far too confusing and it all changed constantly. Except for the loud banging. That was new. And insistent. It seemed to come from a dark room somewhere in the dream, until it turned into the *whomp whomp* of helicopter blades. I was in the helicopter, soaring over shadowed lands. *Bang! Whomp whomp. Bang! Bang!* Suddenly, the chopper tilted, my seatbelt disappeared and I tumbled out of the door. My worst nightmare! My hands stretched into the air as I desperately reached for something to halt my fall. There was nothing. As I twisted and fell, I saw Mr Monday far below, looking up at me. He was holding an old-fashioned fireman's safety net, ready to catch me. I heard his voice faintly as he yelled, 'Don't worry, it's vintage!'

But the closer I got to the ground, the further away he seemed.

Bang! Bang! Bang! The sound wouldn't stop, and my body jerked mid-air. Slowly, the banging sounds pulled me from the dream's chaotic depths. I struggled beneath the layers of sleep, against leaving Mr Monday behind. My heart ached that I couldn't bring him with me. The feeling of loss was acute as I woke up, the bright light of the morning piercing through the last layer.

I blinked and looked around, totally confused. I was in my own bed. I put my hand out, hoping to feel Mr Monday snuggled down in the sheets beside me. But the bed was empty; the sheets were cold. It had seemed so damn real. I couldn't process anything. I was still trying fight off sleep and figure out what the hell was going on.

The noise, though, didn't fade away like my dream. It kept on going. I shook my head and rubbed my eyes. I pushed the covers back, not wanting to leave the cozy warmth of my bed. I stood up a little too quickly and had a head rush, then stumbled through the bedroom into the living room. Yes. The sound was coming from the front door.

'Stop, stop! I'm coming already!'

I unlocked the door and hauled it open, then froze, realizing my mistake. I never opened the door without looking through the peephole first. I blamed it on my being half asleep, and on the person with a death wish who was standing in the hallway, disturbing my beauty sleep after a crazily tough week.

'Finally.' A deep voice filled the dark hall.

'What are you doing here? And who are you anyway?' I asked. I rubbed my eyes to get the last bit of sleep out them. Gradually, my vision cleared, and I blinked harder. He was in the shadows, but I could see enough of him to be able to guess that he was from Diamond. I stepped closer and tipped my head back to look up at him. He took a step forward, and the sunlight streaming in the windows from my apartment fell on him. He. Was. Huge. With his long blond hair that fell to his shoulders, rock-hard muscles and vibrant blue eyes, he looked like a Viking god, ready to carry me off on his longship. Holy Lord! In my sleep-dazed state, I was ready to start packing.

I collected my thoughts. It was Mr Monday who I wanted to sweep me off my feet. Yes. Him. Okay, I tried to refocus on the beautiful man in my hallway watching me silently freak out. Even though I knew he must be from Diamond, I wasn't going to let him off that easy or roll out the red carpet. I was going to make him work for whatever it was he was here to do.

'Who the hell are you? And what are you doing banging on my door first thing in the morning? It's Saturday, for crying out loud! A day off. A day for sleeping in – which I was, by the way.' I tried to make my voice sound firm and tough, but it still had the thick sound of sleep.

'I know it's Saturday. It's play day and –' he glanced at his watch – 'ten o'clock in the morning. "Sleeping in" time's over.' He walked past me into my apartment.

'Excuse me? You can't just walk in here. I don't even know you.' I blinked, taken aback at the way he had just barged into my home. 'Hey, you there. Far enough. And damn right it's a play day, and I want to play my way, in bed!'

As soon as the words left my mouth, I wanted to sink into the floor. I'd meant that I wanted to sleep, but the way his gaze swept leisurely down my body, reminding me I was wearing only shorts and a tank, no bra, made it clear that the mystery Viking's mind had gone somewhere else. I weakly muttered, 'You know what I mean.'

'The best play days are spent with someone else.' He smiled wickedly, a dimple appearing in his cheek, and my knees went weak. 'So come on, get ready and let's go.'

I shook my head and raised my hands, waving them back and forth. 'I'm not understanding this. You're throwing too much at me so early in the morning.'

'It's not early.' He strode over to my bookcase, perusing the titles. Over his shoulder, he said, 'You do have a very sexy morning voice right now, though. I like it.'

'What?' Who was this man, this very bold, bossy and yes, I'll say it again, gorgeous man? 'Sexy voice . . .' I shook my head, then stared right at him. 'Yeah, you just woke me up. And, no, I'm not going anywhere. It's Saturday.'

I walked over to the couch, flopped on it and promptly gave a big, lion-like yawn. I tried to talk to him midway through, which only resulted in the garbled words, 'See, yawning here.' I pointed at myself and the yawn stretched out even longer.

He jerked his head back and gave me a bemused look, before manfully deciding to ignore my gibberish. 'Anyway, it might be Saturday, Tess of the Tests, but that doesn't mean it's a day off for you.'

'What are you talking about? I should be done for the week.' I stretched out on the couch and snuggled into the pillows. I knew I had two more tests left, but surely they would be on Monday and Tuesday, right? That made perfect sense to me, and having the weekend to myself would be heaven. I could use the time to figure out once and for all what I was going to do about my revenge plot.

'Mr King told you there'd be seven tests over seven days. He never said they'd be business days. CEOs are on call 24/7. You should be thanking me. There'll be no budgets today. But if you'd rather sleep in, I'll just go back to the company and tell them you're finished with the interview process.' Mr Saturday, the fiend, started to head towards the door. Put on the spot, there was really only one thing I could say.

'You promise there'll be no budgets today? No long columns of numbers that never seem to end?' He laughed, his eyes crinkling, and my apartment seemed almost to shake from the sound. 'Yes, Tess of the Mathematically Illiterate, I promise there will be no financial problems on this test.'

I sat up, preparing to head to my bedroom to get ready and take one last, longing look at my bed, but I paused because I just had to be sure. 'How do I know I can trust you? You could be a stock analyst in disguise.'

Surprisingly, my neighbor didn't bang on the wall when Mr Saturday let out another loud laugh. In about another forty years, he'd probably be a killer Santa Claus. He reached out and took my hand. 'I'm the VP of Marketing, darling. Would I lie to you?'

I rolled my eyes, because wasn't that really what marketing was? Wrapping up the truth in a glossy, pretty package and drowning it in advertising hype? Tugging my hand free, I replied, 'Fine. Let me just grab a quick shower and—'

'Not to worry.' He waved his hand as if to dismiss my concerns. 'You can have a shower where we're going.'

I sat up and swung my feet to the floor, a tingle of alarm skittering down my spine. 'Okay, that sounds really weird. Where the hell are you taking me?' I narrowed my eyes and lifted my chin. 'Maybe I should see some ID before I go anywhere with you.'

'Well, that's closing the barn door after the horse has bolted.' He carried on chuckling.

'I really don't find it funny at all.' I held out my hand. 'Prove you're from Diamond, or you can leave right now. Without me.'

He stuck his hand into his pants pocket, moving with a confidence and grace that seemed only to make him that much more masculine. He wasn't even dressed in a suit like the other Mr Days-of-the-Week. Sure, it was a Saturday, but still. On the positive side, it meant I could be casual, too.

He pulled out a folded envelope and put it in my hand. 'I think this should explain things.'

I looked at the crumpled-up envelope resting in my hand. 'Really? I hope it does clear things up. At least as far as you're concerned.'

I tore it open, pulled out the wrinkly letter, and a business card with Mr King's details on it. The paper bore the same emblem as the note I got on Thursday. In the same scrawling hand, it read:

Tess, I'm so pleased you made it to the sixth test. Enjoy brunch on Diamond before Mr Saturday takes you to begin the test. Good luck!

'Hmph.' I blew out a puff of air and looked up at him. 'This really doesn't prove anything, you know. Look at the state of this envelope. You could have taken this from the real Mr Saturday.'

'You can't be serious.' He tipped his head to one side and gave me a quizzical look. 'You certainly are an interesting woman.'

I shrugged my shoulders. 'I am who I am. And nothing will ever change that.'

'Well, Tess of the Paranoids, sometimes change happens when you aren't looking.' With that cryptic statement, he clapped his hands together, then looked at his watch. 'Let's get moving. The brunch reservations are in fifteen minutes. You can shower at the appointment after that.'

I rubbed my eyes, trying to get out the last little bit of sleep, and stood up. 'So what do I need to bring with me?'

'Nothing. Your purse, I suppose, if you're so inclined.'

I gave him a sideways glance. 'My mom always told me to carry mad money. You know, like when you have to take off in a hurry, always make sure you've got money, so that you can jet.'

'Now I know where you get your suspicious mind from.' He wagged his fingers at me. 'I think you should get changed. You look amazingly sexy in your jammies, but they're not really suitable for where we're going.'

Grrr. I knew I had to fall in line if I wanted to keep going with the tests, but I was so over these men giving me instructions with no context. With a false sweetness, I asked, 'Is there perhaps a dress code at our destination?'

He ignored my saccharine sarcasm. 'It's a play day, so just wear your most fashionable comfy clothes. Come on, get going and get dressed. Or I will dress you myself.'

I drew in a gasp and gave him a stern look. 'You most certainly will not.' I turned around and tossed my head. 'You are a pain in the ass.'

His laugh followed me into my bedroom, and I slammed the door shut on it. It felt good for a fleeting moment . . . until I heard him still laughing on the other side. Quickly, I pulled on a shorts and T-shirt set, thrust my feet in sandals and fluffed my hair out. I swung the strap of my bag over my shoulder and opened my bedroom door.

'All right, then. I suppose you want me to follow you.'

He looked up from his phone, smiled, and nodded when he looked at me. 'Now, don't you look hot? Even dressed down, you sure can take a guy's breath away, give him all kinds of delightful ideas.'

I rolled my eyes. 'Don't be a pig.'

Mr Saturday gave a cheesy half-bow before taking my arm and escorting me out of the apartment. 'Come on, milady Tess, we've got places to go.'

After the week I'd had I definitely felt I deserved a treat. Mr Saturday whisked me off to a very exclusive building in an equally exclusive neighborhood. He turned and drove down a laneway beside the building; beautiful, arching trees lined the drive into a private parking area that clearly belonged to this lovely gracious place. I knew it was somewhere special.

'What is this place?' I asked, admiring the fantastic architecture.

After parking the car, he leapt out and walked around to open my door. 'This is where we're having brunch. A nice, relaxing start to the day.'

How did he know that a bit of relaxation was all I wanted?

I let him help me out of the car, and we wandered up a cobblestone pathway lined with colorful flowerbeds. Ornate wrought-iron benches were tucked away in secret and private places. A small waterfall graced the end of the path, just before a brick staircase that led up to fabulous leaded-glass doors.

'This is so lovely.' I could feel my edginess wafting away on the summer breeze. I sighed happily.

'I can't imagine how stressful it must be, to go through all those tests. You deserve some moments of serenity.'

I took back every bad thought I had about Mr Saturday. We continued into the building, his hand resting on my lower back. This place was five stars all the way. It smelled as gorgeous and clean as it looked. I'd never been able to afford to patronize a place this posh before. This was a brand-new experience for me. One that I would probably be able to repeat on my new CEO salary. All the possibilities that lay ahead built up until I was close to bubbling over with excitement.

'This way to the dining room.' A charming hostess greeted us with a demure smile and showed us to our table.

The restaurant took my breath away, from the champagne-colored walls to the gilt-edged mouldings, all the fresh flowers and the sparkling crystal, the gleaming silver and rich damask tablecloths. All the tables were strategically placed for privacy, and ours was in a rounded alcove with floor-to-ceiling windows that looked out on to the gardens. It was all exquisite. All the tension of the past week evaporated. I felt giddy with my luxurious surroundings. A wonderful sense of peace filled me and I settled into a comfortable chair at the table we'd been shown to. This would be my future. No more pinching pennies, no more strict budgeting, no more praying that unexpected expenses wouldn't crop up. If I got the CEO job, I would be financially secure, and no one would be able to take that away from me. A waiter came by to ask what we'd like to drink, and returned so quickly with our tea it was as if he had wings. I shook my head in wonderment.

'Why are you shaking your head?' asked Mr Saturday as he reached for the teapot to pour. It was a very odd thing to watch such a masculine man handle a delicate piece of bone china.

'Hmm?' I added some milk to my tea and stirred with a dainty silver spoon.

'Why were you shaking your head?' His hand dwarfed his cup, but he handled it so elegantly it looked protected rather than overwhelmed.

'I was just thinking about everything. What I had to go through to get here. And where I am now.' I took a sip from my cup. It wasn't coffee flown in from Costa Rica, but it tasted just as good as the tea Mom and I had shared the last time I visited her in England. Which was a while ago. I wish I could get the courage to fly more often. I really missed her at that moment. The waiter drifted to the table, quietly inquiring if we were ready to order brunch. We did so, and it seemed like mere moments later that he and an army of impeccably dressed busboys brought out a huge English breakfast.

Immediately, we dug into the food. Mr Saturday ate with unabashed pleasure. I watched him over the rim of my tea cup.

He was a devilishly sexy and wild-looking man. A daredevil. Yet he held an air of sophistication which was rather surprising, considering his outwardly rebellious appearance. I did have to admit, though, he was very liberating to be with. The kind of guy who would take you to the edge and back. Accept you for whoever you are and not try to change you. I suspected he didn't toe the line very well.

Was I getting too used to being around sexy, hot men? I was bringing a piece of toast that I'd dipped in egg yolk to my mouth when I thought of Mr Monday. My hands paused halfway and my belly tumbled. When would I see him again? Did he know about this test? He usually escorted me, but nothing about today was typical. I glanced at Mr Saturday, but he was very focused on the plate in front of him and, thankfully, didn't see my hesitation. If Mr Monday didn't know I was here, that meant I might not see him today.

I put down my fork, desolate. I didn't have his phone number. I couldn't reach him. He would have to find me. After the passionate kisses we had shared yesterday, I badly wanted more, my body on the edge of constant arousal. I could still appreciate Mr Saturday's good looks, but it was like admiring the skill of a painter yet not wanting the painting.

My appetite gone, and lost in the turmoil of my thoughts, I sipped my tea while Mr Saturday decimated the remaining food. I put my teacup down shakily, and it rattled on the fragile saucer, knocking the silver sugar spoon on to the tablecloth.

'Easy now,' Mr Saturday said, his eyebrows raised. 'There's no need to wreck the joint.'

I touched my fingertips to the cup and saucer, hoping to steady them. I let out a sigh. I was ready for this brunch to be over and my test to begin. He must've read my mind, because at a small gesture of his hand the waiter appeared with the check. Mr Saturday handed him a black credit card. I couldn't make out his name, but I could see that 'Diamond Enterprises' was embossed on the card. Once the bill was taken care of, he announced, 'Time for the first appointment.'

He stood and pulled my chair back. His fingers briefly traced over my shoulder, and I shivered a little.

'Cold?' he asked me. His voice was low and held an edge of sexiness.

I wasn't cold; it was his touch that had caused me to react as I had. But I wasn't going to tell him that. I glanced up at him and smiled, slinging my bag over my shoulder again. 'Where are we going?'

His grin was triumphant. 'Nowhere! The rest of this facility is a world-class spa. I did promise you a shower, after all.'

My fingers gripped the strap of my bag tightly. I may have dreamt about being financially solvent, but I wasn't there yet. 'I can't afford any treatments at a place like this.'

Mr Saturday waved away my concerns. 'No, no, it's my treat. You just concentrate on relaxing.' As I stepped away from the table, I saw the receipt he had just scribbled his signature on. Our breakfast had cost well over a hundred dollars. I was shocked. If the breakfast was any indication, any spa treatments I took were sure to cost a fortune. Knowing that gave me an unsettled feeling in my stomach.

'Are you having a treatment?' I asked, trying to distract myself.

He let out a great bellow of laughter. 'Good God, no! I have had a mani and a pedi a time or two over the years, but it's not high on my priority list. The spa has some squash courts, and I plan on working some frustration out while you're enjoying being pampered.'

I raised my eyebrows. 'Really? Squash, and then what will you do?'

He shrugged his shoulders. 'Who knows? Maybe I'll go swimming, or perhaps take a sauna. Maybe I'll even have a massage.' He gave me a wink. 'They do have couple's massages here, you know.'

I was shocked by his suggestion. Not quite sure how to handle it, I just let it slide. The image of us lying naked side by side on the massage tables, covered only in sheets, became locked in my brain. I could imagine the low lighting and almost feel the masseuse manipulate my muscles, hear the calming music and smell the soothing scents that wafted on the air around us. And while it sounded absolutely divine, it was extremely inappropriate. For me and Mr Saturday, anyway. For me and Mr Monday, on the other hand . . .

I followed Mr Saturday through the gracious halls. It must've been a home at some point in time, and then been renovated. The spa reception area was beautiful, as was the young woman who greeted us. This seemed to be the week for me to interact with very attractive people.

'Miss Canyon. Your aesthetician is waiting for you.'

'They are? What am I having done?'

'Your facial awaits,' the receptionist said with a smile. I turned to Mr Saturday. He was so incredibly close that, if I wanted, all I needed to do was move forward slightly and our lips would be touching. The whole week had been filled to the brim with handsome men, titillating my emotions, throwing me off kilter, making me feel more turned on than I'd ever been. My body was highly tuned to their every little nuance. I was sensitive to each little thing, all of the men so different. Being close to Mr Saturday was no different. It didn't matter, though, how hot he was. He wasn't Mr Monday.

I smiled and took a step back, hoping to appear casual. 'A facial – I haven't had one in so long.' I raised my hand and touched my cheek. 'I think my tired skin will be very happy to be pampered,' I told him, and smiled at the young woman.

'Come this way, then, please. We'll get you set up with a locker and you can get comfortable.'

I turned to face Mr Saturday. 'Thank you,' I said.

Mr Saturday leaned down and whispered into my ear, his voice seductively low, his breath fluttering my hair. 'You're welcome.'

He leaned down and put his lips on my cheek. My immediate reaction when he pressed a kiss to my skin was startling. I had to reach out to hold the counter, curling my fingers around the edge so I wouldn't stumble.

I looked into Mr Saturday's eyes and felt a touch of confusion at what I saw. There wasn't much emotion in them; his gaze was almost calculating, as if everything that was happening had been carefully planned out. His loud laughter and easy smile had done a good job in keeping me grounded, but I suddenly had the feeling I was being manipulated. That thought helped to chase away any arousal that had snuck through my defenses. I followed the receptionist to the treatment area. I didn't even have the urge to glance back over my shoulder and see if he was still there. I didn't care if he'd left.

After storing my things in a locker, I was taken to a room, and sat in a chair. Being pampered like this was something I've never been able to do – I'd never had either the money or the time. I became so relaxed as the beautician worked on my face, neck and shoulders, I felt as if I was melting into the chair. I hadn't been this calm in years. The aesthetician was good, and she was quiet, as if she sensed that I really didn't feel like talking. I appreciated the lack of conversation. It allowed me to clear my mind further and not think about anything in particular. I was surprised when she gently touched my shoulder and roused me from the snooze I had fallen into.

'We're done. Take your time. There's no rush,' she said, in a very soft and gentle voice. She left the room, and I stayed in the chair for a few moments, enjoying the solitude. A few minutes later I left the room and was immediately greeted by another young woman. She escorted me into an exquisite sitting area with a serene view of the garden outside. I tucked my fluffy white robe around me and up under my chin. She indicated the sideboard laden with fruits and glass pitchers containing a variety of beverages.

'Please help yourself. We have a variety of infused waters.' She picked up a sparkling tumbler and handed it to me. 'Make sure you drink. You need to replenish your fluids after your treatment.'

'Thank you.' I took the glass from her and walked over to the pitcher of citrus water. I lifted the silver toggle of the nozzle and filled my glass.

She left, and I was alone in the room. A few minutes later, another couple came in, wearing matching robes. They seemed very intimate, whispering and constantly touching each other. They found a seat as far away from me as possible and cuddled up together. She rested her head on his shoulder, and he wrapped his arm around her. They seemed very romantic, and the flash of envy I felt at their expressions of tenderness surprised me. They must be between treatments, I thought.

I wondered what Mr Monday was up to right now. It would've been nice to spend the day with him, not Mr Saturday. We'd started something the other night that hadn't been taken to its conclusion. I needed it to come to one, one way or the other. Otherwise, I would continue to think about him and to wonder about us. I didn't like the tinge of loneliness that rolled over me.

I placed my glass on the table beside me and rested my

head on the back of the chair. Gazing out of the window to the pretty gardens beyond, I took the time to appreciate where I was. It was nice to have this break from the pressures of reality, but I knew things between me and Mr Monday and me couldn't be fully resolved until the tests were over. After today, there would be only one left, and my fate would be decided. The serenity I'd found disappeared under my rising anxiety about today's test.

'There you are.' Mr Saturday's voice snapped me out of my quiet thoughts. I think I almost resented him for disturbing me.

'Here I am,' I replied. I wanted him to go away, but I also wanted to get cracking on today's test. 'Is that it?' he asked me, a pinch of humor in his voice. 'Just "Here I am"?'

'Sorry, it's all I've got. Remember, you woke me up out of a sound sleep this morning. And I've had a very busy week.' I forced a yawn to prove my point.

'Yes, I did wake you up. So you could be pampered and spoilt.' He looked vaguely satisfied, as if he just won an argument.

I stood, the folds of the robe brushing against my bare legs. The small movement caught his eye, and I became very self-conscious that, beneath it, I was just in my underwear. Holding the lapels of the robe closed, I said, 'Well, the morning was a lovely treat, a great "play day", but I'm ready to get to work now.'

Mr Saturday's shoulders went back a little, and he crossed his arms as he gave me a bright smile. 'The play day's not over yet! You're scheduled for a pedicure next.'

Oooh, that did sound nice. I did my own nails at home to save money and because I was constantly changing the color, and I could afford a pedicure only every once in a while. I was really tempted. 'No, no, I can't accept that. The facial was generous enough. I can't let you pay for me to get a pedicure.'

He raised his eyebrows in a look of surprise. 'Oh, don't worry. Diamond is picking up the tab for everything.'

I took an involuntary step backwards, my flip-flops making a squeaking sound against the floor. 'Why would Diamond be paying for me to go to the spa?'

'A CEO has to know how to relax, right? It's not good for the company if they get burnt out. Besides, I often come here with clients and claim it as a business expense.'

'But I'm not a client.' Mr Saturday claimed regular spa visits on his expense reports? I began to get an uncomfortable feeling in the pit of my stomach.

He lifted his hand and lifted his shoulder. 'Potatoes, po-tah-toes. And you have the note from Mr King, right? So, clearly, he knows about today.'

'That's true. But it still doesn't make any sense. Why do I deserve to be pampered and spoilt today? I'm no different from the next employee.' I had to admit, though, the reminder about the note from Mr King was reassuring.

Mr Saturday shrugged before going over to pour himself a drink of the fancy water. 'You don't give yourself enough credit. Look at what you've done this week! You've obviously earned the right to be pampered, and of course Diamond should pay for it, since they're the reason you're so stressed out in the first place. Today is your day.'

'If you say so.' His reasoning made sense, and some of my excitement about the impending pedicure returned, but I still had a nagging feeling that I was missing something.

I watched him tilt his head back and lift the glass to his mouth. His throat muscles worked as he swallowed the water in a few big gulps. There was no denying he was a very attractive man. He also gave the impression that he was always ready to have a good time. I liked that about him. It was uplifting and rather refreshing after the other men I had met this week. They had all been rather intense and brooding.

'If I'm going to go have a pedicure, will we start the test after that?' I decided I did want the chance to relax a little more, but I didn't want to lose sight of the bigger picture.

Selecting an apple from the fruit on offer, he bit down with an audible crunch. The couple sharing the room with us seemed visibly annoyed about the noise we were making. After he finished eating, Mr Saturday said, 'Oh, yeah, yeah. Don't worry. I'll make sure you do what needs to be done.'

'And you're sure it's okay that Diamond is paying for all this?'

Taking my elbow, he began to herd me toward the door. He looked at me and I met his gaze. 'There's no need to feel concerned about being here. Think of it as an executive perk.'

I shook my head, in both disagreement and anger. 'I never could truly understand the high salary earned by some people, compared to the low salary of others. What justifies that?' He was silent as I continued. 'Why do sportspeople make millions of dollars when first responders get paid a fraction of that? To me, it makes absolutely no sense. Hard-working people are laid off left and right, while execs keep their high salaries and bonuses, all at the company's expense. It seems so unjust.'

He let me go so he could raise his hands up in defense. 'Whoa, now. Don't shoot the messenger. I didn't know that you'd missed the memo, Tess the Naïve, but the world isn't fair. There are people in Third World countries who don't have access to clean water and, out on Long Island, there's an above-ground pool in every yard. Sportspeople wouldn't be getting millions if people weren't willing to shell out hundreds for a ticket to the game.

That's how the system works. There will always be people who have more than someone else. So wouldn't you want to be a member of the "haves" rather than the "have-nots"?'

Yes. I'd been a 'have-not', thanks to Diamond firing my father, and I didn't want to go back to that. I'd worked my ass off, first by getting my masters in library science, and now by going through this crazy interview process. Didn't I deserve to be a 'have' for a change? Yes. But didn't everyone deserve clean water?

I stayed silent, struggling with my inner conflict of fair versus unfair. When he realized I wasn't going to respond, Mr Saturday looked at me contemplatively for a moment before giving me a bright smile.

'All right, then,' he said. 'Enough of the serious talk. We're here to shed all that negativity and rejuvenate. Time for you to get to your pedicure.'

As we exited the room, we were greeted by yet another gorgeous woman. She walked over and rested her hand on my shoulder, rubbing it lightly, and then massaged up my neck. It was glorious and, if it was any indication of what a massage would be like here, I was definitely considering treating myself.

'Miss Canyon, please come with me. We're ready for you.'

I nodded to Mr Saturday. 'I guess I'll see you later, then.'

'Yes, you will. Enjoy yourself.' He looked thoughtful, but he was still smiling. This man must have some kind of happy pill to keep him so optimistic. Then I remembered something my dad told me a long time ago: never trust anyone who smiles all the time. So I assessed Mr Saturday from a new perspective, unsure what to think about him.

I lifted my hand in acknowledgement of his words as I followed the woman down a wide hall to a room containing a bank of chairs. Everything about this place had been carefully thought out. Even the view from the treatment chairs was breathtaking. It wouldn't be hard to sit here all day and be pampered. Pedicure. Manicure. Facial. Massage. Steam rooms and rainforest showers. The list of ways to spend an absolutely perfect day here was endless. I climbed into the chair but, as comfortable as it was, I couldn't bring myself to relax.

'Would you like the massage feature turned on?'

'Oh, yes, please.' The rolling mechanisms under the soft leather of the chair were heavenly. Hopefully, this would do the trick. Surrounded by comfy pillows and soft music, and looking at the serene view through the windows, I sighed. This was the height of being spoilt. The aesthetician filled the foot sink built into the chair with hot, soapy water. A wonderful scent – sage and citrus – carried on the air from the water. Gently, she lifted my feet and put them in. I groaned in delight.

'Oh my God, that feels wonderful,' I said, as she rubbed the backs of my calves.

'I know, it's just divine, isn't it?'

I nodded in agreement, barely able to form words.

'Could I get you a glass of wine? Or perhaps a different beverage?' The hostess had appeared next to me, holding a little silver tray. She lifted a dish filled with a variety of nuts and dried fruit off the tray and put it within arm's reach on the table.

'Thank you,' I answered when she handed me a card with beautiful script on it. I was surprised to find it was a wine list. Wow, could this get any better? Having a pedicure, wine and tasty snacks all together was almost too good to be true, even if it was a bit over the top. I scanned the list to see if there was anything familiar and in my price range. I did know a little bit about wine. I recognized some of the names. When I saw Sequoia Grove, my mouth nearly started to water. It was one of the most delicious wines I'd ever had. I debated with myself. There were no prices, and I didn't want to appear gauche by asking. Ah, hell. It couldn't be more than twenty dollars a glass, so I ordered it.

She smiled at me with approval. 'Very good choice.'

I wasn't really hungry, but I wanted to taste the little nibbles in the bowl that had been placed beside me. The nuts had been nicely toasted and were deliciously buttery. My pedicurist sat on the stool in front of me. It was much more comfortable-looking than the other low stools I'd seen in salons and spas. This showed me that the spa cared about their staff, and I liked that. After my time with Diamond, I'd developed an appreciation for businesses that took care of their employees.

'I'm Tiffany,' the girl said to me. 'If you need anything at all, don't hesitate to ask.'

'Thank you, Tiffany.'

She shook out a towel and lifted one of my feet. Her hands were both gentle and firm as she began her routine. I've always loved my feet being rubbed, and her hands were magic.

'Do you know what kind of polish you would like? French, or a color?' I took the card she offered, which had pages of colors on it. I was in absolute heaven. There was matte finish, sparkle, holographic, glitter and bling. I was stunned by the endless possibilities they offered for nail art, and wanted it all! Where had all this choice been all my life? I was a nail-polish aficionado so this was a dream come true.

'Oh my goodness, how can I possibly choose?'

'I know,' she said. 'Everybody has trouble deciding.'

I settled on a gorgeous OPI purple polish, and then the hostess returned with my wine. I sipped it, delighting in the taste, while Tiffany performed miracles on my feet. But the nagging feeling grew stronger and my attention drifted back to the problem at hand. What Mr Saturday was doing with his expense reports was not much different to what my father had been accused of. I wondered what his real name was and if I would see it on the list I had printed out.

Continuing to participate in the spa day felt almost like an approval of what he was doing. Yet if I left, then I could be running the risk of failing the test, even though I didn't know what it was. And I hadn't decided what to do yet with the evidence I'd found. I could leak it to the media, anonymously, of course. The business papers would salivate over definitive proof of upper-management wrongdoing and misappropriation of company funds, but if I let the information out into public then I was putting the well-being of the company's employees and their families at risk. If I became CEO, though, I could make things right internally. Which meant I absolutely had to pass this next test. Which meant staying.

For the first time, I wondered if Mr King was aware of the expense-report abuse. Yes, his note had mentioned brunch, but it hadn't said anything about the facial or a pedicure. I suddenly thought of Jenny, who I'd met on Wednesday. *What if the money Mr Saturday is spending today could be the difference between the daycare center being set up or not?* Yes, I had worked hard, but should my 'perks' come at the expense of other people? I made a decision then and there. I simply couldn't continue with this spa day in good conscience. Once Tiffany had finished rinsing my feet, I leant forward.

'Tiffany, I just remembered something. We need to stop.'

'Is something wrong?' Concern marred her pretty features.

I shook my head. I didn't want to let her think she had done something wrong, or that I was upset. 'No, no, I just remembered something I've forgotten to do. I really must go.'

She looked startled. 'But we're not finished yet.'

'I know.' I checked my watch to make what I said more

convincing. 'I lost track of time, and I have to leave now.' I got off the chair and stepped down to the floor, slipping into my flip-flops.

'Are you sure? Did you want to reschedule?'

'Give me your card, and I'll reschedule when I can. I'm sorry for the inconvenience. You've worked magic on my feet, and I'd like nothing more than to stay here and have you finish.' I started to edge towards the exit, wanting to get back to the locker room and grab my—With dawning horror, I suddenly remembered something I really *had* forgotten. The evidence of those falsified expense claims was still at Diamond, just lying there, hidden only by a blotter. I had convinced myself last night that it would be fine over the weekend but, as Mr Saturday had proved, there was no such thing as a weekends for some Diamond employees. I no longer needed to pretend. There truly was an urgent matter at hand.

I couldn't get out of there fast enough. The burning urge to run back to Diamond Enterprises was nearly suffocating. What if somebody had found the envelope and the information in it? I would be screwed. Totally and royally screwed. Everything would be over. How could I have been so stupid! I dropped a twenty-dollar bill on the table beside the chair and dashed out of the room.

Sprinting out the front doors, I was thankful that a cab was right there. I hopped in and gave the address. 'Hurry, please.'

I checked my bag to make sure I had my latest key card and breathed a sigh of relief. In my haste to leave the spa, I hadn't thought twice about Mr Saturday. I puffed out a breath of air. What would he think? I'd totally abandoned him, and probably disqualified myself from the CEO job, but I couldn't, in good conscience, continue. I decided I would find out his real name and look into his expenditures, see just how much he manipulated the system.

The drive seemed to take an eternity, but finally we came to the building. I gave the cabbie instructions to wait. I did my best to walk into the lobby at a normal pace, when all I really wanted to do was run like hell and retrieve that envelope. A different security guard was on duty. I hadn't seen him before, and I hoped he wouldn't give me a difficult time for arriving on a Saturday. So when he addressed me by my name, I was stunned.

'Hello, Ms Canyon, it's nice to meet you.'

'And you, too. I just have to go upstairs to get something I forgot yesterday.'

'Of course. If you don't mind signing in—'

I did so, then hurried to the elevator, grateful that my key card worked. I rode up and stepped out on to the twenty-third floor. It was hushed and quiet. Nobody was here, and I ran to the office I used yesterday. I nearly cried with relief when I saw the envelope was still where I had left it, under the blotter. I grabbed it and was relieved it was still sealed shut. Which meant that nobody had discovered my proof that expense reports were being falsified.

'Holy shit,' I whispered, and let my shoulders slump. 'What drama.'

Now that I had the paperwork in my hot little hands, I couldn't wait to get home. I needed a drink. Briefly, I mourned my unfinished wine. As I rode the elevator back down, I wondered if Mr Saturday had noticed I was MIA. I had no way of contacting him, and I hadn't thought to leave a note. Tiffany would probably tell him I'd left in a hurry, and I really hoped he wouldn't come to my apartment again.

Thankful that I had asked the taxi to wait, I jumped in. I had him stop just before my street, where there were a few convenience stores. I splurged on two nice bottles of wine. Hello, wine night! Did I care that I was going to drink alone? Nope. Then I stopped at the wonderful Italian grocery, where I grabbed a loaf of bread, some cheese and a tray of antipasto. When I got home, I was going to treat myself to my own spa day. One that was legitimately paid for.

I was never so glad to get back into my little apartment. I was surprised at just how much time had gone by; it was late afternoon. I pulled down the blinds and lit candles scented with sage, rosemary and lemon. They helped to re-create the smells of the spa. I chose some music that would give the same ambience.

With the antipasto in the fridge, a bottle of wine open and breathing, I went into my bathroom and drew myself a bath. I poured my favorite oil under the steaming hot water and sprinkled in some bath salts. I inhaled the wonderful scent as it rose on the steam.

'There,' I said, standing back and looking at my handiwork.

My bedroom was still in chaos after the rush this morning, so I quickly made my bed so it looked inviting. Not that I was expecting company, but I always liked it to be just so. I shucked the clothes I was wearing and tossed them into the wicker hamper. Naked, I padded into the kitchen and poured myself a nice full glass of wine. I grabbed a couple of pieces of cheese from the fridge and headed to the bathroom.

Finally, I lowered myself into the tub; it was a lovely deep one. I leaned back and let the hot water wash away my stress. After a long soak, I dried off, and slipped on my red satin robe, tying the sash around my waist. I liked the sultry feel as it whispered over my skin. Rather erotic and sexy. I was feeling good and wishing for a little bit of man time.

Mr Monday time. I regretted, not for the first time, that I had no way to contact him.

Before I left the bathroom I opened a drawer. The array of

nail polish I had collected shone back at me like a brilliant rainbow. I looked through it, debating what color to paint on my toes. Ah! I wanted mermaid colors. I selected a beautiful turquoise, a deeper blue, and I also picked up my little container of sparkly rhinestones. I fancied having some bling on my toes. I took everything into the living room and organized the bottles neatly on my coffee table, which was in fact an antique weighing scale.

With everything set up perfectly and me looking forward to my own private spa night, I sat on the couch and leaned back, balancing the wine glass in my hand. I finally felt myself begin to truly unwind.

A bang on my front door startled me. I sat up and held my breath. Maybe they'd go away. No such luck. The person on the other side banged again. Who the hell? I immediately thought of Mr Saturday. I stood and debated whether to answer the door. I could hide and hope he went away, but he certainly hadn't given up this morning. Oh, I hoped it wasn't him. I walked over to the door and looked through the peephole.

Oh my God. My heart leapt into my throat, and I glanced around the room glad I put the papers underneath the couch earlier. It was presentable, except for my pedicure paraphernalia all over the table. The knock at the door was louder this time. I tried to still my pounding heart and drew in a deep breath.

Mr Monday. He was here.

I pulled the door open, and we stood there, staring at each other. He gave me a slow smile and my heart raced at the look he gave me. It wasn't until his gaze slid down my body that I remembered I was in my slinky robe. The silky fabric suddenly held a whole new sensation for me. I felt my nipples harden and press against it. I flushed and grew hot. All it took was a steamy look from this man and he had me aroused in a flash. That I was standing almost naked in front of him only heightened the mood.

'Well, look at you.' His voice held a sexy edge, and my heart tripped.

I nodded, incapable of words. I was so stunned, surprised; pretty much close to brain dead at that moment.

'There was no need to get dressed up for me.' The timbre of his voice held all sorts of sexual innuendo.

Good Lord, I could barely breathe.

I smiled back and stepped aside, hoping he would take it as an invitation to come in, because I didn' t trust my voice the least little bit. Once he passed by, I swallowed and cleared my throat. 'You caught me at the right time,' I said to him.

He turned around, and I nearly died at the passion in his eyes. 'I'll say I did. Timing is everything. And, obviously, mine is spot on today.'

I held up my wine glass. 'Can I pour you some?'

I shut and locked the door before walking into the kitchen, not waiting for him to answer. I wasn't going to let him go that easily now that he was here. He followed me and stopped behind me as I faced the counter to reach for a glass. I froze when he leaned around me, the heat of his body enveloping me, and placed a bag on the counter.

'Great minds think alike. Wine.'

I turned my head so I could see his face, and smiled. His presence filled the space, and dwarfed it. Electricity almost crackled between us in the small room. I refilled my glass and, just as I was about to pour his, I felt his hand on my hip. I instantly and very involuntarily reacted to him. My knees wobbled and I wavered, leaning back against him.

'You smell good.' *Ohh.* His voice was deep and next to my ear, fluttering my hair. His hand moved slightly, sliding over the silky robe until he touched my belly and pulled me firmly back against him. I barely breathed, and froze, waiting to see what he was going to do next. His hands remained maddeningly still on my body. I desperately wanted him touch me more. He moved his hand the tiniest little bit, gently squeezing his fingers a more tightly on me.

'Did you just have a bath?'

I nodded. 'Yes, I just got out.' My voice was raspy with desire. And I didn't try to hide it.

'I can tell. Your hair is a little damp, and I can smell your soap.' He nuzzled my neck, and I couldn't keep my head steady, letting it tip to the side so he could have better access. 'I'm glad you got ready for me.'

'Me, too.' But all I could manage was a whisper. I turned in his arms, unable to stand having my back to him any more. I needed to see him. His hand slipped around my waist with the movement and he splayed his fingers over my lower back, just low enough that I felt his fingers at the top of my ass. All he had to do was slide his hand lower and grasp my silk-covered cheeks. I wrapped my arms around his neck and pressed against him. 'I'm so glad you came. I wasn't expecting you.'

'Well, then, I'd certainly like to see what it would be like if you *were* expecting me.' His husky voice did all kinds of good bad things to me. Heat grew between my thighs, making me acutely aware I had no panties on. I was naked, and all he needed to do was slip his hands under the robe to find that out for himself.

If we kissed – who was I kidding? – *when* we kissed, I knew it would be even more powerful than the kiss we had shared yesterday. And the day before. We definitely needed a three-peat and if he didn't make a move soon, I would. I knew the passion he was capable of and how strongly it affected me. I craved him.

The air between us heated, and I swear the hair on the back of my arms rose up as if lightning were about to strike.

Then he did what I had so longed for him to do. He gave me the longest, sexiest look as he raked his fingers through his hair. I was breathless and drew in a big sigh, arching my back when he placed his hands either side of my face and lowered his head for a kiss.

It was as if he wanted to absorb me into his very soul. I was enthralled. He wasn't close enough; I needed to push away the thin layer of heated air that separated us and press myself against him. Only he had on too many clothes for me to be able to properly feel his heat. I wasn't prepared when he stepped back. All my weight was on him, and so I stumbled. He was breathing heavily, his eyes half closed and his hands still holding my cheeks. We were connected, fused together, and I never wanted it to break. We paused, hovering in a strange place of suspension. I was lost in my body, loving how I felt under his touch. He seemed to be in a similar state of pause. Slowly, our breathing returned to normal. I had my eyes open, watching him. His eyes were closed and, when he opened them, I saw such tenderness, bordering on something even deeper, reflected in their depths.

The moment broke when he reached into his pocket and pulled out a key card. 'You deserve it.'

I reached out and took the card. 'But I left the spa early. I didn't complete the test.'

'The spa *was* the test. It was a test of your ethics.' He tucked a strand of my hair behind my ear, his fingertips lingering on my cheek, but I was too irritated to appreciate it. All those executives defrauding the company and they were testing *me* on ethics?

'Ethics? Really?' I said dryly, crossing my arms and tapping the key card against my elbow.

He nodded. 'I'm quite serious. A few years ago Diamond created a code of ethics that it requires all employees to follow. The CEO would be expected to lead by example. A shift within the company came after some rather unethical practices were uncovered. They had to be addressed.'

'So Mr Saturday taking advantage of company money at the spa, blathering on about perks and me getting what I deserve, it was all a test?' In my current emotional state, I felt that a company-wide code of ethics was too little, too late.

Mr Monday chuckled. 'Yes. He was only trying to see if you'd fall for the glitz and glamor and take advantage of what your status could be in the organization. He's actually one of the most upright and honest men I know.'

I shook my head and turned away. I knew these tests were designed to manipulate me, but the hypocrisy of this one really bothered me. Walking to my purse, I dropped the key card in it and waited for Mr Monday to make his excuses and leave.

Instead, he drew in a breath. 'What are your plans for this evening?' he asked, and I had to think about it for a moment. I had completely forgotten what I had planned to do tonight. Being so close to him, and with only the wispiest silk between my bare flesh and his hands, was mind-numbing, far too distracting to think clearly.

I looked around and then back at him, suddenly remembering. 'Well, I was going to stay in. Have my own spa night.'

He glanced over his shoulder at the coffee table. 'I see.' His hands dropped from my face and slid down to my shoulders. He pulled me a little roughly toward him and I let out a small gasp. I wanted him, in every way possible, and stared up at him as his gaze bore into me. I waited, holding my breath for what was to come. But rather than a kiss, he whispered in my ear, 'How about I help you with that?'

He was going to stay? I shivered and stared up at him, still caught in the sweet ferocity of his grip. I didn't care that he was holding on to me so tightly he might leave bruises. That meant he was marking me as his. At least, that's what I chose to think.

'O-okay,' was about all I could muster. We were so close, and I could see everything. He was an open book. I could tell by looking at him that, for the first time, there was nothing being held back. His mask was gone. The man I was seeing right now, standing before me, was the man I'd been looking for all week. Something had changed him. I was thrilled to be able to see inside this man, who had worked his way under my skin and into the broken pieces of my heart. 'Help me how, though?'

He let me go, sliding his hand down my arm until he took my fingers and led me into the living room. He indicated the couch with a nod of his head. 'Sit down and get comfortable.'

I did as I was told, starting to quiver with anticipation. I fingered the sash of my robe, remembering my thoughts yesterday about Mr Friday's tie. Maybe . . . ?

My robe came only to my knees standing up, so when I sat on the couch it rode up my thighs, exposing me to him. I watched as his gaze dipped down. He reached and touched my leg. I couldn't hold my head up and let it drop back. A soft sigh came from my parted lips. Something wonderful was happening here, and I was filled with anticipation and hope.

He sat at the other end of the couch and reached for the items on the table.

'What's your favorite color?' he asked as he inspected the different bottles.

I watched him pick them all up individually, give them a shake and put them back down.

'I'm not fussy. I like all of them. But I felt like an oceanic theme tonight.'

He picked up the little container, which was divided into even smaller compartments.

'What are these?' He peered through the transparent cover.

'Bling,' I told him.

'Bling? What do you use it for?'

'To put on my nails. I like sparkle. Any kind of sparkle.' I smiled at him, and warmed under the look he gave me.

'I'll have to remember that.' He winked at me and put the container back down on the table. He took one of my feet in his hands. I watched his large hands as he massaged the arch and then moved down to my toes. He cradled my heel and pressed his fingers along the back of my ankles and up into my calf.

'You're good. You must have had lessons,' I murmured.

He shook his head. 'No lessons.'

'Then how can you be so skilled at this?' I asked him as his hand stroked upwards to my knees. 'It's not hard. All I have to do is watch your face, see how your body reacts under my touch. Feel you. Know you. Discover what it is you like.'

I smiled at him, and he turned his attention to my other foot. 'Do you have any idea how sexy what you just said is? Mmm,' I moaned. 'I could have you do that all day.' I closed my eyes and felt as if I'd melted into the couch. I felt so relaxed and wonderful. Not only was he excellent with his hands, he certainly had a way with words.

'So how does one paint nails with an "oceanic theme"?'

I kept my eyes closed, enjoying the touch of his hands on me, wishing they would go higher. That they'd slide underneath the robe. I could barely lay still and had to bite my lip in order to concentrate on what he was saying and not squirm with desire. 'You don't have to. Do whatever color you like.'

'You'll trust me to make a decision like that? I've never done this before; it could go horribly wrong.' His voice was teasing, but I was very serious when I answered.

'I trust you.' I opened my eyes a little, and the look he gave me made my heart swell. I'd never seen this expression before on him – or on any man, for that matter. The closest was when my father looked at me with love. Before he got fired and consumed with his own bitterness. But I put that thought out of my head. I didn't want to be filled with sadness. I only wanted to think of Mr Monday right now, and what he was doing to me. Holding my feet and stroking them. Driving me crazy with his touch and then promising to give me a pedicure. No man had ever done that for me before.

'Okay, then. I'll definitely do something, but you'll have to tell me how to put the bling on.'

I quickly ran through the process I used. He raised his eyebrows in shock. 'Got all that now?' I laughed.

'It seems like a whole lot of work for toes.'

'Too much? Because I can do it myself.'

He shook his head and picked up my foot. 'No, I said I would, and I always keep my word.'

Mr Monday again rubbed his thumb along the arch of my foot. I moaned as he increased the pressure. He was killing me, and I think he knew it, getting pleasure from hitting all my hot buttons. It was as if my nerves were on fire and all connected. My body burned with need.

The look of intensity and concentration on his face and the way he had the tip of his tongue poking out between his lips made me giggle. He glanced at me from beneath his brows.

'Just what are you laughing at, missy?'

'You.' I smiled at him, loving how this evening was playing out.

'I'm the one in control here. Even if I have no clue what I'm doing.' He waggled his finger at me. 'Remember. I'm in charge.'

I raise my hands in supplication and then rested them across my belly, lacing my fingers together. 'I surrender myself to you.'

'Hmm. Is that right? It could prove to be a very interesting night indeed.' His voice held an air of curious air of intrigue.

I closed my eyes, trying to show my trust in him.

'You don't want to watch what I'm doing?'

I shook my head. 'Nope. What did I just say? I'm in your hands.'

He chuckled again, and it reminded me just how much I liked the sound of it. My eyes now closed, he readjusted his grip on my foot and began my in-home pedicure. He was gentle and took his time. I must have drifted off as he soothingly tended to my feet. I started, awake now, when he moved out from under me, shifting back to the corner, and rested my feet on the couch.

'You're all done,' he said.

'Thank you.' I sat up and looked at my feet. 'Oh my God, you did a great job! I definitely do have mermaid toes.'

I swung my legs off the couch and stood up.

'Where are you going?' he asked me.

I looked down at him as he sat with one arm slung across the back of the cushions and his free hand holding his glass of wine. Yes, he did look good enough to eat, something that I totally planned on doing later on.

'I'm a little hungry. And I forgot the food in the kitchen.' He was about to get up, and I stayed him with my hand. 'No, don't get up. Let me take care of it.'

A few moments later, walking gingerly to avoid smudging, I had all the food arranged on the coffee table. Thankfully, he had cleared away all of my nail-polish paraphernalia.

'This is nice,' he said, and leaned forward. I was captivated by the fluidity of his movement. The way his muscles rippled and played as he reached for the food. I could watch this man all day, for the rest of my life.

'I like this. It's perfect for a night of grazing and sipping wine.'

He nodded his head. 'Yes, I agree. I don't do this at home. But I like your style.'

This was the first time he had ever made any reference to his home, or his life away from Diamond. It raised my curiosity again. Where did he live? And the big question – was he single? I hadn't really given much thought to his relationship status. But now that he was here in my home and everything seemed to suggest that he would stay the night, it weighed on my mind. There were some questions I needed answers to. Especially the single part. I would never – ever – in a million years, be the 'other woman'.

'You know what I find a bit one-sided?' I broached the subject, trying not to be too confrontational. He picked a few more items off the plate and popped them in his mouth before glancing at me. 'What?'

'That you seem to know everything about me – and I know nothing about you.' He gave me a rather cute lopsided smile and picked up another piece of Calabrese sausage. I could tell he was avoiding answering the question.

'Giving yourself time to come up with a really good reason?' I asked, and took a sip from my wine glass. I looked at him over the rim, waiting to see what his answer would be.

'No mystery. Just no reason to talk about it. Trust me. We'll discuss everything later.'

The conversation was going in a direction I really didn't want it to, despite me being the one to bring it up. I quickly decided that I could let it slide, because I knew that if I carried on and pressed for more answers it would change the dynamic of the night. But there was one thing I had to know.

'Okay. Tell me this, though. There's no one waiting for you to come home?'

He looked away, suddenly appearing sad, before he turned back. He picked up my hand, pressing a kiss to its back, saying, 'There's no one waiting for me. If there was, I wouldn't be here.'

I nodded, happiness warming me. I hid my smile behind my wine glass. 'Then I will hold you to that promise. We'll talk about everything later. Right now, I just want you all to myself and to enjoy our time together.'

'I think that sounds like the best idea yet.' He leaned over, took the bottle of wine and held it out to me. I offered my glass and he filled it, then topped up his own.

I relaxed back on the couch and perused the mini picnic I had spread out on the coffee table. I filled a small plate with cheese, bread and meat. We fell into comfortable silence for a while, listening to the music. He lifted my feet back on to his lap and began to stroke the soles. I was in heaven.

'I like your apartment,' he said.

'Thank you. I do, too. Small, but it's me.'

'Yes, very much you.' We gazed into each other's eyes, and the attraction grew even more deliciously between us.

He lifted my feet and stood before putting them back on the couch. I watched him prowl around my apartment, looking at things. I liked the fact that he had an interest in the bits and pieces of me. He seemed genuinely interested in who I was. As he moved around my apartment, he switched off the lights, leaving us in the warm and romantic glow of the candles. My heart started to beat more rapidly with anticipation, especially when he stopped and paused in the doorway to my bedroom.

He looked inside the room and then back at me, giving me one of his sexiest smiles. My belly somersaulted and I held my breath, wondering what he was going to do next. He waggled his eyebrows comically, and I giggled. I wiggled my fingers for him to come back to me. He did, and dropped to his knees at the end of the couch. He placed his hands on my ankles and, this time, his touch was scorching. He moved my feet apart and moved closer to me, still on his knees. My robe rose a little higher on my thighs and parted, allowing him to see more of me. I was glad of the darkness. I flushed, and I didn't really want him to see that I was nervous. He wasn't looking at my face but was focused on his hands as they gently stroked my bare skin, over my knees, to my thighs.

My eyelids fluttered as desire for him swept through my body. I gasped when he lowered his head to place a kiss on the inside of my knee, cradling it in his big hand. Feeling his touch, finally with no barrier between us, was something I'd been craving for so long. And now it was happening. His skin felt so wonderful next to mine. He stroked me gently, his hands creeping higher and higher. His gentle touch and his feather-light kisses had more of an impact on me right now than if he'd been demanding. I was beside myself with pleasure and could barely stop myself from becoming a quivering mess.

He was getting closer and closer to where I wanted him most. Buried deep, hard, and thrusting into me. I moaned and grabbed at the couch with my hands. I didn't know what to do with them. I was becoming very agitated and restless. In all the right ways.

He lifted his head and we looked at each other, silent for the briefest moment, until he spoke. 'You' re trembling.'

I nodded. 'I know.' All I could manage was a hoarse whisper. I watched him push my robe aside to kiss my hip, but he didn't break eye contact with me.

'I like that.'

Oh my God. That was one of the most erotic things anybody had ever said to me. His hands slipped over my hips, then across my belly, gently tugging on the sash to pull my robe open. I was now completely bare to him, framed by red silk. I could barely contain myself as he gazed at me.

'You are absolutely stunning.' He rose up on his knees and leaned down to kiss my belly button, rolling his tongue through the sensitive indent and sending exquisite shots of desire to my clit and my nipples. I was quickly becoming overcome.

I shoved my fingers into his hair and pulled him tighter to my belly. He left a trail of fire as he kissed and licked his way up to my breasts. His hands cradled each side and pushed them together as he buried his face between them. I heard him inhale.

'You smell so good.'

I shivered when his lips moved closer to the peak and gasped, arching my back involuntarily when he drew my nipple into his mouth. I'd never felt anything so wonderful as he suckled and flicked his tongue on my sensitive flesh. I held his head tighter, my hands tangled in his hair as my breasts ached for him.

My nakedness against his clothing caused friction that only increased as I rubbed on him, lifting my hips against his erection. He groaned and pressed his hips into me. He leaned over, balancing his weight on one hand, his hair falling over his eyes as he gazed at me. His expression told me everything I needed to know. He was into me as much as I was into him. Perhaps more so.

He ran his finger across my collarbone and down the valley of my breasts, then he covered one, holding it tenderly and sweeping his thumb over my nipple. I nearly exploded; my body lit up like a sparkler. I clutched at him, tugging desperately on his shirt, and wrapped my legs around his hips, digging my heels into his ass. I tightened my legs so he was trapped and tilted my hips, desperately needing him deep inside me. I couldn't lie still. It was as if my body had a mind of its own, trembling and jerking as he did all these wonderful things to me. My body felt so alive.

I needed a short breather, but he didn't give me one, kissing a scalding trail along my collarbone until he found that sensitive hollow under my chin. He ground his hips into me, the fabric of his pants becoming damp against my wetness. I matched his cadence. It felt so naughty, to be completely naked while he was still clothed, as if he were completely devoted to my pleasure and wanted none for himself.

I turned my head to find his mouth and we met with an intensity that took my breath away. We kissed as if for the first time. Frantic, desperate, exploring. It was as if we'd become one, and we separated just long enough to catch our breath before falling into each other again. Then he reared back, licking his lips, eyes glazed as he stared down at me. I couldn't believe this man was with me.

I made a little sound when his hand burned a trail of fire over my flesh as he helped me out of my robe, leaving me fully exposed to him. Electrifying me further, he trailed his fingers over my belly button, drifting down to give the barest brush against the delicate skin at the crease of my thigh before swirling lower to dip into my sensitive folds. He backed up on his knees so he could fully see me. I felt his gaze as if it were touching me. Slowly, a smile curved his lips.

'You're a redhead.'

My eyes opened wide, and I touched my hair. I'd been so careful dyeing it and my eyebrows, but I never expected I would be in a situation for somebody to see my pussy.

'I wanted a change,' was all I said. I hoped he would be satisfied with that.

'This explains why you're so fiery.' He growled the words and lowered his face, pressing his mouth to my belly and grabbing my ass with one hand. He lifted me as he moved lower, closer, and then his chin brushed the delicate hairs, which amplified the sensation. I moaned and froze, waiting for his next move.

The candlelight glinted off his dark hair. I couldn't pull my attention from him as I watched him move lower between my thighs. Then the sweet wetness of his tongue found me. My knees fell open wider, allowing him deeper. With one hand under my ass and the other resting on the inside of my thigh, his tongue slipped through my folds to find the sensitive nub, an assault on all my senses. It was excruciatingly wonderful. I rolled my hips, unable to keep still.

My fingers dug into the sofa cushion beneath my writhing body. His talent knew no bounds, and my orgasm began to build. I couldn't keep quiet and moaned when he slipped a finger inside me, curling it and thrusting in time with the lapping of his tongue.

I was unable to catch my breath, and tried to hold off as long as possible, loving what he was doing to me. Tension grew inside me, and I welcomed it. My orgasm was building, his hand was on my butt cheeks and he lifted me more firmly against his mouth. I couldn't help it as my knees closed on him in the last moments before release nearly ripped me apart. I'd been holding my breath and I cried aloud as he drew my orgasm out.

He didn't give me any time to calm down before he drew another delicious orgasm out of me. I was like a rag doll, and it seemed like an eternity before my body settled down. Little tremors of delight overtook me every few seconds, and he pulled me into his arms, cradling me and brushing my hair to the side. I opened my eyes and looked up at him. He gazed down at me with a tender look on his face.

I reached my hand up to his cheek and ran my thumb over

the scar. 'How did you get this?' My voice was weak and breathy. I wrapped my arms around his neck and he snuggled me into his lap.

'I fell out of a tree at camp. Needed ten stitches.'

'A tree? How bourgeois of you. You didn't feel like using the climbing wall?'

He smirked, pressing a kiss to my head, and I sighed in contentment.

'There was always a line for the wall. I've never been good at waiting.'

'Long lines aside, did you enjoy camp? I've never been to one.'

I shifted a little closer, and he ran his hand down the curve of my back.

'No, I hated it. I barely saw my parents as it was, so being away from them for two months and not seeing them at all was horrible.'

'You never saw your parents?'

'My father worked really long hours and my mother was always involved in some high-society or charity event or other. They loved me, they just . . . didn't have much time for being parents.'

My heart broke. Things had changed when my father got fired but, growing up, my family had been close and I had always felt deeply loved as a child. Not knowing what to say, I changed the topic.

'Well, the scar makes you look even sexier, if that's remotely possible.'

He chuckled, and I hugged him tighter. We sat like that for a few minutes until I recovered. I noticed he was still breathing raggedly. I shifted on his lap, feeling his erection pressing against my bottom. His hard length made me ache for him all over again. Never in my wildest dreams did I think I was capable of multiple orgasms.

'I want you in me,' I told him.

'God, woman, you're driving me crazy.'

I began to undo the buttons on his shirt, but got too impatient and pulled until his shirt ripped. Neither of us cared.

'I want to see you naked. I want this more than you can ever know.'

He sucked in a breath and reached for me. He pulled me down on to the couch beside him, and I dropped my hand to the front of his pants. I quickly undid his belt, then fumbled with the button and zipper. He swept my hand away, swiftly undoing his fly. He lifted his hips and shoved his pants down. His cock sprang free. Finally, he was naked. And he was magnificent. Just as I knew he would be. I touched his chest and ran my hands across the fine sprinkling of hair. He dropped his head back and sat still as a statue. I explored him, much as he had me.

Finally, I curled my fingers around his thick length, stroking and cupping his balls, liking the sounds that came from him. He flexed his hips and pumped into my hand. But I wanted him inside me.

'Condom?' It was all I could manage to say, because I was so aroused my voice would barely function. He leaned forward and picked his pants up off the floor, digging into the pocket. I smiled at him. 'A good little Boy Scout, always prepared.'

'Honorable, truthful and reliable, that's me,' he replied, and I watched as he quickly sheathed himself. Then his arm whipped and grabbed me around the waist, pulling me on top of him.

I rested my hands on his shoulders and balanced on his powerful thighs. My legs spread wide and fully open for him to see. I shivered when he looked. I grabbed his cock and raised myself up.

'Ride me, baby.'

I dropped myself on him just as he thrust his hips up. He filled me, my muscles accepted him, and instinct took over. He wrapped his arms around my waist, pulling me towards him. I sat forward so that my breasts were right in front of him, and he turned and pulled my nipple into his mouth as I bucked my hips, riding him as he'd instructed. I was going to come again. I rode him harder, my breath ragged, and my orgasm was even more powerful than before. I collapsed over him, and he held me tight as I quaked until I went limp on him.

He flipped me with a swiftness that surprised me. As he hovered above me, his eyes were closed, his muscles corded and the strain of his arousal was etched on his face. I locked my heels behind his ass as he drove into me. I grew wet all over again and reached my hand down between us to swirl my fingers over my clitoris.

He groaned and thrust. I'd met him move for move and couldn't believe that I had such an amazing man above me, bringing me to such delicious heights over and over again. Like right now. It was going to happen again. Only this time I was going to come with him, deep inside me.

'You're making me come again. I-I can't believe this.' I couldn't hold it back. My body was completely overwhelmed by all the excitement, emotion and release.

'Keep coming for me, baby.' He looked at me intently, and I was lost in his gaze. 'I'm so glad I found you.' He crushed his lips on mine. Had I heard him correctly? Was it my imagination? I didn't know, because he was sweeping me away. Then he groaned, and I rose to meet his final thrust. The power of his orgasm draped around us as he let out a great roar before stilling and then collapsing on me.

Our breathing was ragged, and I heard his heart thumping. We laid like that for a few moments, the weight of him comforting me. I didn't want to break the spell. I ran my thumbs up and down his back, before he let out a long sigh and then rolled off me. Silently, he gazed down at me. There was no cause for words right now. He covered me with my robe and gave me a kiss before walking off to the bathroom. I watched him go and then stretched like a Cheshire cat. Contented. Sated.

I hadn't felt this happy in years. And all because of this man who I knew only as Mr Monday.

MR SUNDAY

MR SUNDAY

I'd been watching my Mr Monday sleep for about the last fifteen minutes. I liked how he looked in my bed, the rumpled sheets tucked up around him and his head cradled between the pillows. I wanted to reach out and brush away a strand of hair that had fallen across his forehead, but he was sleeping soundly and I didn't want to risk disturbing him. He looked very relaxed, as if whatever had been weighing on his mind had vanished under the layers of sleep.

I sighed with utter contentment. We'd made love all night and ended up in the shower, which definitely wasn't built for two, before finally tumbling into bed. I didn't even remember falling asleep, only waking up in his arms a quarter of an hour ago. We fit together so perfectly that, when I opened my eyes, I hesitated to disentangle myself from him.

I lifted his arm, which was draped over my hip, and slipped out of bed quietly as I could. I pulled on a pair of yoga pants and a matching T-shirt, then left the room, quietly shutting the bedroom door behind me. All we'd eaten last night was the antipasto plate – and each other – which wasn't enough to carry me through. I was starving and in desperate need of a coffee. Too bad I didn't have any Costa Rican; all I had was store-bought. It would just have to do. At least I could make him a nice homemade breakfast: pancakes, bacon and Canadian maple syrup. I got everything ready as the coffee brewed, then poured a cup and took it into the living room. Finally, I would have an opportunity to go through the evidence from Diamond. I had a big decision ahead of me, and going through the paperwork might help me make it.

I felt reluctant to look at the papers, even though I knew I needed to digest all the information in order to make a sound decision. I grimaced. It was Sunday, and there was one test left. Would it be today? I would have to wait until Mr Monday woke up to find out.

I settled in a comfy, overstuffed chair beside the couch. I curled my leg under me, reached for the envelope I had hastily hidden on Saturday beneath it and pulled it over to me. Inside this unassuming envelope was paperwork that could bring down – or, at the very least, make life miserable for – Diamond Enterprises. I looked through the bedroom door; Mr Monday was sleeping like a baby. He clearly had some kind of connection to Diamond. All the other Mr Days-of-the-Week had been head of their respective departments, so what was Mr Monday in charge of? Looking back over the week (had it really been only six days since we met?), the only thing I could be sure of was that the other men reported back to him on my progress. He always knew how the day before had gone before I had the chance to say anything. Last night, he'd asked me to trust him and said that he would answer my questions at another time. Just when would that time be? I had to wonder if it would ever come.

I ran my fingers along the edge of the envelope. I felt like I was touching a loaded gun. Ignoring my feelings of unease, I ripped it open. I was just about to pull the papers out when I heard Mr Monday stirring in the bedroom. The last thing I wanted was for him to find me with a bunch of incriminating paperwork on the company he worked for. It wouldn't look good on a personal level and certainly not on a professional one. I just managed to cram it back under the chair before he came through the door.

'Good morning, sunshine,' he said when he saw me. He had the biggest smile on his face. Well, he'd earned that smile after all the sex we had last night.

I'm pretty sure I had an equally big smile on my face. I stood and walked over to him. He wrapped his arms around me and gave me a big hug, and I squeezed him back. We stayed like that for a few moments, simply enjoying each other's presence. I murmured against his chest, 'There's coffee.'

'I bet it wasn't flown in fresh from Costa Rica this morning,' he said, and chuckled as we walked into the kitchen, our arms still around each other.

'No, I'm sorry to say it's not. And I was thinking exactly the same thing when I was making it.'

'Well, I guess we can make do.'

I poured him a cup and handed it to him. This time when our fingers touched, we looked at each other and smiled. We knew things about each other now. Intimate things that only lovers know. I liked the special bond that had grown between us. I was still basking in the afterglow from our night together, and I was ready to begin another marathon of lovemaking, secluded away in my apartment. I looked up at him as he leaned easily against the door jamb of my tiny kitchen.

'I like you being here.'

'I like being here.' He pushed away from the jamb and leaned down for a kiss. His hand cupped my cheek and held me in place and he thoroughly, passionately, kissed me. My heart thrilled at the possibility that we were embarking on a relationship, that *more* was finally in reach. In the back of my mind, though, I was worried that perhaps my desire for revenge would affect my desire for him. Could I have both him and revenge?

'Do you like pancakes?' I murmured against his lips.

'I love pancakes.'

'Then I shall make you some.'

He didn't let me go right away and caught me in a tight embrace. 'Thank you,' he said against my hair as he pressed his lips to me.

'Thank you? For what?'

He leaned back to look down at me. 'For being you.'

I tipped my head to the side and gave him a wondering look, surprised. 'I'm just me, you're right, and I don't know what I've done, but you're welcome.'

'What you've done is keep me grounded this week. It has been a tough time for you, too, I know. We've both had a difficult time.'

I took his hand and led him to the tiny table tucked under the kitchen window. I barely fit in the chairs, they were so small, and they were totally impractical but I thought they were cute and wanted them for my apartment. He eased himself on to one and his eyebrows rose as it groaned under his weight.

'Uh oh,' he said as he settled himself delicately on it.

'Just don't move around too much, you should be fine,' I told him.

I turned on the stove and pulled the bacon from the fridge and started it cooking. While it sizzled in the pan, using the ingredients I'd already laid out, I whipped up some pancakes. I felt very domesticated, making him breakfast. It wasn't that I felt my place was in the kitchen, it was that I liked taking care of my man – especially since I was planning on him taking care of me in the bedroom later. I spun fantasies of what future Sundays might hold, but he looked pensive. Gone was his relaxed, sleep-pressed face. The weight of the world seemed to have returned to his shoulders. I supposed that was no surprise, since sleep is our escape from all the things going on in our lives, our chance to heal and rejuvenate. Yet, looking at him now, I knew the rejuvenation process had never even hadn't even begun.

I put a plate in front of him and sat down across the table. 'What would you like to do today? Shall we play mermaid and fisherman?' I asked with a flirtatious grin, and sent a silent wish that we could just stay inside and be alone together.

At my role-playing suggestion, he paused in drinking his coffee, then set his cup down with a firm clink. Shooting me a scorching look, he said, 'As appealing as that sounds, we have something to do today.'

My heart sank. Just when I thought we might be able to hide away from the world . . .

'Well, I suspected as much.' I fiddled with my bacon, suddenly no longer hungry.

He reached across the table and covered my hand in his. 'There's no need to fret.'

I looked up at him. 'I'm not fretting. I enjoyed myself so much last night I just didn't want it to end.' I smiled, but I felt shaky. I grabbed my coffee to take a sip so I could hide the fact that I was beginning to get upset.

He squeezed my hand. 'Tess, I definitely want a rain check, but you have one last test to complete. Finish your breakfast and go and get dressed. No need to dress up, it'll be a casual day.'

'You're still telling me what to do,' I said. I forced myself to eat, thinking that I'd better have a few bites of food before we left. My last test! This was it. This would determine my entire future. I couldn't help but sneak a quick look at the chair in the living room. Well, it wasn't the only thing that would determine the future. I needed to figure out what to do about my revenge.

'Of course I'm still telling you what to do. Your assessment isn't over yet.'

I shot a look at him. The tone in his voice seemed different, and it made me wonder about our night together. Did it mean as much to him as it had to me? Had I imagined the tender moments, when in reality all they had been were him satisfying his lust? I got up, put my plate in the sink and disappeared into the bedroom to get ready.

One last test, I told myself. Let the chips fall where they may.

For the first time all week, our drive into the office felt slightly awkward. I was upset by this because I had really seen myself finding a happily ever after with Mr Monday, and now I wasn't so sure where we were heading.

'This is as far as I can take you.' He gave me a smile, which lightened my heart slightly, since in it I saw a hint of the feelings he'd shown me last night.

There was no doorman today, probably because it was Sunday, and I stared into the empty lobby. 'So this is it, then? What comes next?'

'Trust me. All I ask is for you to trust me.'

'That's a lot to ask without giving me any details or explanations.' Blind trust was never easy to give but, for him, I'd try.

He reached over and took my hand, squeezing my fingers. The warmth of him was what I needed right now and it helped me to shunt aside my unsettled feelings.

'Remember: you've done everything this week without any

details or explanations. And you've done well. Don't begin to second-guess yourself now.'

I pressed my lips together and nodded. 'I'll do what I can.'

'That's my fiery girl.' He leaned over and kissed me. Our lips lingered together and I was glad we still had that magical spark. He lifted away and I opened my eyes, catching a softened look on his face.

I got out of the car and cast one last look at him over my shoulder. He hadn't roared off yet. Instead, he sat there watching me as I walked into the building. He raised his hand, and I waved back before stepping through the doors into the lobby. I fixed the strap on my pink purse so it sat more securely on my shoulder. Inside the elevator, I took out the card that Mr Monday had given me last night. In our lingering goodbye, he'd forgotten to tell me what floor I should head to, so I did my patented button-mashing until one lit up. We were going almost to the top floor today, just two down from the penthouse. There was something wonderfully metaphorical about that. I'd almost made it to the top.

For the first time, when the elevator opened, a man was waiting for me. He must have been in his early to mid-forties and was just handsome as the previous Mr Days-of-the-Weeks, in a mature sort of way. He was a very sexy silver fox, but I sensed an even more abstruse aura about him. He glared at me with fathomless dark eyes, a stern twist to his mouth. I knew this man was no-nonsense. Instinctively, I could tell he wasn't one to cross. I certainly didn't want to be on his bad side.

'Ms Canyon, welcome back to Diamond. If you'll follow me, please?' He turned without waiting to see if I did as he asked, obviously expecting I would. And he was right.

This floor must be one of the lower executive levels, I thought, as it wasn't open-plan. It was all very nicely decorated, attractive enough for clients to be entertained there. There were small groupings of chairs and tables, and a large conference area that looked like a hotel lobby. I couldn't get over the opulence apparent on this floor. Money was clearly no object, but then, I had to give credit where credit was due. Most of the staff had very nice workstations, the restrooms were a cut above and the staff lounges on each floor were nicely stocked with all manner of drinks and snacks. We hadn't had anything like that at my old job. It always came down to money, didn't it?

I'd left the evidence hidden in my apartment, but I felt the weight of it. What would my father say if he could see me right now? Would he be proud of me? Would he regret that it had come to this? Which path would he advise me to take? The one that was fair or the one that was right? Leak the papers, or effect change from within?

Mr Sunday cleared his throat and I could barely stop myself from jumping. 'Please come into my office.'

I did. It was a monstrous size. His office was decorated completely differently from the rest of the building: it was all modern, chrome and glass – very cold and austere. I looked at Mr Sunday and realized that it suited him perfectly. He walked to the far side of his office, where a stretch of windows opened to the city below. He had his own mini conference table as well as very uncomfortable-looking guest chairs. This was not a place anyone would want to linger.

I chose the seat farthest away from the windows.

'Would you like to have a coffee or another beverage?'

While his words and tone appeared genuine enough, there was nothing at all welcoming about the man. 'No, thank you, I'm fine,' I said.

'Excellent.' He sat down, crossed his legs and undid the lower button on his jacket. 'How was your week?'

I was a little startled by the question. I hadn't expected any inquiry into my feelings or well-being. I looked at him and realized he really didn't care how my week had been. This was all just formalities and small talk. 'Fine. Thank you for asking.'

'Good, good. Glad to hear.'

I was right. I could practically see him checking 'make small talk' off a mental to-do list. I realized I was still clutching my pink purse so I set it down on the floor beside my chair. Any time he wanted to give me my test wouldn't be soon enough for me.

'So, then. First, I'd like to congratulate you on making it this far. To come from an unassuming background and get this close to the CEO chair, why, it's a remarkable feat.'

He was insulting me. It was all dressed up in polite words, but it was an insult nonetheless. I held on to my temper with both hands. 'Thank you. I'm grateful for the opportunity, and it's been quite the learning experience.'

'That's a good thing. I believe even old dogs can learn new tricks. Even one so very young for CEO.' He looked at me with those dark eyes and I had to really fight back a shiver, of rage or fear, I couldn't tell. I was pretty sure the bastard had just called me old and he was older than me! Not to mention following up with a backhanded jab at my age. I bit my tongue so I wouldn't blurt out something I'd regret. 'Tell me, what have you learned?'

I had to be careful here. There was a trap somewhere. It's not easy to explain what you have learned from a certain experience. It's personal, and not everyone will learn the same thing. It all flows together, every new experience building on the completion of the experience before it. Yet I had to think of something. I hoped whatever it was it wouldn't provide him with ammunition to use against me.

'The main thing I've learned is to go with the flow. To assess opportunities as they present themselves, and to view obstacles objectively and devise solutions accordingly.'

'I'm impressed. You are able to express yourself articulately, and you grasped the particulars nicely.' He nodded, as if I were a child who had just demonstrated they were rather bright. If I got the job, I would fire this man, I swear. He went on, 'But there is one thing I'm curious about.'

A chill ran up my spine. I had a bad feeling about what he was going to say next. 'And what is that?'

'I'm curious how you found out that the KevOptics proposal was a farce?'

I blinked in confusion. I hadn't been expecting that question at all. It felt as if Mr Sunday was angling for something specific, but I would play it cool and hide Carol's involvement, as I'd promised.

'Research. I'm a corporate librarian. Or I was.' I shrugged my shoulders. 'I looked for anomalies, I cross referenced, I compared. Whenever I found a red flag, I dug a little deeper. Eventually, there were a lot of red flags and they all added up to KevOptics being an unsound company.'

He narrowed his eyes and looked at me. I was waiting for the next bombshell to drop. Then he nodded. 'Excellent skills to have.'

There were no insults that time, and that made me suspicious. What was this guy's game? Could he have had a stake in Kev-Optics, or have an ulterior motive for wanting Diamond to take a hit? All I knew was that I needed to tread very, very carefully.

He pointed to a folder on the conference table. 'On the table are some files containing some sensitive information. Please go and get the one on the top.' I looked over at the table and stood up, then glanced back at him, my brows furrowed. 'Go on, then.'

He flicked his fingers at me as if to hurry me up, stopping just short of telling me to go fetch. Would he give me a treat when I brought it back? He was so fired.

I picked up the file and brought it back to Mr Sunday. He gestured for me to open it. It was an in-depth company profile, and I gasped when I saw the name EGL Communications. Northbrook's competitor. I glanced at Mr Sunday and lifted the folder. 'What is this?'

He looked at his fingernails, glancing at me out of the corner of his eye. 'You've proved you're a smart girl. Read it and tell me what you think.'

In all honesty, I didn't want to know what was in this file. I had a really bad feeling that I wasn't going to like what was coming next, but I was curious so I pulled out the chair and sat. I rested my elbows on the table and pressed my fingertips to my forehead.

I read.

I sat very still, moving only to flip a page and read more. My heart started to beat faster the more I read. This company was going to be a very valid competitor of Northbrook, Diamond's new subsidiary. If the information in this file was correct, they were going to give us a run for our money and we would have to be very strategic to outmaneuver them. It was good information and I wondered how he'd come by it.

'How did you get this?' I turned in the chair and asked him straight out. I had a feeling this was insider information, and the implications of that chilled me to the bone.

'It doesn't matter how. What matters now is what you do with it.'

And there was the bomb.

'Let me understand.' I tapped the file and stared him down. 'What matters now is how I deal with this?' I heard the tone in my voice; it was steel, and I was glad to see that it made Mr Sunday sit a little taller in his chair.

'Correct. That company needs to be eliminated as competition.'

I was shocked. He wanted the company taken down, just as I wanted Diamond taken down: two completely separate companies that were tied together by a silken thread. I sat back in the chair and put my hands on my hips.

'And you intend for it to be removed as a rival?'

He reached into the inner pocket of his jacket and pulled out a folded sheet of paper. 'With this.' He held the paper out to me, fully expecting me to come and get it from him.

I sighed as I stood but, once again, I was motivated by curiosity. I snatched it from him and opened it. My eyes widened when I read it.

'But, based on the information in that file, this is all wrong. These are lies. Complete inaccuracies.' His smile sent a cold chill down my spine. 'Exactly.'

'This could ruin EGL. Just think about the people who work there. What will they do if it shuts its doors?'

'That is not my concern. My concern is for Diamond. And that –' he pointed to the letter in my hand – 'is the way to make it happen.'

I lifted my hands up questioningly. 'How, exactly?'

'By leaking it, of course.'

My heart dropped. It was exactly what I had been planning to do to Diamond. I felt as if I were looking into a funhouse mirror and was suddenly confronted with an unflattering portrait of myself. I had been leaning towards giving up my revenge, but I hadn't committed to it. So what was the difference between me and Mr Sunday?

'And I suppose that is what I have to do? Leak this information to the media?'

He nodded, and gave me that nasty smile again. Everything was spiraling down into a black vortex. With a sudden clarity, I knew I couldn't do this. I couldn't be responsible for the downfall of a company whose only crime was succeeding too well. EGL's innovations were impressive, and that made this man want to shoot them down in flaming glory.

'I won't do this.' My words rang out in the office, sounding a lot more confident than I felt.

Mr Sunday's smile faded, and he folded his hands together, resting his index fingers against his lips. After a few incredibly uncomfortable moments regarding me as if I were a lowly ant, he finally said, 'The Northbrook chip doesn't work. Not yet, anyway.'

'What?' I asked feebly.

'The chip doesn't work. After the meeting on Tuesday, the lead researcher was brought in, and she revealed more accurate results of the testing. They'll need significantly more time before they have a product ready to go to market. You closed a deal for a worthless company.' His words were sharp, tiny daggers slicing at my skin.

'I . . . I didn't know. How could I?'

'You were able to find out what was wrong with the KevOptics deal, were you not?'

I shot to my feet, pacing around in my agitation. 'I had more time then, and access to a computer. Mr Tuesday gave me only the barest of warnings before we had to get into the car to go to the meeting. There was no time!'

'So it's Mr Tuesday's fault, then?'

'N-no. That's not what I said.' My mind was in turmoil as he continued to hammer at me.

'Hmm. Regardless of whose fault this glaring error is, it needs to be corrected. We need to buy time for R&D to make the

Northbrook chip viable, and the way to do that is by preventing anyone else hitting the market first. You claim to want to be CEO – well, you have to be ruthless. Diamond must come before everything. Your bravery, cleverness, compassion, inquisitiveness, adaptability, ethics, body, soul – all of you must be devoted to Diamond, and Diamond alone.'

I was past being concerned about showing weakness, and I sank back into the chair, burying my head in my hands. What should I do? Maybe I was supposed to say no? But the test on ethics was yesterday – surely they wouldn't do the same twice in a row? And it made sense for a CEO to be ruthless. How else would anyone survive in this cut-throat world? What should my decision be? What could I do? If I said no, if I refused to do this, then the past six days had all been for nothing. I'd have no job, no income. And potentially no Mr Monday.

I choked back a sob. There was still my revenge. I could say no and take revenge on Diamond for destroying my father, for ruining my childhood, for putting me in this position in the first place, but . . . no. No. Diamond had wronged my family, whereas EGL was guilty only of being too smart, but it was all the same in the end. Lashing out because of a hurt. Inflicting pain because of pain felt. No. I'd learned a lot about myself this week and I didn't really like what I'd discovered. I'd been blinded by my grief and, deep down, angry at my father for causing it all. There had been so much negativity, but I was done with it now. I was done with all of it.

'I'm sorry.' My voice came out muffled through my hands, and I lifted my head, letting my hands fall weakly into my lap.

He gave me a quizzical look. 'Sorry for what?'

I shook my head. 'I won't do it.'

He stood up. He seemed to tower over me. He was trying to

look intimidating, but he didn't frighten me because I no longer had anything left to lose.

'You . . . won't do it?'

I stood, too, forcing him to take a step backwards. 'You heard me correctly. I. Will. Not. Do. It.'

'Well. You're of little use to us, then.' He held his hand out and I stared at it, bemused. Did he want me to shake it? 'The key cards, please.'

'Pardon me?' I was now really confused.

'The key cards. You need to return all the key cards you were given this week.'

I went over and picked up my purse, brought it to the table and put it down. I blinked rapidly when I felt the hot prick of tears. No way would I cry before this man. If I was going to give myself a pity party, it would be on my own. I slipped my fingers into the side pocket that held the key cards and pulled them out.

'Here you go.' I did my damnedest to keep my voice a monotone. I wouldn't give him the satisfaction of letting him see how upset I was. Over the past week, going for the CEO position had become more important to me than my revenge. Now, I had neither.

'Thank you.' He took the key cards, walked around to his desk, opened the drawer and dropped them inside. Bizarrely, he picked up his phone, dialed, said, 'Red light,' and then hung up. Turning to me, he said, 'Security will be here in a moment to escort you from the building.'

'Are you serious? I'm being escorted out like a criminal?' I couldn't believe it. This was more offensive than being given this last test. My greatest regret was that I wouldn't be able to fire this guy.

Moments later, a distressed-looking Stanley was standing in the doorway. Mr Sunday was back in his chair, looking for all the world like the lord of the manor. He said insincerely, 'All the best to you, Ms Canyon.'

I wasn't one for burning bridges, but I couldn't return this man's false pleasantries. I didn't reply but hitched the strap of my purse over my shoulder and sailed out of his office. I didn't bother to wait for Stanley and strode angrily back to the elevator. I pushed the call button as Stanley caught up with me.

He said quietly, 'I'm sorry things didn't work out for you, Ms Canyon.'

His sincerity touched me, and I found myself fighting back tears again. 'Thank you, Stanley.'

When the elevator came, Stanley swiped his card, getting us to the main lobby. I stared at the floor indicator, watching the numbers tick down, and I desperately wanted Mr Monday. I wanted someone to tell me everything would be okay. Would he be waiting for me? If he wasn't . . . I still had no way to contact him. I'd be alone. Again.

The bell pinged indicating arrival at the lobby, and I closed my eyes tightly. Please, I wished, please. I felt a puff of air against my face as the doors slid open. I stepped forward and opened my eyes to see . . . no one there.

I was crushed.

With a sad nod of farewell to Stanley, I exited the building and stood in the empty driveway. What was I supposed to do?

Well, at least I knew – for my sake, for my mother's sake – that my father was innocent. It wouldn't bring him back or spare us from the years of pain, but the knowledge did give me a small measure of comfort. Since I couldn't very well stand here all day moping, I began to walk away, heading for the street. Given that I would have to start economizing, it looked like I would be taking the subway home. Behind me, I heard the sound of a car as it drove into the covered driveway. I thought nothing of it, but then I had to stumble back when it veered and cut me off.

'Hey! Are you trying to run me over?' I snapped at the car, and slapped the hood.

The rear passenger door opened and I was stunned, speechless.

'Tess. Come with me.' The look on Mr Monday's face was imploring, and it made me pause for a fraction of a moment. Oh, how I wanted to go with him.

'It's all over. Done. Out on my ear, escorted by Security. How embarrassing is that?' I didn't wait for him to answer and started to walk away again. I wanted to be far, far away from Diamond.

'Tess, wait.' He came after me and grabbed my arm. Facing him, I wrenched my arm out of his grip. 'Why? What more do you want from me?' I searched his gaze, waiting for some sign that he wanted me for me, but there was nothing. I sighed and shook my head. When I turned away he grabbed my arm again and, this time, he wouldn't let go.

He pulled me around and yanked me until I was against his chest, my hands grabbing his shoulders to steady myself. His face lowered to me and I could see hurt, anger and determination in his gaze. 'Tess, you need to come with me.'

He didn't wait for my answer and escorted me back to the car. I didn't fight him, despite the fact I was practically being kidnapped. I don't know why I didn't leave run away – maybe it was because of what I saw in his eyes or the way he had looked at me just moments ago. I was feeling so emotional, angry, hurt, pissed off – everything jumbled together – and the anger started winning. I wanted a real relationship with him. I wanted him to be the person to soothe my hurts, but he was going to have to prove he wanted to be with me.

I looked out of the window, trying to ignore him so that he knew just how pissed off I was, but it was hard to not feel his presence, to experience the scent of his skin in the back of the limo. I flashed back to the first night in the helicopter, to when he put the blindfold on me. It had all started then. And I still had no idea who this man was.

I shimmied closer to the door, trying to put more space between us, and I heard him chuckle. I flashed him an angry look, then turned back to the window.

'You should really go back to being a redhead, you know. Your temper doesn't suit a brunette.'

'How can you say stuff like that? You have no idea what I just went through. That man was positively wicked. When I refused to do something morally repugnant, he fired me.'

'You were not fired. You couldn't be fired because you were never hired.' I heard the humor in his voice, but I wasn't ready for it.

'It's not funny.' My voice was a sheet of ice.

'Tess, Tess, come on.' He took my hand. I tried to yank it away, but he held me too tightly. 'Get over here.' He pulled me across the seat – very ungracefully, I might add – until he had his arm around my shoulder.

He put his finger under my chin and tipped my face up to his.

'Stop it,' I told him. I wasn't ready to give up my anger yet, and his tenderness was cracking the shell of rage around me. I tried to turn my face away, but he held me prisoner.

'Tess. You need to calm down.'

That only fired me up more. 'Stop telling me what to do! Be calm! Be patient! Trust me! I am done taking orders from you. Do you have any idea what just happened back there?'

He nodded. 'Do you really think I wouldn't?'

'This is nuts.' I shook my head and pulled away from him.

This time, he let me go, and I was a little sad that he did. No wonder men were confused by women, I thought.

'What's nuts?' he asked me. He leaned back on the seat and rested his arm along behind me.

I waved my hand. 'All this. Everything I've done this week. Today, up there.' I jerked my thumb in the direction of Diamond, 'That man!' I turned and looked at Mr Monday. 'You should fire him. It was the first thing I planned to do as CEO.'

Mr Monday laughed and dropped his hand to my shoulders to pull me against him. I came willingly this time.

'You don't have to tell me about him. I know all about him.'

I shook my head. 'But what he asked me to do—'

'All part of the test.'

'Yeah,' I spat out. 'A test that I failed.'

He gave me a squeeze. 'Are you sure about that?'

I looked up at him. 'What do you mean? Of course I failed, he took all the key cards back. I was escorted out by Stanley, which mortified us both. I call that a failure.'

His smile warmed me. He shook his head. It looked like he was about to say something but, instead of talking, he cupped my face between his hands and covered my mouth with his.

The last thing I had expected at this moment was to make out in the back of the limo, but he felt too damn good to push away. I sighed into his mouth and wound my arms around his neck. Instantly, my anger was replaced with desire. I responded to him quickly and crawled on to his lap. He was just what I needed right now, and I think he knew that before I did. He knew me better than I realized. The kiss grew heated and he groaned, shifting me off him so I was lying back on the seat.

He lifted his head and looked down at me. My heart swelled as I looked into his eyes. Reflected in them was the man I had gotten to know last night. Last night's Mr Monday was completely different from the man who had escorted me to each test this past week. I felt he had allowed himself to relax, dropped his work persona and had shown me the man behind the mask. I let out a sigh and kept my fingers laced at his nape. I didn't want to let him go, I wanted to keep our connection, because it made me feel that I was no longer adrift in the world.

'Are you calming down a bit now?'

I nodded. 'But only if you mean my anger, because if you keep this up,' I said, pulling him down to me for a quick, promising kiss, 'it'll be a long time before I really calm down.'

'Then who wants to calm down?'

'Not me.' I shook my head and lifted my chin to the side as he buried his face in my neck. He continued his exploration and left a sizzling trail as he moved up to my jaw and covered my mouth, so close to mine. He smiled down at me, and it finally reached his eyes. I'd even go so far as to say that he had passionate and heart-throbbing eyes, like in the old cartoons.

'C'mere, you.' I pulled his head down again and we moved together. He was a magnificent kisser, and he had definitely figured out all my hot buttons last night.

The rocking of the limo had us swaying against each other. I don't know how it happened, but suddenly I was clad only in my bra and panties. I laughed, and could hardly believe the deep, sultry sound that came from me. I pushed him back and slid off the seat, taking a quick look to make sure the privacy glass was in place.

'Don't worry, that's the first thing I did.'

'So you had this whole thing planned all along?' I teased him, and reached for his shirt so I could pull it over his head. 'There's been enough unfairness going on today so, if I'm going to be naked, you're going to be naked as well.' His shirt was tossed away, falling on top of my clothes.

'Can he hear us?' I whispered, and pointed at the driver.

'No.'

'Great, now get these off,' I told him as I unzipped his pants and yanked them down. 'Ohh, I love looking at you.' I leaned forward to press my hand to his chest. He had just the right amount of chest hair, and his muscles were so perfectly defined. I leaned forward and buried my face in his chest. 'Mmm, you smell so good. I could eat you up.'

'I'd like to be eaten.' His hand held my head and I pressed my lips to him. He lifted me so easily and shifted until I was between his knees. I slid my hands over his firm flesh, enjoying the combination of the way his hair tickled me, his iron-hard muscles and his unbelievably sexy scent. He overwhelmed me. I reached out my tongue, flattened it against his belly and found his belly button. He let out a hiss when I prodded into the sensitive area, then I moved lower.

My hands trailed down his side and stopped when they bumped over the waistband of his boxers. I flattened my palm on the fabric and lightly skimmed across it, drawing in an excited breath when my hand found the hard ridge of his cock. I ran my fingertips up and down his length, my mouth lingering on the enticing trail between his belly button and what lay still hidden. I pulled at the waistband, dragging it down slowly, exposing him to my hungry mouth and gaze.

He helped me push his pants further down, and my fingers closed around him. I held him in my palm, squeezing and stroking from the tip of his cock to the base. I didn't think it was possible for him get any harder than he was but, when I lowered and took him into my mouth, he did. He gripped my head a little tighter, moaning, a deep, gravelly sound, and I loved it. He held me in place and slowly pumped his hips as I rose in time with him. I cupped his balls again, and alternated between holding them and rubbing my fingers across the flesh until they tightened. I wanted to give him the same pleasure he'd given me last night, but I could tell he was holding back. I flicked my tongue on the sensitive underside of his cock. He shuddered. I liked having this power over him. Liked being able to make his great and powerful body tremble under my touch.

'Tess.' He groaned my name and sucked in a quick breath when I swirled my tongue around the tip. 'Like last night,' he said, and leaned forward to grab for his pants. I knew what he wanted and let his cock pop out of my mouth so I could help. He pulled a condom from the pocket, quickly slid it on himself and pulled me on to his lap before I could blink. 'Ride me.'

I didn't need any encouragement. It was my favorite position. He held my hips as I reached between us, pulling my panties aside, and grabbed his cock, positioning him at my opening. I moaned as I slid down on to him, and he filled me. I worked my hips on him until we were rushing towards our frantic release. His hand slid up my back and pressed me toward him. With his teeth, he pulled aside my bra so my breasts were bared to him. He sucked a nipple into his mouth while his free hand rolled the other one between his fingers. Sensation barreled up the backs of my legs and flared out of my hips to pool in my belly as my muscles clenched. I had no control over my movements except to keep riding him.

Our sex sounds filled the back of the limo and the road seemed to get a little bumpier, which only enhanced our movements. I held my breath, waiting, and my body coiled in on itself before exploding into a muscle-clenching spasm. He pumped his hips harder and drove into me, pushing me down on him. His hand slipped between us and he found my clitoris, swirling his fingertips. I could barely keep myself upright as my muscles tensed again. He gave one last hard thrust and pressed deep on my sensitive flesh. I dropped my head down and bit his shoulder to keep from crying out. He buried his face in my neck and we clung to each other as wave after wave of relief washed over us both.

We tumbled to the seat in a heap. He cradled me in his arms and I held him as we slowly came down from our sexual high.

'Are you thirsty?' I asked him in a soft voice, still weak after the body rush. He nodded, and I slid off, fixing my bra and panties. 'We were pretty creative to be able to do that without taking these off.' I handed him a tissue, which he used to dispose of the condom.

'Where there's a will, there's a way,' he said, and lifted his hips as he pulled his boxers back up from down around his knees.

I rummaged through the cabinets and found bottles of water.

'This certainly is a sight. You in your lingerie on your knees in the back of the limo. I think I could get used to this visual.'

'Cheeky,' I said, and smiled at him. Then I tossed him some water. I opened mine and drank it down. I was parched.

Grabbing my clothes, I got dressed, then flopped on to the seat. Today alone had been a crazy, emotional roller-coaster ride. Coupled with the rest of the week, it was a miracle I was still sane. I rested back, my body so relaxed I thought I might fall asleep.

Then I realized we'd been in the limo for a while. 'Where are we going?'

I looked out of the window but didn't recognize anything.

'I suppose it doesn't really matter any more. Since we're already on our way there.' He looked at me, and I saw sadness reflected in his eyes again, 'We're heading to the place I took you on Monday evening.'

I sat up and looked out of the window, looking for anything that was familiar. But then, we'd arrived by helicopter, at night, so I wouldn't. 'We are?' I turned back to Mr Monday. 'Why are we going there?'

'To finish up some final business.' He pulled his clothes on. I already missed seeing his naked body. 'Final business? What do you mean by that?'

'Just as it sounds. There is some final business to take care of.'

This really didn't make any sense to me. I wasn't going to be CEO, so why on earth were we returning to Mr King's mansion by the sea? But I had learned from the past week that, no matter how much I asked, he would never give me an answer. He was always watching for some mythical 'right time', and I knew the time was not right, so I stayed quiet. The afterglow of sex had made me mellow, and I wanted to stay that way.

We turned up a long driveway to, I assumed, the house. It was very evident that this estate dripped money. The house appeared around the final turn, and we drove around the circular drive to the front of the building. It was manicured and wild at the same time, with a mature forest skirting the neatly mowed, lush lawn. I absolutely loved the mix. The helipad must be somewhere else on the property. I wasn't the same woman who had come here six days ago but, if you'd asked me how I'd changed, I wasn't sure I'd be able to pinpoint it. I did feel lighter, though, freer.

Mr Monday got out and reached for me. I put my hand in his, and he helped me from the limo. My legs wobbled, and he slipped his arm around my waist. 'Steady now. Find that courage I know you have.'

I looked up at him and smiled. 'I'm not frightened. I just had spaghetti legs after our mind-blowing sex.'

He laughed. I hadn't seen him look this relaxed in a while, other than last night, and I was glad. He led me from the car and up the wide, shallow limestone steps, the most amazing purple-and-pink flowers in beds alongside. I was agog at the massive and ornately carved front doors with their leaded green glass. Inside, I was simply blown away by the grace, beauty and warmth of the house. It was completely different to the entryway from the other night. Much more homey, even if it was magnificently grand.

But there was a different energy in the house today. I heard voices and the hustle and bustle of people rushing around.

'What's going on?' I asked, and hung back, suddenly feeling nervous.

'Actually, there's lots happening here today, and you need to be here for it.' He smiled down at me and I drew comfort from the tenderness in his gaze.

'I do? I'm not sure why.'

'You'll find out soon enough. Just have some patience.' He took my hand and gently tugged me along.

'Trust me, patience is something I've learned to have over the years. If I hadn't, I would never have survived this week or your constant "I'll tell you later's".' I raised my eyebrows at him.

He looked a little sheepish at that. I didn't say any more, and instead looked around as we walked through the house. The voices grew louder, and there was laughter. Cutlery clinked on plates. There was the most wonderful aroma of food in the air. This was very weird indeed.

'This really is a lovely home. I bet Mr King raised a family here. I think I'm envious of growing up in a house like this.'

'Don't be envious of what you never had. It could've been worse than what you did have.'

I looked at him and was surprised that he'd expressed such a deep sentiment. 'Look at you, getting all philosophical.'

He shrugged. 'We all have our moments.' He gazed down at me and it looked like he was about to say something, but we were both distracted by the hub of activity. Mr Monday let go of my hand. I found that a little odd, but I accepted it. I had no idea who else was in the house; obviously, he didn't want anybody to know that we were an item. If we were an item. We hadn't discussed terms yet. What I did know was that I wanted us to be more than whatever it was we were right now.

'Through here.' He turned the handles of some double doors and pushed them open. The room was jam-full of people. Some I recognized from the Diamond offices, but most I didn't. I was hesitant, not knowing what to expect with all these people, especially with Mr Monday being so mysterious.

I noticed the light pouring through the windows. They were lined with green glass here, too, casting an emerald glow on the floors. Through the shifting crowd, I could just make out a grouping of photographs. I squinted, as best I could, and realized I was looking at photographs of Mr King. There was one of him that looked as if it'd been taken recently, but there was also an amazing array of pictures from when he was a child, right through to his later years. I noticed there were vases of flowers among the photographs, stunning arrangements, with small note cards clipped to them. Then I knew. I reached out and grabbed Mr Monday's wrist. I almost tripped on a thick, luxurious rug, I was so taken aback. He had brought me to a funeral. To Mr King's funeral. I stumbled against him.

'What's the matter? Do you feel ill?' He took a step toward me and I could tell he was genuinely concerned.

I shook my head and looked up at him. 'This is a funeral?'

'No, no, it's not a funeral, exactly. More like a combination wake and memorial service. Let's go in there.' He nodded to a door off to my left and took my elbow. It didn't matter how innocent his intentions were, it always electrified me whenever he touched me.

I followed him through the crowd, many people nodding to

him and giving him grave looks. He seemed to hustle me more quickly through the crowd until we were safely locked away in the room.

'Will you tell me now? Everything you've been putting off telling me? Is this why you've been so unhappy?' A lump of dread formed in my throat. I had no clue what to expect. No idea at all.

He took a big breath and held it in for a minute before blowing it out. 'In a moment.'

I grew frustrated. He was always stalling. 'Just tell me what is going on. I'm getting alarmed.'

'I know, and I'm sorry.'

I was really getting annoyed with all this surreptitious activity. 'If there's one thing that really bugs the hell out of me about Diamond, it's all the damn secrets.'

'Well, maybe you can help fix that.'

I shook my head. 'Enough with the cryptic bullshit! Please, please, just tell me what's going on.'

He walked over to the wall and pulled a cord, like he had the first night, when he called for the nurse to take Mr King back to his room. Moments later, the door opened and in filed some very familiar-looking men. I gasped.

'I don't understand.' I looked at Mr Monday, confused.

'Tess, please come and stand beside me. I have a lot to tell you.'

I had no energy to argue any more so I did as he asked.

'I know you felt betrayed by what happened today, but let me assure you: everything will be fine.'

'Okay.' I shrugged. 'That still doesn't tell me a whole lot.'

'I understand. Each of these men was charged with testing you on a specific character trait. At the end of each test, they reported to me on your progress.'

'To you? Why not to Mr King? He's the one who wanted me to do this.'

'A moment.' Mr Monday looked over my shoulder, and I turned around as he began to speak. 'Gentlemen. This is your final opportunity to voice any concerns before the announcement is made.'

'Announcement?'

I had no idea what was happening. It was vaguely surreal, and rather overwhelming, to see these men out of the context of my tests. I felt as if I had just woken from a dream they'd all been in.

One man disengaged himself from the crowd and walked over.

'Mr Saturday,' I said.

'Actually, his name is Lane Ryder.'

'Tess of the Triumphant! It's good to see you.' Lane took my hands and held them warmly. 'You were a blast to be with yesterday.'

'Really? I ditched you. How much fun could that have been?'

He gave a laugh, the same as yesterday. I smiled with relief. There were no hard feelings. 'And that's what made it right. The fact that you left and didn't feel that what we were doing was honest. Good luck in the future.'

'Thank you.'

One by one, the men approached, and I finally learned their names. Mr Tuesday was Steve Black. Mr Thursday was Robert Hall. Mr Friday was Zoltan Gray. All of them were very gracious and complimentary towards me. Mr Sunday wasn't there, and I was glad of it. I was still upset about him and his awful behavior.

But one man was missing. Mr Wednesday. I looked around but couldn't see him. Mr Monday leaned down and whispered in my ear. 'Who are you looking for?'

I didn't really want to tell him. It felt awkward to be looking for a man I had kissed when I was standing beside the man I had just made love with.

A deep voice behind made me smile. 'I think she's looking for me.'

I spun around and, yes, it was Mr Wednesday. I was tempted to give him a hug, but I didn't think Mr Monday would appreciate it. Instead, I held out my hands and he took them. 'Yes, I was looking for you. I wanted the chance to say goodbye.'

He shot a glance at Mr Monday before squeezing my hands gently, then letting them go. 'I wish you all the best, Tess. You did an amazing job this week.'

Before he could disappear again, I said, 'Hey, everybody else has told me their name except you. Spill it.'

He drew in a breath, which expanded his impressive chest. 'Rourke. Rourke Stone at your service, ma'am.'

I smiled at him. 'So pleased to meet you properly, Rourke. Oh, and is that a country twang I suddenly hear in your voice?'

'You caught me,' he said. 'It doesn't normally sneak out.' Rourke took a step back and gave Mr Monday a nod. 'I should let you be getting on with it. See you later.' I watched him go, and my heart felt a bit lighter.

I turned to Mr Monday and seeing the look on his face filled me with joy. He was happy.

'What are you smiling about?'

'Come with me.' He took my hand and led me into another room.

'I remember this place.'

'I thought you would.'

The last time I was in this room, I met Mr King and fell down the rabbit hole. Was it really only six days ago that all this began? But it was over now, so I wasn't sure why he looked so pleased or why this was all happening during a memorial service.

'Turn and watch the screen, please.' Mr Monday pointed to

the wall behind the desk, where a large flat-screen television was mounted. The remote was in his other hand.

'What is this?' I looked at him and was disappointed to see that his happiness had morphed into sadness again. 'What's wrong?' I stepped closer to him and reached for his free hand. He curled his fingers around mine.

'You'll see in a moment.' He stared at the TV and his voice was soft.

I let my gaze linger on him a bit, concern swelling inside me. A voice pulled my attention away and I turned to the screen.

'Oh!' I was startled when Mr King's face appeared on the screen. He looked frail and grey, tired with sunken eyes, and I was surprised at how rapidly he had declined since my initial visit. 'Hello, Tess. Six days ago, I set you on a quest to take seven tests, to prove your worthiness. Unfortunately, I cannot be with you today. My doctors have advised me that I don't have much time left. I may not make it to Sunday –' I snapped a look at Mr Monday, and my heart nearly broke at the expression of absolute sadness on his face – 'which is a very high probability. Tess, I know who you are. Your father was a good man, but –' Now, I was staring at the screen, my jaw dropping to the ground – 'things went very wrong for him. By the time we had discovered the truth, he had passed away. I am truly sorry we were unable to right that wrong. Yet I kept you on my radar. I wanted to help you, but I knew of your hatred for this company and that you wouldn't accept financial assistance. We arranged for you to receive bursaries and scholarships. I couldn't change the past, but I could help you with your future. When I saw you had applied for the executive-assistant position, I knew this was finally my chance to make things right. I had put far too much focus on the almighty dollar and lost sight of the people within the organization. I realize that now. I was out of touch, hearing only what the executives were telling me and accepting it without question, and I regret that.' He began to cough and I glanced at Mr Monday, then back to the screen. There was a brief blip, as if the recording had been stopped and then resumed. 'My son, Daxton, will explain the rest. I always believed. Tess, believe in yourself, too.' Mr King struggled with the words, and then the video went black.

I turned to Mr Monday. 'Daxton? He has a son?

Mr Monday nodded.

'But I've never met him. I would remember a name like Daxton.'

'Maybe it's because you were never introduced to him by his real name.'

'W-what do you mean?' My heart beat more quickly and I didn't dare consider the possibility. Could it be—? 'Y-you?' He turned to me, and we stared at each other. My eyes widened.

'Call me Dax.'

I shook my head, unable to digest it all. In the space of five minutes my entire worldview had shifted. They'd known, all along, who I was? They'd known what I had planned to do? And Mr Monday was the son of the former CEO, Mr King? I was astounded. And kinda angry.

'You should have told me.' My voice was tight. I was so close to losing my cool that I physically clenched my hands into fists.

'I couldn't. You have no idea how many times we argued about it.' He nodded his head to the now dark TV screen.

I put my hands up, palms out, as if to ward off any new revelations. I didn't want an explanation . . . or did I? Then it all clicked. Mr King was dead, and he was Daxton's father. Immediately, my anger dissipated and I turned to him, sliding my arms around his waist. I knew what it was like to lose your dad. It was heartbreaking, and I didn't think you ever truly recovered. Tears filled my eyes as I remembered my father. Mr King's confirmation of my father's innocence had healed my last remaining emotional scar. But Mr King's death was still raw for his son.

'I'm so sorry. It's not important now.' I looked up at him as he wrapped his arms around me. 'When did he die?'

'Very early Thursday morning.'

'Oh! That's why—'

He nodded. 'Yes, that's why I didn't come for you.'

'Oh, honey.' I rested my cheek on his chest and listened to the steady thumping of his heart.

'He was old. Sick. But he'd led a very good life.'

I rubbed his back soothingly. 'Regardless of his health or age, he was your father, so it still hurts.' His arms tightened, and then he let me go. 'You're right. When we got his diagnosis, it was one of the hardest things I'd ever had to face. We'd had a turbulent father-and-son relationship, but the diagnosis seemed to wake him up somehow, and he started to see things in a new light.' He drew in a deep breath. 'And it made me see that my dad was actually human – fragile, for lack of a better word – and not the unapproachable superhero I'd always viewed him as. We had a very small window to make up for such a vast amount of lost time.' Dax gave me a hug before stepping away from me. 'But now there is something we have to do.'

'What?'

'We're having a board meeting before the celebration of Dad's life, and you need to come.'

'Me? Why?'

'Trust me?'

'Always.'

We went through the doors into that wonderful hall I remembered from the other night. Rather than go through the main doors, we rounded the stairs and went out on to a vast patio that ran the length of the majestic house. The view beyond took my breath away. A solid-iron railing ringed the yellow brick patio from the cliffs below. A lovely breeze blew in off the ocean and I lifted my face to it. Closing my eyes, I enjoyed the feel of it as it whispered over me, and I drew in the sweet sea air.

'Nice, isn't it?' Dax murmured next to my ear.

'Mmhmm, it is.'

'Maybe you could get used to living on the edge here?' I heard a lilt of humor in his voice and opened my eyes to look at him. He was smiling down at me, and my heart somersaulted in my chest.

'I could.' I furrowed my brows when his smile widened. 'What are you up to?'

He took my hand and we walked around a curve in the patio to a stunning gazebo. The shocking thing about it was the way that it was tucked under the trees but perched right on the edge of the cliffs. 'Are we going in there?'

'Yes, the board of directors have convened and we only have about fifteen minutes for this meeting.' I wavered. 'I can't go in there. Look where it is.'

'You'll be fine. I'll be beside you.'

I kept my gaze on his back and followed him into the make-shift board room. Once inside, I was able to ignore the fact that we were balanced on the edge of the cliffs, but barely, so I focused on Dax. It almost felt weird not thinking of him as Mr Monday.

'Thank you all for coming this morning,' he said. 'This shouldn't take long, as Mr King put everything in order prior to his death.' Dax turned to the elderly gentleman on his left. 'Peter, as chair, I now turn the meeting over to you.'

Peter nodded and stood. 'First, a moment of silence for Fraser King.' The only sound for a brief time was the rushing wind and the crashing of the waves below. 'Now, next on the order of business is to appoint Daxton King the new CEO of Diamond Enterprises.'

I shot a look to Dax, who was sitting beside me. The full impact of who he was crashed down on me. It was hard to take it all in, so I sat there rather incredulously. Why had I gone through all those tests if Dax was always next in line?

The chairman of the board sat down and Dax stood. I looked up at him, and pride swelled inside me, nearly bursting out of my chest, drowning out my uncertainty.

'As you know, before Dad died he set up the Diamond Enterprises charitable foundation. He had been searching for a candidate to head the foundation, someone with a solid moral character who was innovative and flexible, with compassion for people, but was also tenacious enough to fight for what they believed in. He never got to the chance to offer the position to his chosen candidate, so now I'm here to do that as CEO, on Dad's behalf.'

I held my breath and stared at him. Dax turned to me.

'I give you Tess Canyon. Dad has been watching Tess for a number of years and, after she was put through a grueling interview process, it became clear she was the perfect person. Dad's last business act before his death was to make sure that Tess was put in place as head of this foundation.'

I sucked in a surprised breath. 'Oh my God, you can't be serious?'

He nodded and smiled at me. 'Yes, very serious.' He turned back and looked at the rest of the board members around the table. 'Please, welcome Tess to our family.'

Everyone stood up and clapped. I was speechless. I had no idea what to think, it was so completely unexpected. I smiled and nodded at everybody around the table, thanking them but feeling rather overwhelmed by this new turn of events. I was glad nobody asked me to do a speech.

Dax sat down beside me, and I leaned over to him. 'I-I don't know what to say.'

'Just say yes.' He smiled and gave me a wink.

'Yes,' I whispered.

He took my hand under the table and squeezed it. 'There might be some more questions I hope you answer yes to.'

Suddenly, my future looked a whole lot different to me. I was stunned by the turn of events. The momentary flash of disappointment I'd felt when I'd realized I wouldn't be CEO had gone just as quickly. I think I even felt a bit relieved. Perhaps, deep down inside, I had known it wasn't the right fit for me. But this new twist! I was eager to find out the details about the position as head of the charitable foundation. And I was even more excited about the future I could have with Dax. I couldn't wait for the meeting to be over. Finally, after the board members had filtered out of the gazebo and into the house, we were alone.

'There's so much to talk about,' Dax said to me, and pulled me into his arms. 'But we have people waiting for us at the memorial celebration. After that, there'll be a good old-fashioned Scottish wake.' He led me inside. 'Now, I have to do something and if you'd come and wait with me while I do it, I'd like that.'

He took my hand and led me back into the house, up the grand staircase to another level that was absolutely stunning. Beautiful paintings lined the long hall.

'Ancestors?'

'Yes. Hundreds of years of them. And there's more at the home we have in Scotland.'

'You have a place in Scotland, too?'

He nodded and looked at me. 'A castle, actually.'

I opened my eyes wide and nodded. 'Oh, of course. Naturally, you'd have a family castle.'

He laughed and opened a door halfway down the hall, and we went inside, to an amazing bedroom suite.

'I am in absolute sensory overload here. You're throwing so much at me today, I can barely grasp what's going on.'

He turned and swept me into his arms. I melted into him as he kissed me and his hands roamed over my body. He kissed along my neck and whispered into my ear, 'As long as we're together, we'll be able to do anything. Now, give me a minute. I'll be right back.'

I nodded and watched as he disappeared through the door into what looked like a dressing room. I turned and looked around the room. This must be his bedroom. It was bigger than my whole apartment. I wandered over to the double French doors and opened them, sucking in a breath when I saw the view. A beautiful balcony ran the length of the room. I forced myself to walk to the railing, and curled my fingers around it. I held tight and looked out. Below was the beautiful patio we had just been on. Beyond that were the cliffs that fell away to a striking view of the ocean. It was a glorious day, the sky was blue, and little white dots of sailboats bobbed out on the waves.

'Oh my! To think that some people live like this.'

'Do you think you could live like this?' I spun around when I heard Dax's voice.

'Holy shit. You're in a kilt!'

'That I am, lassie.' He put on a thick Scottish brogue and I burst out laughing.

'You look fabulous. And you have the best legs in town, I swear.'

He smiled and walked toward me. I knew nothing about Scotland, or Scottish culture, but seeing him in his kilt and that gorgeous white shirt and with his dark hair blowing wild in the breeze off the ocean, I couldn't have imagined a more stunning man. I wanted to claim him for my own.

I couldn't look away from Dax, he was so amazing in his kilt and tartan. I drew closer to him and spoke in a low, husky tone. 'I've always wanted to know what's under a kilt.'

'Have you now?' Dax tilted his head sideways, his gaze thick and filled with passion. I loved that look on his face, and it totally ignited me. 'Then we'll have to remedy that at the earliest possible moment.' He scooped me into his arms and slayed me with the most wonderful kiss. I hung in his arms, my muscles suddenly useless. Moments later, he lifted his head and stared into my eyes. 'Now then, hold that thought.'

I blinked and drew in a shaky breath. 'O-okay.'

'You ready? We really do have to go down now. We'll have all the time in the world later.' Downstairs, Dax settled me by the window with a drink, kissed me on the cheek and said he had to mingle. I understood completely, and it afforded me the opportunity to see him in action. To understand the man he really was. Daxton King. Not simply Mr Monday. My heart swelled with pride as I watched him move among the guests. Some pretty well-heeled ones, too, which blew my mind. I was travelling in a rather elite circle all of a sudden.

'Tess?'

I turned and stood a little taller when I saw Mr Sunday. I narrowed my eyes at him and wondered what he could possibly have to say to me.

'Hello.' I said, refusing to let my guard down, even though he was smiling.

'I'd like to properly introduce myself to you. Malcolm Fox.' He stuck his hand out, and I had no choice but to take it. I didn't want to appear rude in the middle of a wake. Hesitantly,

I shook his hand. 'You should know that Mr King was looking forward to working with you,' he said.

Of all the things he could say, I hadn't expected him to say that. I wasn't surehow to answer. I knew now that Malcolm's behavior earlier today had probably been put on, all part of the test, but it still felt odd to have him say such kind words. He continued, 'There were numerous candidates shortlisted, but he had you at the top of the list. He knew you would be the one to pass the tests with flying colors.'

'I don't know what to say.'

He raised his glass slightly, making a small toast to me. 'I felt I owed you the introduction and a bit of an explanation, because you made it very obvious how you felt about our meeting.' The smile he gave me was startling. Then his eyes shifted as he looked over my shoulder, and I turned to see what had caught his attention.

Dax was approaching through the sea of people. Our gazes met and my heart did a little double-time beat.

'All the best, Tess,' Malcolm said.

'Thank you,' I replied, not turning away from Dax. I heard Malcolm leave and was relieved. Even if it was all fake, being around him was still uncomfortable. I watched Dax weave through the crowd, getting waylaid from time to time. He was gracious and gave each person the appropriate amount of attention. Every now and then, he'd glance at me and I'd nearly melt at the passion I saw. Passion that was for me. For us.

No fairy-tale godmother could ever grant a better wish than what was happening right now. I had my heart's desire, even if I hadn't truly known what it was until today. I was so much better suited to be the head of a charitable foundation than CEO of a profit-making company. I'd realized more than ever now that it was about the people, and this was a way to help those in need. A way to assist others in achieving their dreams.

I suddenly wanted to call my mom. I needed to tell her everything that had happened. But I supposed that could wait until tomorrow. It would be a new day, a day that would mark the beginning of a different and exciting future. Right now, though, the day and night belonged to me and Dax.

* * *

Finally, back in his apartment that overlooked the sea, we were alone. I leaned my back on the balcony railing, unable to tear my gaze away from his superb form in that to-die-for kilt. I reached for him and let my fingers run over the glorious fabric he had tucked intricately all around him.

'I think you're going to have to give me a bit of an education on this whole get-up.'

'Any time, lassie.'

'Lassie, I like that.' I smiled as I tugged him a little closer to me. 'How are you doing?' I asked him. The past few hours had been a strain for me. I could only imagine how draining it had been for Dax.

'Fine. Much more bearable because you were here with me. I'm looking forward to you being around a lot more, and to changing the world with you.' He stepped into me and lowered his head, his lips close to mine. So close, but not touching.

'I'm glad,' I whispered, and stared up at him. 'But I still don't know.'

'Don't know what?' He brushed his lips over mine oh so softly but the electricity between us was high voltage.

'What's under a Scotsman's kilt.'

His slow grin turned me inside out. I inched my hand lower, letting it drop to his hip, flexing my fingers on the kilt. I could see he was getting a considerable erection. I stepped into him now, and it prodded my belly. I itched to wrap my fingers around him.

Keeping eye contact, I slid my fingers until I had bunched the kilt up. I smiled and licked my lips. He grinned and didn't move a muscle when I reached under and rested my palm on his powerful thighs. I drew in a soft breath as he gritted his teeth at my touch. 'I want to discover you. Touch every part of you, taste you . . . love you.'

'Woman, keep up that talk and you'll do me in far too soon.' He closed his eyes and placed a hand at the back of my head, thrusting his fingers into my hair. I took this as approval and pushed my hand up under his kilt. I leaned forward and placed my lips on his.

A tremor shook him and his cock jumped under the fabric as I moved closer to my prize. I shivered with delight at his uncontrolled reaction to me and deepened our kiss. The breeze off the ocean tempered the heat of our flesh.

I chuckled when I curled my fingers around his hard cock. 'So it's true a Scotsman doesn't wear anything under his kilt.'

'Was there any question?'

I shook my head and pressed my lips to his again. I winced when Dax curled his fingers, gathering my hair into his fist, but I didn't stop him. The bright flash of pain quickly subsided into a throbbing ache that drove my excitement. I tilted my head and opened my mouth wider. He responded and held me tight to his loins so my hand was trapped between us. I breathed him in, loving the familiar scent of his warm flesh.

I cradled his thick length in my palms. He growled and thrust his hips toward me. I lifted my head away from his kiss and we stared at each other. Feeling power surge through him, my desire ripened. I felt his thigh muscles bunch as he held himself in place, and that aroused me to fever pitch.

He pulsed his hips slowly, his cock sliding deliciously in my hand, and he grunted with each deep thrust. The sun beat down and the breeze picked up. The scent of the sea mixed with our heated bodies; it was intoxicating to me. Dax held my head and moved his hips in time with my strokes.

Then he pulled back and lifted me into his arms.

'What?' I was confused and startled.

He carried me under the awning and put me down. I watched him as he pulled off his tartan, licking my lips as he unbuttoned his shirt and tossed it down. Standing only in his kilt and those crazy socks, he was simply magnificent.

'You drive me crazy.' He backed me up to the smooth stone wall of the mansion and braced his hands either side of my head.

His hair fell forward and I reached up to take his face in my palms. 'As you do me.'

He smiled, and it was my undoing. I reached for him, desperate to be naked. He swiftly had my clothes off, then buried his face between my breasts. Taking my nipple into his mouth, he laved them until they were pinpoints of sensation. I squirmed under him and thrust a knee between his legs.

'Your kilt.' I panted the word out.

'What about it?' He glanced up at me, and I shivered as his tongue played with my nipple after he spoke.

'It will get crushed.'

He shrugged.

'You don't want it to get wrinkled.'

'If it worries you, then there's one solution.' He stood back and removed the kilt with deft fingers. He carefully laid it over the other chair and turned to face me. I simply couldn't believe how perfect he was. Gorgeous in every sense of the word. And he was mine.

I reached out for him. 'Come to me.'

He did, and this time he pinned me against the wall, lifting one leg and dropping his hand between my thighs. I gasped when he pressed his finger into me, rubbing the heel of his hand on my clitoris. My head dropped back and I was lost in the most incredible feelings as his fingers slipped inside me. He curled them and thrust deep. I'd never been touched like this before and his power had me quivering and whimpering uncontrollably. My whole body was feeling, unlike it ever had before. He had found my g-spot and my mind blanked out as I came hard. Waves took me and, again, I was a rag doll in his clutches. If I made any sound, I was totally unaware of it, and his mouth closed on mine, silencing any possible moans of ecstasy. As I came back down to reality, my thighs felt wet and I realized what had happened for the very first time ever for me. Before I could feel even the least bit self-conscious, he whispered in my ear, 'You are mine.'

I nearly cried at the overwhelming emotion sweeping through me. Instead, he carried me off again when he reached between us and I felt his cock at my opening, and then he filled me. He held my ass and I looped my arms around his neck, raising my hips as he flexed, filling me completely. My head spun with yearning.

'Oh my God,' I whispered, my body shivering with delight, and stared at him. Loving how his passion played across his features, I slipped my fingers into his hair.

Our gazes locked and we met each other's thrusts with a ferocity that took my breath away. My back against the warm, smooth wall steadied us. He lowered his face and caught my lips. I wound my arms around his neck tighter, as if never to let him go. His tongue reached for mine and, with his, it played a seductive dance. If I could have spoken, I would have said, You are mine and I am yours.

We raced along, our frantic breath carried away on the sea breeze. I was going to come again and my orgasm was oh so close. I tried to hold off so we could come together. Yet I wasn't able to as the glorious rush spiraled down into my belly and bloomed as Dax thrust inside me. I clawed at him, and my muscles trembled uncontrollably. Then he groaned, deep and gravelly. I met his last few deep plunges as he came, filling me with him.

The sound of his roar mixed with the sudden playing of the bagpipes below. I shivered at the combination of the power of this man and the haunting sound of the pipes.

Dax collapsed on to me, and I was breathless between him and the wall. We stayed like that for a moment as his breath came in great gulps. He moved and scooped me up into his arms. How he could manage to carry me after all this was mind-boggling. We crawled on to the wide chaise, and he pulled me to him so I was curled up next to his side. Sated and satisfied, I pressed a kiss to his chest. We were quiet. Our heartbeats slowed, and our breathing returned to normal. The bagpipes continued to weep their memorable tune.

He wrapped his arm around my shoulders and looked down at me. 'You didn't answer my question.'

'Your question? I don't remember.'

He laughed. 'Think back. You said something and then I said something.'

I thought quickly and then I remembered. My eyes opened wide.

'I remember what I said now. And to answer your question, yes, I think I could live some place like this. As long as it is with you.'

He pulled me tighter and I slung my arm over his waist. I laughed with delight when pressed his lips to mine and then whispered, 'There's no place like home, lassie. No place like home.'

I had found my home. This whirlwind of a week had been like nothing I'd ever experienced. A simple job interview for a position as an executive assistant had taken me on an incredible journey. I'd broken free from the chains of the past, defeated the shadow on my father's legacy and found an amazing future with my very own Prince Charming. Relieved of all the anger and regret I'd been clinging to for all those years, I felt impossibly light.

What more could a girl ask for? All that was left was to live happily ever after.

Read on for a bonus *Working Girl* read.
Tess finds herself whisked away for a
fabulous Valentine's Day adventure!

I opened the handwritten note, crossed my legs and smoothed it out on my thigh. My heart swelled and I smiled when I read the words again.

Come away with me. Be ready at 9 a.m. Don't pack anything.

That was all. No X's or O's, no profession of love. No name or initial. Just instructions. Demands. Expectations. And I was going to do exactly what it said.

I touched the bold script with my fingers. I knew who it was from and I could almost feel his energy captured on the page, as though it had absorbed his very essence. He'd touched this thick ivory sheet of paper, had written the note to me. He'd folded it and put it in the envelope that had been slid under my door last night before I got home from work. My heart fluttered and heat rushed to my core. He didn't even have to be in the same room with me and I got wet for him. Seeing his handwriting gave me shivers. Maybe that's because I knew what those hands could do when they touched me. I sighed and rested my head on the leather seatback as a wave of raw desire swept through me. If only he was here on this jet with me right now.

I'd waited in my vestibule at the designated time. We hadn't combined our homes yet. Part of me was ready to live with him, but the other part still wanted to experience my new-found sense of independence. And he respected that. When the long, sleek limo had pulled up curbside I expected him to be waiting for me in the back seat. But it was empty except for some fine Costa Rican coffee and delicious New York bagels.

I looked out the window of the private jet I'd been whisked away on and smiled. He was full of surprises, my man. I loved that about him. And it was so much better flying in his jet than in that damned helicopter.

My trust in him was obvious. I was here, traveling to an undisclosed location with no idea what to expect when we landed. Was it wrong to be so terribly excited about whatever was to come?

I looked out the window. We were above the clouds and every now and then a flash of turquoise peeked through a break in the puffy layer below. The sun streamed in, beautiful, golden, hot. I turned my face so the rays hit me dead on and my thoughts about him raised my body temperature more than the heat of the sun ever could. I squeezed my thighs together and pressed my hand to the sheet of paper still resting on my lap. Where was I going? Somewhere tropical if the color of the water below was any indication.

This was an adventure I hadn't expected. It was fortunate I had a lull for a few days at work before my next project began. But then he'd have known that as well.

'Excuse me, Miss Tess.' I turned to the flight attendant.

She held out a long box. It was white with a beautifully tied silk ribbon.

'Oh my. What's this?' I took the box from her. It was heavy

and I quickly put the paper on my leg into my purse and set the box on my knees.

She gave me a mysterious smile and shrugged her shoulders before placing a glass of champagne on the table before me.

'I have no idea. But I was told to give it to you at this precise moment. If you need anything, please ring for me. I'll be in the galley for the rest of the flight.'

'How much longer?'

'I can't say for sure.'

'Ah, the mystery continues. You're sworn to secrecy.'

She widened her eyes and nodded her head slowly, smiling. Her grin was contagious and I found myself returning it before she turned and disappeared to the back of the aircraft.

I fingered the bow the middle of the box. I was pretty sure roses were inside. Tomorrow was Valentine's Day. Our first one together. I knew he'd been keeping something secret and this whirlwind flight must be it. More and more, he was revealing a deep romantic streak. I'd fallen hard for him – there was no denying that. I'd do just about anything he asked of me.

I gently pulled on the bow and it slipped undone, the wide red ribbon puddling in my lap. I held my breath as I lifted the lid off the box. An exquisite scent rushed up at me and I inhaled the perfume. Inside nestled a rainbow of long-stemmed roses. I was awestruck. He knew I adored roses, but could never pick a specific color as my favorite. It looked like every conceivable color was in this box. I lifted out one that was on top, a gorgeous coral, and buried my nose in the velvety petals. I loved how they felt next to my skin.

I saw an envelope tucked between the stems and tissue paper. Putting the rose down I picked up the envelope and quickly opened it.

A color for each the wonderful sides of you and to all those I've yet to discover. Look closer – you might find something exciting.

My heart leapt. What else could be in the box? I dared not let my imagination run wild. Don't jump to any conclusions, I told myself, but my fingers shook as I gently moved the roses aside.

When I saw it I burst out laughing. Part of me had thought I might find a ring inside, but this was just perfect. It would go very nicely with what I was wearing beneath my clothes as well. I was thankful for taking some extra time with my toilette this morning and selecting the perfect lingerie – especially since I was told not to pack anything. I pressed the blindfold to my cheek, closed my eyes and remembered. So much had transpired since that night last year.

The plane banked and began its descent. My anticipation for what lay ahead spiked and suddenly I was nervous. I buckled the seatbelt and watched out the window as the clouds gave way to wispy horsetails and then a lovely blue sky. I looked down at the clear turquoise water below. Small islands and coral heads were scattered among sparkling waves. He was down there somewhere. On one of those islands.

Waiting for me.

The jet swooped low, gave one last seriously tilted bank that had me catching my breath and then zoomed in on a small runway carved out of the local fauna. Palms and thick bushes with bright spots of color whipped past as the jet slowed. When it turned to taxi back up the runway I gasped seeing just how close we were to the ocean. If it hadn't stopped the plane would have shot right into the sea.

The flight attendant appeared when the plane came to a standstill. She didn't look at me or say anything, which I found rather odd. All she did was open the door and disappear into the sunny outside.

'Hmm, that's weird.' I glanced around and stood up. It was like I was on a mystical plane taking me to a fantasyland. I gathered my purse and the box of flowers and paused at the doorway. I was nearly blinded by the bright sun. I blinked.

Heat rushed in. The stairs had been lowered and there was no one else around. I hesitated, suddenly unsure what to do. The engines still roared and I wondered if the jet was going to turn around and head back to New York.

I backed up a little and wondered if I should wait on the plane. I let out a yelp when strong arms slid around my waist and pulled me against a powerful chest.

'What!' I gasped.

Held tight in a set of iron-hard muscled arms, unable to move, I was pinned against the body behind me.

His tantalizing scent enveloped me and that wonderful, deep voice I'd grown to love whispered in my ear. I relaxed against him and sighed, utterly astonished he'd been on the jet the whole time.

'Happy Valentine's Day, my love. Are you surprised?'

This time he let me turn around in his arms. He took the rose box from me and carefully placed it on the table under the window.

'What do you think?' I lifted my face to him and gazed into his eyes. What I saw in them made my heart melt. 'Where were you? It's not easy for you to hide on this plane.'

He chuckled. 'I was up in the cockpit.'

'Flying the plane?'

He nodded. 'I know you're not much of a Valentine's Day girl, but let me try and sway you otherwise.' He smiled. 'A little bit of romance, flowers,' he nodded at the box he'd just put down then winked at me, 'and adventure. Have I got your attention so far?'

'Yes, you have. Wait, you're a pilot . . . and "So far" . . . you mean there's more?' I asked him.

'Of course.' His voice was almost a whisper and whiskey smooth with desire.

'You're overwhelming me all over again,' I whispered.

Our gazes locked, he lowered his head and his mouth covered mine. My eyelids fluttered shut. It wasn't a sweet kiss, not innocent, but hungry, like he was burning up for me. As I was for him. He pulled me tighter until I felt every muscle and bulge. His tongue found mine, and I melted against him. It didn't matter how many times we kissed. It was always like the first. He left me breathless and craving more.

He broke the kiss and pressed his forehead to mine, his breathing ragged. It sent a deep sexual thrill through me that almost buckled my knees.

'I didn't know you could fly,' I said inanely.

'There's still lots we need to discover about each other.'

I nodded and swallowed. 'Where are we?'

'Does it matter?' He pressed his lips to my temple and kissed me down to my ear. I couldn't hold my head straight and let it fall to the side where he dove in to find the curve of my neck.

I moaned and shook my head knowing he was expecting an answer. 'Mmm, no, I guess it really doesn't.'

He chuckled and lifted his head to catch my gaze. 'That's my girl.' He took my hand and picked up the box of flowers. 'I hope you found it.'

'What? Oh, yes,' I murmured. I knew exactly what he was talking about – the blindfold. My brain started to work again, rising up through the spell of desire he never failed to cast over me. 'And what's this about not packing anything? How am I supposed to survive for however long we're here without a bag?'

'Don't worry. You'll have everything you need.' He stepped out of the plane, paused to look over his shoulder at me and gave my hand a tug. 'Come. No time to waste.'

I laughed and followed him down the steps into the hot tropical sun.

No indeed. No time to waste.